Roma Aeterna

Roma Aeterna

The Fifth Art West Adventure

Ben *and* Ann Witherington

PICKWICK *Publications* · Eugene, Oregon

ROMA AETERNA
The Fifth Art West Adventure

Pickwick Publications
An Imprint of Wipf and Stock Publishers
199 W. 8th Ave., Suite 3
Eugene, OR 97401

www.wipfandstock.com

ISBN 13: 978-1-62032-591-9

Cataloging-in-Publication data:

Witherington, Ben, 1951–

Roma Aeterna : the fifth Art West adventure / Ben Witherington III and Ann Witherington

iv + 224 p. ; 23 cm.

ISBN 13: 978-1-62032-591-9

1. Archaeology—Fiction. I. Witherington, Ann. II. Title.

PS3605 W55 2013

Manufactured in the U.S.A.

Cover photo courtesy of Mark Fairchild. Used with permission.

1

Life and Death

S HE WAS FADING FAST, and Grace Levine had the sinking feeling that nothing would prevent her mother Camelia from passing away. Life and death situations tend to strip away pretense and pride to highlight what really matters in life—life itself. In fact, Grace was wearing her Hebrew necklace engraved with the word Chai—"Life." Granted Camelia was now 87 years of age, and granted she had been in declining health for a year or so, nonetheless, she had lived well past the biblical three score and ten (70) years, but this still did not make things any easier for Grace.

Grace's mother was her anchor for much of her life. No amount of fame from her career as a scholar of Aramaic epigraphy, or her marriage to the millionaire Manny would ameliorate the loss of her mother. Grace's mother was the bedrock of Grace's childhood home. Grace's father died of a heart attack when she was very young, and she hardly remembered him. It was mother Camelia who taught Grace to ride a bike; mother Camelia who applauded when she sang at her *bat mitzvah*; and mother Camelia who blessed her choice of Manny Cohen for a husband. Grace had never been all that good at personal prayer, but her friend Art West had prayed fervently over the phone for Camelia. As the tears flowed down her face, she was thankful she had such a devout good friend. If nothing else, it made her feel like she was not alone; her family and friends loved her and would be praying.

At the moment her friend Sarah, the owner of Solomon's Porch coffee shop on Ben Yehuda Street, was sitting with Grace, silently supporting her at Sinai Hospital. The doctor emerged from the room to report that Camelia's pulse and blood pressure were gradually going down. He asked if Grace wanted Camelia put on a breathing apparatus. Grace quietly said no. Her mother would not want to prolong the dying.

One of the most puzzling things about the death of a loved one is that life goes on while death is happening. Sometimes it seems that life is quite disrespectful of death. For some reason Robert Coffin's poem, "Crystal Moment," popped into Grace's head: "Life and death upon one tether, and running beautiful together." People in the waiting room at Sinai were talking, texting, laughing, all quite oblivious to her private sorrow.

"Mrs. Levine, you can come in now," said the nurse quietly.

"*Todah*," murmured Grace.

The room in which Camelia was housed was full of busy, somewhat noisy monitors. Even here there was no complete silence or total rest. Camelia had said precious little in the last 48 hours, and Grace noticed how very pale she looked, as if the blood had drained out of her face. In fact she looked like an ancient and wrinkled angel as Grace came over and took her hand once more.

This time her mother squeezed her hand back and opened her eyes. Amazingly, she also opened her mouth, but for several agonizing moments nothing came out. Finally, what she said took Grace completely by surprise. In Hebrew she recited a familiar benediction, "May God bless you and keep you and make his face to shine upon you and grant you his peace." Then Camelia smiled.

This was almost more than Grace could take, and tears were streaming down her cheeks. "Thank you; you are my biggest blessing, ever since I was born. I owe you so much. I'm sorry for all the grief and anxiety I sometimes caused you. I . . ."

But Camelia did not want to hear a *mea culpa*; she put her bony crooked finger over her lips to silence her daughter. Then she closed her eyes, sighed deeply, and never took another breath. Gradually her grip on her daughter's hand loosened and Camelia passed over into eternity. As the nurse ran into the room, it was now Grace who put her own first finger over her lips and then said, "She's gone, let's leave her in peace."

A calm came over Grace, and she realized how very exhausted she was. She told the nurse her husband would call in a bit, and the arrangements would be made with her synagogue. Yad Vashem, the Holocaust museum in Jerusalem, would be notified since Camelia survived a German concentration camp. After the war, Camelia immigrated to Boston where she married. When Grace was born, a knitted Red Sox hat was put on her head in the hospital. She had been a Red Sox fan ever since.

"Sarah, the ordeal is over," she said as she emerged from the ICU. The two women looked at each other and recited the traditional blessing.

Barukh atah Adonai Eloheinu melekh ha'olam, dayan ha-emet.

"Blessed are You, Lord, our God, King of the universe, the True Judge."

Grace added, "Let's go have a drink to the life of my mother." Leaving the hospital, Grace noticed how bright the sun was, how the birds were singing, and how life went on despite Camelia's death. Camelia had led a rich full life after overcoming the obstacles of war. All the *chutzpah* Grace had she owed to her mother.

Surprisingly, as she crossed the long parking lot heading for her red Miata she experienced a series of flashbacks. There was Grace at five on the ground next to the swing set, with her mother bandaging her knee. Then there was Grace at ten standing on the stage after winning the regional Spelling Bee with her mother cheering in the front row. Her brain fast-forwarded to two years ago when she was rescued from a kidnapping, and her mother was there to wrap her arms around her.[1] And then once more she saw the wrinkled face of her angel in the hospital, so peaceful looking in death.

Finally, it struck her like a bolt of lightning that she would never be anyone's parental angel. She was 48-years-old and would not be having any children. Indeed, she was scheduled for a hysterectomy in a few weeks due to uterine fibroids.

Sarah noticed Grace wobbling as she was walking and grabbed her before she completely passed out and fell. It was all she could do to drag Grace the remaining five yards to the car and get her into the passenger's seat. Grabbing her water bottle, Sarah splashed Grace's face.

1. This story is told in the second Art West adventure, *Roman Numerals*.

She came to and asked weakly, "Where am I? Don't I need to get back to the hospital? What will mother think?"

"It's alright Grace," said Sarah softly, who was crying herself. "It's time to go home just now and I will drive. You just close your eyes and relax." Grace didn't need any further encouragement. Grief, exhaustion, and sleep overcame her. Sarah pulled out of the parking lot with the air conditioning on full blast to overcome the early August heat.

2

So Much for Vacation

AUGUST HAD TURNED INTO September providing some relief from the extreme heat of summer in Charlotte, North Carolina. Art and his fiancée Marissa had settled into a comfortable routine, staying with Art's Mom, Joyce, and her lodger, Jake Arafat, the budding basketball star for the Charlotte Bobcats. While there was not yet a hint of fall in the air, nevertheless it was cool enough on the back porch to enjoy sitting in the shade, sipping sweet tea, smelling the magnolia, and chatting with a more noticeable Southern drawl. Art could not remember the last time he had spent five weeks in a row in Charlotte with nothing pressing to do, and he was genuinely and surprisingly enjoying being a man at rest.

During the Fall semester at Duke University, due to start later in the month, he would give a number of special lectures on archaeology and the Bible as the D. Moody Smith Visiting Professor of Bible, but for now he was a gentleman of leisure. He sporadically left his cell phone on; he only checked his email once a day. It was not at all like him. He blamed this on Marissa who seemed to have a calming effect on him. Joyce West noticed the change this attractive Turkish archaeologist had brought about in Art's life, and she was grateful. She had convinced herself long ago that Art was too married to his work to ever find a living soul to love, but then serendipity happened and no one was more pleased than Joyce. Mentally she was already thinking about the wedding. . .and grandchildren!

"Soooo, you're thinking maybe the wedding will be next summer, Marissa?" asked Joyce carefully as she sipped her tea while sitting in the old rocker on the back porch.

Marissa smiled at Joyce, and elbowed Art in the ribs, making him sit up and pay attention. "Yes, I've been talking to my parents, and they think next June will work well. There really is no suitable place to have it in Ankara, so I was thinking Istanbul where most of our relatives live and where there is a fairly significant Christian population."

For some reason Joyce had been hoping the couple liked Charlotte so much that they would decide to have the wedding in the Queen City, and so she sighed, realizing that was too much to hope for, especially since the bride and her family were doing the lion's share of the planning. Just when Joyce was about to ask four more questions, the phone in the kitchen rang and rang with an insistence that could not be ignored. Finally, Art jumped up and trotted in to pick up the phone. "Hello! Art West here!"

"Hey, Art! It's Charlie Miller, your old seminary classmate. I've been involved in a dig in Rome this summer on the back side of the Vatican, which has produced some surprising, some would say shocking results, and I need both some advice and some help."

Immediately this conversation had Art's full attention. Charlie and Art finished one-two in their seminary class and Charlie had gone on to Yale to do a top-drawer degree in biblical archaeology, studying under Wayne Meeks and others. His specialty was social archaeology, the archaeology of the mundane, ordinary life. Charlie was short and wiry, perfect for wiggling into nooks and crannies at dig sites. In their seminary days, they shared a room on a summer dig. Art had a few pictures of Charlie, every one of which had a camera in his face. Charlie was famous for taking ten photos when one would do. On occasion, Art used Charlie's pictures to illustrate his books.

"What set your radar off?" asked Art, his right leg beginning to jiggle with excitement as he sat down in a kitchen chair and crossed his legs.

"I've found a grave, and not just an ordinary grave, but the grave of a saint and his family, all buried together in a single cave, not far underground."

"So far I'm interested but not jumping up and down. Who do you think this saint is?"

"The names we have been able to decipher so far are as follows. I am going to read you the inscription—HIC IACETUR ANDRONICUS ET JUNIA APOSTOLI CHRISTI.

Marissa was startled first by the outcry emanating from the kitchen, and then the sound of the phone hitting the floor. Running into the kitchen she yelled, "What is it Art? You look like you've seen a ghost!"

Art was too mesmerized to answer. Stooping over and picking up the phone he said, "You're telling me you found the tomb of Andronicus and Junia, Paul's co-workers, and that this couple's epitaph includes reference to their being apostles?"

"That's exactly right," replied Charlie. "But I haven't told you the best part! The inscription on the ossuary itself goes on to say that Junia was originally one of Jesus' own female disciples in Galilee!"

"Holy smokes! The Jewish equivalent of Junia is Joanna, and a few NT scholars believe there might be a connection. You may have the living proof! Now I'm really pumped! But it sounds like you've already made this landmark discovery. Why would you need me?"

"There are several problems. I haven't told a soul but you about this. We only got the initial phase of the dig completed this week. We've done all the photographing and cataloguing of the four ossuaries here, but I am thinking this will not merely come as a surprise but a shock to many in the Vatican, especially since this tomb is directly beneath the back wall of the Vatican.

"My fear is that someone will try to bury this tomb and its remarkable contents rather than reveal to the world there were women apostles in the early church. I am equally afraid of what will happen to the dig if I simply go to the rabid press who are always looking for ways to tweak the nose of the Catholic authorities in Rome. The dig is not technically on Vatican soil, but the back of the cave is in fact beyond the imaginary line of the wall and so under and thus within Papal territory. In short, it's partially in two different sovereign states. We dug under the Italian authority of the Ministry of Culture here. The site was discovered as they were putting in a new sewer line down the middle of the road behind the tourist entrance at the back door of the Vatican. A further complicating factor is that I became a Roman Catholic a couple of years ago.

"What happens if there is a jurisdictional dispute over the artifacts? What happens if the Vatican claims the ossuaries as holy relics,

since at least one of them was over the line in Papal territory? What if
my loyalty to mother church is questioned? I'm over my head here. Art,
you know people here. You have connections. Could you come and
help me with this on a short-term basis as a consultant? Oh yes, and
one more thing. We found several small hand lamps decorated with
fish symbols. I'm not sure why the lamps are there in the first place, and
the fish symbols surprised me as well! Maybe Christians were already
making their own lamps in the first century?"

With Marissa sitting right beside him and rubbing his back as
she heard and saw the excitement building in Art's frame, Art said, "I
would definitely like to do that, but I need to talk to my fiancée first.
Fortunately she's right here. I'm putting the phone down for a moment."
The words came spilling out.

"Honey, it's Charlie Miller, the archaeologist, on the phone. He
wants me to come to Rome for a short while, and here's why. He seems
to have found the tomb of the first Christian power couple, Andronicus
and Junia, and they are both clearly identified as apostles on the lintel
over the tomb door! As you might imagine, this find is going to create a
sensation in Rome. Charlie is a shy person. He's never really dealt with
the media or ecclesiastical big wigs, so he wants me to consult. What
do you think?"

"I think you should go—but only for a week or so. I'll stay here
for now and finish up the paper I've been writing. My deadline is fast
approaching." Art smiled at his beautiful bride-to-be, gave her a quick
kiss, and turned back to his phone conversation.

"Charlie, I will do my best to get on a plane tonight out of Charlotte.
I'll call you later today when I have details if you will just give me your
cell number. I will probably stay in a hotel off the Piazza Navona. I'll
call you when I'm settled. And I will call my antiquities expert."

Hanging up the phone and kissing Marissa again on the cheek
he said, "Thanks honey, this is important, no doubt and I should call
Father Salta at the Vatican and let him know I am coming and I will
need to talk with him in due course. We have to tell some trusted in-
sider at the Vatican about what has been found."

Online, he found a flight from Charlotte leaving at 6 p.m. and
landing in Rome at 9:30 the next morning. "Perfect!" he exclaimed as
he booked the last available seat and printed up his boarding passes.

"Marissa, where's my suitcase?" The time for lying on the couch was suddenly over!

3

A Long Night's Journey into Day

THE NINE-HOUR FLIGHT TO Rome can be tedious but Art was enjoying the new capacity to work on his laptop, check email, watch live
TV and movies, and make phone calls as well during the flight. Using
his FF miles he upgraded to business class and when he got tired he
would be able to get some sleep.

Art had not paid attention to the newspapers in recent days but
the headline in the New York Times online edition grabbed his atten-
tion: 'Challenges to the Vatican on ordaining Women Priests in Three
Countries." The article was written by someone who had interviewed
Art various times, Laurie Goodstone. Quickly scanning the article,
Art's eyes focused on two paragraphs. The first read,

> In a 1994 declaration seen as intended to end the debate, Pope
> John Paul II issued an apostolic letter, *Ordinatio Sacerdotalis*,
> saying that the church "has no authority whatsoever" to ordain
> women. Among the reasons the church gives is that the apostles
> of Jesus Christ were all men, and that that has been the church's
> practice all along.

Art said quietly, "This new archaeological find could put an end to that
rationale." Reading on he learned,

> More than 150 Roman Catholic priests in the United States have
> signed a statement in support of a fellow cleric who faces dis-
> missal for participating in a ceremony that purported to ordain
> a woman as a priest, in defiance of church teaching.

The Rev. Roy Bourgeois has received letters from the Vatican threatening dismissal for his role in a ceremony that purported to ordain Janice Sevre-Duszynska, far right, as a priest. The American priests' action follows closely on the heels of a "Call to Disobedience" issued in Austria last month by more than 300 priests and deacons. They stunned their bishops with a seven-point pledge that includes actively promoting priesthood for women and married men, and reciting a public prayer for "church reform" in every Mass.

And in Australia, the National Council of Priests recently released a ringing defense of the bishop of Toowoomba, who had issued a pastoral letter saying that, facing a severe priest shortage, he would ordain women and married men "if Rome would allow it." After an investigation, the Vatican forced him to resign.[1]

"Wow," breathed Art quietly. "The timing of Charlie's discovery couldn't be much worse. I wonder if he has read this article in the *Times*? I guess the door is left open a crack for Catholic women because no *ex cathedra* pronouncements have been made by any Pope saying 'Women shall never be Catholic priests.' I wonder how Pope Jerome will react to all this?" Art's thoughts wandered back to the task at hand of helping Charlie.

"Okay, Jerusalem is 7 hours ahead of Charlotte. So, given our flight time . . . Yes! Now I can call Kahlil and catch him at breakfast or at least before the shop opens, if I'm lucky!" Pulling his smartphone out of his backpack, Art dialed his old friend Kahlil el Said in Jerusalem.

1. This information comes from a real *NY Times* article written by Laurie Goodstein, "In 3 Countries, Challenging the Vatican on Female Priests" (July 22, 2011) http://www.nytimes.com/2011/07/23/world/23priest.html.

After three rings a deep baritone voice said, "*Salam aleichum*, who is calling?"

"And *aleichum salam* to you as well old friend. It's Art West. Do you have one final adventure left in you? I'm now on a flight to Rome. It looks like a remarkable tomb has been found right next to the back wall of the Vatican. It involves some possibly important first-century hand lamps, maybe the first Christian lamps ever made, and since you know more about those ancient equivalents of the flashlight, I thought I'd invite you to join me for a little fun in Rome!"

Art could hear the phone being put down and Kahlil yelling into the back of the antiquities shop where he and his daughter Hannah lived. "Hannah, Art is on the phone!" When she emerged, Kahlil continued, pleading almost like a child. "Could you spare me for a few days? Art wants me to come to Rome, and I've never seen Rome! There's an archaeological dig with some interesting hand lamps. He says he could use my help. Imagine!"

Art could not hear the response, but he pictured in his mind Hannah, holding her new born son Samuel in her right arm, smiling wistfully, and telling her father she would be fine while he went off to Rome. A couple of minutes later, Art heard, "I would be honored to join you. Hannah is on our other phone checking the flights. She says there is an early afternoon flight from Tel Aviv which arrives in Rome in only three hours! Allah be praised! Hannah is off to find my suitcase already. Such a daughter! She says you and Marissa need to come see Samuel before long. Pretty soon he may be saying his first words, and since he is named after the prophet, we may need you to interpret!"

Art chuckled. "We do indeed need to come see the baby. We'll talk about it in Rome. You have my cell number so call me when you land."

"Will do. Looking forward to seeing you soon." Art closed his phone, put it away, and decided to take a snooze for a while before he arrived at Heathrow. "I don't think I've ever heard the very reserved Charlie Miller that excited. This is going to be interesting," murmured Art to himself as he closed his eyes.

4

Graffiti Then and Now

Though estimates vary, one conservative count suggests there are some 3,500 graffiti artists (using the term "artist" loosely) in Rome. Of these 3,500, some 1,000 are called "taggers," people who spray paint public buildings and walls, including ancient and historic buildings. Giovanni Fisconi, in charge of the city's clean-up crews, has a team of some 16 people used 24 hours a day to clean up the graffiti which mar both landmarks and modern buildings, but still they can't keep ahead of the "artists." Not since the Vandals first invaded Rome has there been so much "vandalism" going on in the Eternal City. The city authorities, weary of fighting the graffiti battle, decided to build some six miles of walls, specifically set aside for graffiti artists to use, hopefully in exchange for leaving other buildings and walls alone. Alas, this remedy was only a partial deterrent. New graffiti keeps cropping up all over the ancient center of Roma.

This whole matter is complicated by the fact that high quality graffiti sells for thousands of dollars on the local art market in Italy and elsewhere, and there is even a book, entitled *Crusaders and Vandals* that suggests that some of these graffiti artists should be treated as great purveyors of modern art! Others, however, see the graffiti artists as young people trying to attract attention by doing something risky in public. Of course graffiti has a long history, going back to ancient Rome, as the excavations at Pompeii show.

The word "graffiti" in fact means "scratchings" or "writings" on the walls. While the modern graffiti artist claims to stand in the tradition of the ancient practitioners of graffiti, even in antiquity plenty of people were fed up with the defacing of public buildings. One anti-graffiti graffiti from Pompeii in the first century AD reads, "Oh walls, you have held up so much tedious graffiti that I am amazed that you have not already collapsed in ruin."

Standing 6'4" and sporting long black dreadlocks and a jet black goatee to go with his black leather jacket and pants, Boz cut quite a recognizable figure. He was nothing if not flamboyant. He saw it as his personal mission in life to leave his own stamp, or that of his disciples, on all the major tourist attractions in downtown Rome including the Vatican, the Forum, the Coliseum, and Trevi Fountain. Boz trained his disciples to be on the lookout for opportunities to slip in under the cover of darkness and decorate this or that historic wall. One place where devotees of Boz regularly posted lookouts was around the Vatican.

Boz and his gang had nothing but disdain for the lovers of antiquity. In their minds the present was more important than all of the past put together, and the ruins should be seen as pathetic reminders of a dead and gone age and culture. Boz not only hated the past, he hated the lovers of the past—historians, archaeologists, tourists, and the like. On this day, one of his agents, a diminutive figure with a black hoodie and tattered jeans, was watching the dig that had been going on all summer behind the Vatican.

Marco had just reported in to Boz that the "American" as he was dubbed, kept coming and going from the hole in the ground, and now they were apparently installing some kind of steel door with a padlock to keep people out. "I'm telling you there must be something important going on down in that dig site," stressed Marco, holding his flip phone in one hand and fanning himself with his notepad in the other. "Nothing has been taken out of the hole yet while I've been here, but we need to watch this place 24–7 from now on!"

"Yeah, if you say so," grunted Boz who was not greatly interested but agreed to post a lookout. In fact, he believed he had the upper hand on the authorities, because the bureaucracy was so bad in Rome it took months just to get permission to remove or paint over graffiti on the side of a house, never mind on the side of an historic site. And then there was the price tag. Recently, it had cost $40,000 to sandblast some of the graffiti adorning the backside of the Coliseum. Boz smiled at the thought of winning the graffiti war with the talking heads in Rome.

Someday every prominent building in the central part of the old city would be graced with his artwork. And thus far, no one had been able to lay a hand on him, because he only worked at night using his disciples as scouts. Besides, his uncle Guido the lawyer could get him out of any legal mess he might find himself in. He was bulletproof. The one vulnerability he knew he had was that he needed money constantly to finance the buying of paint and the like. He was not above a little black market dealing, if it could get him some more resources to ply his trade, or as he called it "his mission in life."

Father Salta paused once more in front of the famous fresco, reflecting again on its meaning. One of the treasures of the Vatican, "The School of Athens" painted by Raphael (1483–1520) in 1510–1511, was simply full of intriguing figures of note. On this morning, at 7 a.m. no one was present to block his view and appreciation of this masterwork.

Painted during the Renaissance, a time of recovery of lost knowledge and new-found appreciation for the art and wisdom of the past, it also reflected the period in time when Italian society began to question the received dogma it had previously accepted without much question

from the Roman church. It was thus somewhat ironic that a painting of
the likes of Heraclitus, Pythagoras, Plato, Aristotle, Diogenes the Cynic
(pictured lying on the steps in the center of the painting), Plotinus,
Strabo (the famous Greek geographer), and indeed some 49 figures altogether are depicted in this famous painting. But in fact there is a double reference in the painting because it also includes some of the great
minds of Raphael's day. Da Vinci is depicted as Plato, Donato Bramante
as Euclid, Sodoma as Protogenes (next to which is Raphael himself),
and Michelangelo as Heraclitus to mention only a few examples.

Raphael was only twenty-seven when he began working on this
fresco for Pope Julius II. The fact that the face of the painter himself
shows up as the face of a minor figure, Apelles, was well known, but
today Father Salta was studying another more obscure figure in the
painting. Standing in the bottom right hand corner is Ptolemy holding a globe, but beneath him kneeling down and drawing on a slate
with women observing him is apparently Euclid or Archimedes. What
intrigued the Father on this day, as he gazed at the painting with his
magnifying glass was what was on the slate. At first it appeared to be
two inverted triangles, but the more he looked at the drawing, the more
it looked like the Star of David. Why in the world would the Star of
David be on that slate? But then the Star of David could be represented
as two inverted triangles.

Father Salta knew that the painting was based on Bramante's original design for St. Peter's though the concept of the painting was that it
represented Plato's Academy with an All-Star philosophical cast within
it. But where had the priest seen this symbol before in the Vatican? And
what did it indicate? He would have to think about this for a while, but

for now he would set his brain at rest, and just enjoy the style and color of this masterpiece.

In his opinion Raphael never did a finer fresco. Ironic that a work for the Pope was also a tribute to pagan philosophy. Ironic also that frescoes painted on walls are undeniably works of art, unlike the modern wall "art," the graffiti, the Vatican was dealing with lately! For a moment, he was finding all this a bit amusing.

5

All Roads Lead to Rome

ONE OF ART'S FAVORITE novelists, Stephen Saylor, focuses on the Greco-Roman world of the first century AD. Recently, Saylor published a novel entitled *Empire,* the sequel to his equally impressive *Roma.* Art had so enjoyed the latter that he had devoured the former to pass the time in Charlotte awaiting his flight to Rome. So enthralled was he with the novel that he had missed the announcements for his flight, and had to race to the gate for the last call for passengers to get on the plane. He had continued to read the novel for hours at a time on the overnight flight, so engrossing did he find its storytelling.

The most interesting aspect of *Empire* is that it follows the story of a single Roman family through many generations, rather like James Michener's award-winning novel *The Source.* Some members become famous patricians, and some become despised (and then executed) Christians in the first century AD. West loved the historical detail and accuracy of these novels, as well as the plot and characters. What truly intrigued Art was Saylor's vision of how some pagans would have reacted to this new religion called Christianity. Some ignored it, some explored it, some abhorred it, and some just got bored with it. The notion of a crucified god was a deal-breaker for many Romans. Yet strangely, it attracted other Romans from all walks of life.

Art's thoughts wandered back and forth between the novel and Charlie Miller's discovery. What was puzzling Art at the moment was why an ancient Christian family would be buried in a cave, not a catacomb? Granted it would have been well beyond the ancient city boundary, the so-called *pomerium,* and so there was no special permission needed for a burial there, but still it was puzzling. Were Andronicus and Junia somehow elite members of Roman society, or did they have a home on the perimeter of the eternal city? Were they secretly buried beneath their home, or was there some sort of Christian catacomb, as of yet undiscovered, that was connected with this cave that had been burrowed under the edge of the city?

The P.A. overhead crackled and the flight attendant announced that they were making their final approach to Leonardo da Vinci, aka Fiumicino, airport. Zipping his novel into his backpack, Art fastened up the tray table in front of him, and made sure his seat was in the upright position. Da Vinci airport is a good 22 miles from the heart of Rome where Art was heading, and he had managed to snag a good room in his favorite hotel on the Piazza Navona—the D'Medici. The room overlooks Bernini's Four Rivers fountain that was featured in Dan Brown's *Angels and Demons.* He also had the foresight to book Kahlil a room next to his just to make things easy.

Turning on his cellphone as he headed for passport control, he saw the light blinking. The message said that Kahlil was airborne already and would arrive in a couple of hours from Tel Aviv. Art left a message for Kahlil to take the train into town, the so-called Leonardo Express, and Art would meet him at Termini Station.

At baggage claim, Art dialed Charlie's number. "Your first consultant has arrived, and your second is airborne as we speak. Ah, the joys of modern travel! Reinforcements will soon be at hand," promised Art with a flourish.

"Splendid," said Charlie. "We've just finished installing the steel door and padlock on the site so I don't feel like I need to worry about security for the time being. My crew and I have taken over a small B&B near the Vatican."

"Cool. Why not meet us for dinner tonight at the D'Medici. We will go out for gelato afterwards, stroll around the piazza and figure out a battle plan. See you at 7?"

"Excellent idea! You don't know how relieved I am to have some help on this dig. Issues were beginning to pile up," complained Charlie, a well-known worrywart.

"No worries. We will get things on the right track. By any chance do you know my friend Father Peter Salta, the preacher to the Pope?"

"As we would say in good ole North Carolina, you have been hanging out in high cotton, not me. I've been digging holes in the ground. I take it we can bounce some ideas off him without drawing full Vatican attention?"

"That's the idea. Father Peter is just the man so I would like to set up a meeting."

"By all means. Set up a meeting and we can get the ball rolling."

At *Corriere della Sera*, the most famous of Italian newspapers, it was business as usual on this morning. Reporters were frantically typing away trying to meet their deadlines, all that is except one reporter—Adriano Andretti. Adriano covered the old historic sites downtown exclusively, and was always looking for info. One of his regular snitches, Marco, was more than happy to exchange lunch for leads. Today, Adriano raced to the elevator as soon as he listened to the voice message from Marco announcing that something major was going on at an archaeological dig behind the Vatican. People were always finding things under the streets of Rome, and Adriano loved to be the first to report the discovery. Indeed, he had won the Italian version of the Pulitzer Prize for his reporting and ability to scoop the competition. The downside of Adriano was that he had it in for the Catholic Church.

Adriano was a tall thin man, with a penchant for dressing in gray suits and white dress shirts. Impeccably quaffed, his shock of dark brown hair, slightly moussed, was combed back from right to left, revealing his prominent somewhat wrinkled forehead. Although only 45 years of age, Adriano's hair was already showing signs of gray, and it had caused him to shave off his moustache the previous year. Never married, he nevertheless considered himself a real catch. Lately, he had been mulling over the possibility of allowing himself the luxury of taking a wife and silencing his mother's constant nagging on the subject.

Wearing his Gucci loafers, highly polished, he hardly looked like the classic scruffy reporter, and this fact he used to his advantage. The people he interviewed saw him as good company; they opened right up to him like a flower seeking the light. Some days he just walked out of his dull office and into the hustle and bustle of Piazza Venezia. Tourists flocked to this square to visit the Monument to Victor Emmanuel II, the first king of unified modern Italy.

Some of Adriano's best pieces were based on interviews of tourists from around the world. Did they like Rome? Did they like the monument? Did they know that many Romans consider it a monstrosity? Did they think it looked like a "wedding cake" as many Italians have dubbed it? But today would not be spent with tourists. Today he hailed a taxi and headed to Vatican City.

While the taxi driver wove through the notorious Roman traffic, Adriano contemplated the questions he would like to ask the American archaeologist in charge of the dig behind the Vatican—that is, if he could persuade the man to say something. If not, well someone was always willing to brag about the work being done at a dig site. A fistful of euros was always helpful. And fortunately for Adriano, he could be very persuasive. He would explain that anything that helped Rome better recover and understand its past was a good thing, as far as Adriano was concerned. This was all the more ironic considering one of his best sources worked for culture haters. "Ah, yes! This should be a fun visit!" laughed Adriano out loud. But even Adriano, the grizzled veteran of surprising news stories, was not prepared for what he would eventually learn about this dig site.

6

Star Prophecy

Father Peter Salta loved puzzles. Every morning he worked the cross-word in the daily paper and every evening before he went to bed he solved a Sudoku. The only habits more regular than puzzle solving in this priest's life were prayer and saying Mass. He had to admit he was stumped by the unexpected Star of David he found in the painting known as the 'School of Athens.' What exactly was Raphael intending with that symbol?

Curiosity got the best of him as he was leaving St. Peter's after morning Mass. He stopped at Arnolfo di Cambio's bronze statue of St. Peter, whose right toes are now worn and rounded due to years and years of pilgrims stroking the foot. The halo hovering above St. Peter's head was not simply the usual circle of light. Within its circumference was a radiant star with pointed beams in all directions. On closer inspection, the thickest, core part of the star was once again, a Star of David.

Scratching his head, Father Salta found this most odd. Peter, after all, was not the son of David, as Jesus was, so why would artists like Raphael and di Cambio add such an incongruous feature to their works of art? Why indeed!

The symbolism of stars is multi-faceted. He thought about the famous star prophecy in Numbers 24:17: "There shall come a star out of Jacob, and a scepter shall rise out of Israel, and shall crush the borderlands of Moab, and destroy all the territory of the Shethites." This prophecy had a long history of being applied to messianic figures in early Judaism. As a historian, Father Peter knew that the prophecy was often employed during the troubled years that led up to the Jewish Revolt, the destruction of the Second Temple in Jerusalem in AD 70; and the last stand of the Sicarii (the hit men among the Zealots) at Masada in AD 72. Father Peter's internet search showed that the Star Prophecy appears in the Qumran texts, and was a prophecy of great importance to resistance groups during that time, including the Qumran community, the revolutionaries who stood against Rome, and even the early Christians.

"The Star Prophecy was applied to the coming Messiah himself in radical Jewish documents, such as the apocalyptic *War Scroll* found at Qumran. In a *pesher* applied to the text from *Numbers*, the *War Scroll's* writer gives the following exegesis:

> . . . by the hand of the Poor whom you have redeemed by Your Power and the peace of Your Mighty Wonders . . . by the hand of the Poor and those bent in the dust, You will deliver the enemies of all the lands and humble the mighty of the peoples to bring upon their heads the reward of the Wicked and justify the Judgment of Your Truth on all the sons of men."

The Jewish historian Josephus, in his early work *The Jewish War*, "applied the prophecy—perhaps in retrospect, like most successful prophecies—to Vespasian, who was campaigning against the Jewish Zealots in Palestine, and who was to come out of Palestine and rule the world, his flatterer asserted. . . . The prophecy was also applied to Simon bar Kokhba, messianic leader of the Second Jewish Revolt of 132, whose adopted name *bar Kokhba* means 'Son of a Star' in Aramaic."[1]

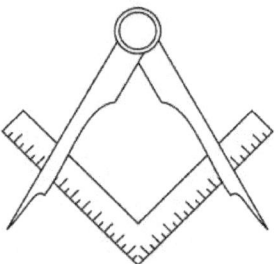

There was as well the star and the Magi story in Matthew 2 that had become a part of the Christian Christmas story. There the context associated the star not with a son of Jacob but with a son of David. Father Peter had done his homework, but he had to admit that the presence of the symbol in these two works of art was strange. "Surely, it doesn't have anything to do with the Masons, does it?" Peter asked himself as his mind flitted from one idea to another. "The Masonic symbol looks a lot like the doodles in Raphael's painting—or maybe not."

---

1. "Star Prophecy," *Wikipedia: The Free Encyclopedia*, http://en.wikipedia.org/wiki/Star_Prophecy (accessed 31 July 2012).

Surely there is no connection thought Peter. The Free Masons didn't arise before the 16th century, so Raphael and Adolfo would have known nothing of these Masonic symbols, one would presume. On the other hand, some claimed a connection between the Masons and the earlier Knights Templar, and they had their share of such symbols as well. In any case, a five-pointed star is not the same as a six-pointed star—and the Star of David is six-pointed!

There was, however, the curious case of the synagogue lintel at Capernaum that includes both a five- and a six-pointed star! Will the real star please stand up! "Are we having fun yet!" laughed Father Peter out loud which attracted not a few tourists. Just as he was leaving by the front door of St. Peter's his cell phone began vibrating in his pocket. Stepping outside quickly onto the front portico of the basilica he took the call.

"Father Peter, it's an old friend, Art West. How are you?"

"Excellent! Are you here in the Eternal City?"

"I am indeed here on a short term basis, and was hoping we could chat in the next few days—whatever suits your schedule." Pulling out his little pocket calendar, Father Peter furrowed his brow and came up with a vacant slot.

"How about a meeting in my Vatican office late Friday morning? I'll send you the address. Maybe we can do lunch afterward."

"I will make it work," promised Art. "We have much to catch up on."

"Indeed! Until then *ciao*," and with that Father Peter hung up. "Art sounded excited. I wonder what brings him to Rome? Well, I'll find out in a few days." The bells above St. Peter's began ringing again, calling the faithful to yet another worship service.

7

Boz and His Band; Charlie and His Angels

WHILE MOST FOLKS ASSOCIATE the Roman catacombs with Christians, many Jewish and pagan bodies were also buried underground on the outskirts of Rome beginning in the 2nd century. Over 40 catacombs have been discovered, each a vast network of passages with burial niches cut into the soft volcanic rock. The best examples attract tourists who are led single file through the maze lest they get lost permanently! The Vatican now maintains and continues to explore the catacomb network—but they cannot police it all!

One of the neglected catacombs became the meeting place for Boz and his disciples. The advantages of this meeting place were many: 1) cool—68°F on the average; 2) scary—most people were superstitious enough to stay away from tombs, especially at night; 3) private—out of sight of the police, tourists, and even the Vatican archaeologists; 4) inaccessible—off the beaten path and nowhere near homes and businesses; and 5) *deathly* quiet. It was from here, well off the Appian Way, that Boz plotted his painting exploits. Since the location was off the beaten track, and the group was able to discuss their plans in a relaxed and extended manner, they saw no need to be too guarded about what they did in and around this abandoned catacomb. They did not maintain it, indeed the entrance way was so covered over with grass and vines and brush that unless one was looking hard, one could miss it altogether.

"So, what's up boss—where next?" asked Philippo, Boz's second-in-command.

"I was thinking about that big ugly Arch of Titus next to the Coliseum," sighed Boz.

"Risky! Too many polizia. I'm telling you, Boz, this American archaeology site needs to be checked out. Something major is going down there," stressed Marco as he chewed on his Sigaro Toscana.

"I think those cigars have muddied your brain. Look, it's not a priority unless you can tell me how that's going to bring in some euros for us."

Marco remained silent, because he hadn't really thought far enough about that aspect of the situation, especially since the steel door would put a damper on pilfering anything.

After a minute of awkward silence Boz continued, "I didn't think so, but keep your eye on the place. You never know what may turn up."

∾

The D'Medici Hotel is a classic 19th century Italianate hotel which mercifully had been upgraded with good air conditioning in recent years. The view from the roof garden was nothing less than spectacular. To the west, one could see across the Tiber (Tevere in Italian) River to Castel Sant' Angelo and Vatican City; to the southeast one could make out the "Wedding Cake" and even the Coliseum. From the Piazza it was a reasonable walk to the Pantheon for culture, or the Campo de' Fiori for food and fun. This was always Art West's hotel of choice when he was in Rome.

The old doorman, Franco, who had worked at the hotel for 35 years, recognized Art when he arrived and helped him with his luggage. Art had plenty of time to go up to his sixth-floor room, unpack, shower, change, and find a great place for lunch on the Piazza. Kahlil would take the train from the airport into the Stazione Termini by late afternoon and Art had arranged for him to have the room adjacent to his own. The D'Medici qualified as a boutique hotel. The rooms were not large, but they were nicely furnished with period pieces. The hotel had recently been bought by the rising Anemon chain of hotels based in Turkey, but nothing essential seemed to have changed that Art could see. This hotel was so cozy, and the staff so friendly, some of whom Art knew by name, that it seemed like coming home in some ways.

Art headed right back downstairs, and began to take a brisk walk to the Train Station. It would take him about thirty minutes to get there, and fortunately he knew a couple of short cuts off the Piazza Navona, so he was in good shape. Charlie would be showing up for dinner about an hour after he and Kahlil returned to the hotel. The heat coming up off the streets was intense. You could even see the heat coming through the manhole covers. Art was hoping for a break in the weather now that September had arrived.

By the time he got to the train station, he was sweating profusely and decided he and Kahlil would take a taxi back. It was asking too much to have a 71-year-old man walk all that way in the heat, dragging luggage. While the Italian trains are not quite as minutely punctual as the German trains, they are nonetheless reliable, and so Kahlil's train arrived on time.

Emerging from the third car, Kahlil looked a little strange in a business suit instead of his usual Arab apparel, but his headgear advertised to one and all that he was not Italian. Art noticed almost immediately that his once luxuriant black moustache was now gleaming white. He was, however, still as tall as ever, towering over Art.

"It's been too long, old friend," said Art with a big smile. "I'm glad we can share this adventure." After Kahlil settled into his room, Art decided, if one cool shower is good, two in hot weather is better. Fortunately the roof garden was now enclosed in glass with shades, and had air conditioning, but they would still have a view. Just when he had gotten dressed again in a new outfit, his room phone rang.

"Have Charlie's angels arrived yet?" asked the quiet voice on the other end.

"I've never thought of myself as angelic! But yes, we'll meet you on the roof for a great meal and a great view, I promise."

8

For Unto Us a Child Is Born

HANNAH COULD HARDLY BELIEVE it. She was a mother with a healthy baby boy. Right about now she was missing her father Kahlil who was in Rome, but so all-consuming was the job of nursing and taking care of an infant like Samuel that she had little time to worry about Kahlil. After she recovered from swine flu and various complications,[1] her pregnancy had gone quite well, with few unexpected developments. Finally in the early summer she delivered a healthy baby boy weighing in at 7 pounds and 9 ounces and now sporting a full head of dark curly hair. The further good news was that Hannah had been able to nurse him for the first several months of his life and she had enjoyed the visits from various relatives and friends to whom she could show off her newfound pride and joy. She felt like Elizabeth in the Bible. Her shame for being childless had been taken away and replaced with great joy, even though this child came unbidden and unexpected. But wasn't that also the case with Elizabeth and Mother Mary as well? Somehow Hannah felt like she was living out a biblical script and could hardly be more grateful to God for this unexpected and untimely blessing, for Hannah was now well into her forties.

Two days ago, Sarah stopped in to dote on Samuel and talk to Hannah about the local news. "David Copperfield is promising to make the Ark of the Covenant disappear, or at least its replica! If he can make the Statue of Liberty vanish then I suppose this should be simple,"

1. This whole story is found in the fourth Art West adventure, *Corinthian Leather.*

laughed Sarah. "So what do you say girlfriend? Can I pry you out of this cocoon of nurturing for an evening's fun? It's not for two weeks and my mother volunteered to babysit for you. So, no excuses!"

"Well, it seems like I have to say yes. As a child I always did like card tricks and games that involved optical illusions. But making the Ark of the Covenant disappear right before my eyes—now that would indeed be magic, or perhaps a miracle if it really happened!"

"As they say, seeing is believing, and the best part is, I have two primo tickets for fifth row seats so we should be able to eyeball everything up close and personal," said Sarah with a note of anticipation in her voice. Hannah had agreed readily and was looking forward to a real evening out with her good friend.

Today, however, was a busy day juggling feeding schedules, paperwork and customer appointments. Kahlil was basically retired, but they still kept their Antiquities Shop for special clients. Hannah was as knowledgeable as Kahlil about most of the items in the shop, and Kahlil still made purchases or sought out items his clients wanted. They were in a position to indulge their hobby rather than worry about making a living. The phone rang in the shop. With Samuel snuggled away in a pouch which hung from her neck, she easily answered the phone.

9

The Story of Andronicus and Junia

CHARLIE, ART, AND KAHLIL settled into a quiet table in a corner far from the very few patrons in the rooftop restaurant.

"*Buena sera*, gentlemen! My name is Carlo, and I will be your waiter for this evening. I recommend the prosciutto and fresh melon to begin your meal! But the vino is to your taste!"

"No argument here," volunteered Art. The others nodded, and placed their wine orders as well. After catching up on all the family news, the three men went silent as they allowed their Italian food to digest. Over a second glass of wine, Charlie finally got around to business.

"Let me tell you briefly the story of this dig. While it is sponsored by the Ministry of Culture, it is funded by an unexpected source, a nun who inherited a fortune from her father, after she had taken her vows, and after she promised away her worldly goods. She decided not to hand over the small fortune to Mother Church. In her mind, one of the most worthy causes of all is changing the male dominance at the top of the Catholic Church. She doesn't much like the celibacy rule either. She wants women priests and married priests, heterosexual I might add. She's convinced this will help avoid future sex scandals. Suffice it to say she is an old friend. I will give you her name on condition that it not be used in public. She is still a practicing nun here in Rome. Her real name is Bernadette Bernini, but her religious name is Sister Thecla, appropriate for someone who believes in women in ministry, don't you think![1] The Vatican knows nothing about the funding which is just as well because I doubt they would approve!

"You may well ask how did she know what I would find before I started excavating? Remember that this site was discovered while putting in a new sewer line in the middle of the street behind the Vatican. The first thing found that stopped construction altogether was a part of the inscribed sign that I read to you. The exposed part simply said 'apostles of Christ' in Latin. Thus far, no problem for the Vatican, and there was no official reaction. Fortunately, I was already here and planning to be involved in another dig near the City Museum of Rome. When I heard about this find, I phoned up the head of the Ministry of Culture and told him I would take it on at my own expense, and turn over everything I found to him. This sounded too good to be true, so he called up the references I gave him, found out I was legit, and since he had already allocated all his money for the digging season, he was happy to give me free reign. In the second week of August I uncovered the inscription stone. That's when I called Sister Thecla. She's immediately likeable, and she was so enthusiastic when I told her about the full inscription she was singing praises to God right on the spot. And yes, she agreed to fund the whole thing, now and next season if it takes that long.

"A week and a half ago I penetrated the burial chamber itself, which seems to be self- contained. By that I mean it's one chamber not connected to any other chambers. It seems then to be the rarest of ancient tombs—a small family tomb with only Christians buried there. Why do I say only Christians? Well, it's not just the pottery lamps that have the *ichthus* symbol on them, the ossuaries themselves have ancient Christian symbols on them. One of them even has the sign of the cross on it, it would appear.

"As for the remains, each of four skeletons is intact—a man, a woman, and sadly, two children. It is possible they were all buried at once, as the ossuaries are all of one sort, and from the first century it seems clear. But here is the real surprise. These ossuaries, like that of Caiaphas have toe-tag inscriptions, by which I mean the person interred is identified on the end of the box and not in an ornamental

---

1. Thecla appears in the second century *Acts of Paul and Thecla* not merely as a colleague of Paul's but an apostle and evangelist of sorts.

script either. No one was meant to see these inscriptions except the family and those doing the burying so they could distinguish them. The inscription on the adult female ossuary is in Aramaic. All the rest of them are in Greek. But the sign on the outside is in Latin. So, I am thinking the Christian community wanted fellow Christians to find this tomb, but Andronicus and certainly Junia, must have been from the eastern part of the Empire." Charlie paused to pour another glass of the excellent Orvieto Classico Amabile, and was going to continue when Art leapt in.

"The reason surely for the eastern inscriptions is, as you surmise, that these persons were from the eastern end of the Empire. I am going to suggest that the Aramaic inscription probably has the Semitic equivalent of the name Junia, which is Joanna. But I will hold my fire until I see the inscription tomorrow. But Charlie you know the controversy about this couple. In the first place, many Christian commentators suggest that Junia was really a man named Junias. The problem is, there does not seem to be any evidence at all in the ancient inscriptions or literary sources for such a man's name. Pagan men didn't tend to be named after female deities anyway. And the evidence for the name Junia is plentiful. Also, the context favors this being a couple, because elsewhere when we have two names together like this in the list in Romans 16 it is a husband and wife, such as the mention of Priscilla and Aquila. The rest of the description of them in that text is very telling. First, they are Paul's co-workers. Second, they have been imprisoned at some point with him. People don't get imprisoned for non-public activities generally, so we are probably to think of their evangelistic work. Third, and most impressively, Paul says they were in Christ before he was. But Paul was an early convert, in the 30s without a doubt. This means these two were surely part of the original Jerusalem community of disciples, or perhaps from the Galilee band of disciples. Either way, they are almost certainly Jews, because the evangelism of Gentiles didn't really get going before Paul's conversion. Fourth, the kicker is that Paul says they are 'noteworthy among the apostles.' Some scholars who don't like the idea of female apostles have tried to suggest the Greek means 'noteworthy to the apostles' but that is not the normal way to read this Greek grammatical construction, and so now comes your discovery and what does it do? It confirms these two persons, husband and wife, were apostles. Since the other two persons in the tomb are children, the sign outside can't refer to them. By the way, what is the gender of the children?'

"One is a male. The other is a female and she isn't named Junia," replied Charlie.

"Perfect, so the name Junia has to apply to one of the adults, one of the apostles. There are a lot of Christians who are going to freak out about this, and to find it right under Vatican's nose, well, it will cause a sensation!"

Kahlil sat back ruminating on all this and swishing his wine around in his glass. "I suppose pretty soon I will get to see the lamps, and we may have more confirmation of the date of these findings, but surely the correspondence between what Romans 16 says, and what Charlie has already found cannot be dismissed as a mere coincidence. But I have a question. Suppose someone suggests that these two persons, husband and wife, are just apostles with a little 'a,' not a capital 'A'? Doesn't the term refer to apostles of churches, that is, missionaries from churches, in some places in Paul's letters and Acts? I seem to recall this being the case."

"Good point," replied Art, perking up again. "But Kahlil, the Latin inscription on the tomb says Apostles of Christ, not apostles from the Roman church, for instance. Wherever Paul uses the phrase Apostle of Christ he means someone who has seen the risen Lord and has even been commissioned by him. Someone like himself. And this has to mean they were there for the resurrection appearances in Jerusalem or Galilee. And this brings me back to this Junia/Joanna.

"I think she is the same woman mentioned in Luke 8:1–3 as one of the original female disciples of Jesus. She is a high-status woman, the wife of Herod Antipas' estate manager, Chuza, but when she went 'walk about' with Jesus not once but several times, he would have considered she had shamed him and been unfaithful, and he would have written her a writ of divorce in short order, as was his right. So, by the time she gets to Jerusalem on the last journey with Jesus, she was presumably again an unmarried woman. As for who Andronicus was, we shall never fully know, I suspect. The name is actually a nickname—something like 'the manly man'—a name sometimes given to slaves. Perhaps he was like Rhoda, a servant in a Christian household in Jerusalem who had become a freedman as a Christian. But this is just conjecture; though, it is certainly quite possible."

"So what do we do about all this?" asked Charlie. "This is a delicious discovery, but it's going to shock a lot of people here in Rome and elsewhere. Those opposing women in ministry aren't going to like it a bit. And since I've become a Catholic I have some reservations about women in ministry as well. Have you devised a plan Art?"

"In fact I have already called Father Pietro Salta, the preacher to Pope Jerome himself. We will meet with him on Friday, and hope he doesn't have a heart attack when we tell him about your surprise find Charlie."

"Okay, but as I say, mum's the word about the source of my support please. Sister Thecla deserves to have her identity protected."

As the wine did its work, the more animated the conversation had become, especially towards the end when they discovered they were the only ones left in the restaurant. Carlo, the waiter, knew one thing for sure—these three were involved in a big archaeological find near the Vatican. He scribbled the names Andronicus and Junia on a blank order form. His newspaper friend, Adriano, would pay for all the tidbits he had gleaned as he discreetly came and went from the table.

10

Heartsick at Home

YES, THE SUN WAS still shining, the seagulls were still squawking, the ocean waves were still lapping the shore in Tel Aviv, but none of these things were helping Grace handle the death of her mother. Food reminded her of her mother; laughter reminded her of her mother; and even her husband's chiding about eating and sleeping reminded her of her mother.

On this morning, Grace was sipping a Bloody Mary on her lovely porch while looking down the street at the bungalow she had bought for her mother to live by the sea. What was the point of life if inevitably and inexorably, all that you truly love just dies and leaves you? Why celebrate or perpetuate the farce of life, if it was always bound to let you down in the end? You have an illusion of togetherness with other people, of family, of friendship, but in the end you are born by yourself and you will die alone. Grace suddenly had new sympathy for the writer of the book of Ecclesiastes, and this morning the one thing she had done was get out her Tanakh and read once more the following words from the seventh chapter of that wisdom book.

> 1 A good name is better than fine perfume,
>   and the day of death better than the day of birth.
> 2 It is better to go to a house of mourning
>   than to go to a house of feasting,
> for death is the destiny of everyone;
>   the living should take this to heart.

3 Frustration is better than laughter,
    because a sad face is good for the heart.
4 The heart of the wise is in the house of mourning,
    but the heart of fools is in the house of pleasure.
5 It is better to heed the rebuke of a wise person
    than to listen to the song of fools.
6 Like the crackling of thorns under the pot,
    so is the laughter of fools.
    This too is meaningless.
7 Extortion turns a wise person into a fool,
    and a bribe corrupts the heart.
8 The end of a matter is better than its beginning,
    and patience is better than pride.
9 Do not be quickly provoked in your spirit,
    for anger resides in the lap of fools.
10 Do not say, "Why were the old days better than these?"
    For it is not wise to ask such questions.

"Epicurean philosophers would have agreed and added 'eat, drink, and be merry, for tomorrow you will die' but Qoheleth would have said even that behavior is pointless. Well, at least I'm still drinking." A profound cynicism had settled into Grace's heart, and when she remembered the numbers of observant Jews she knew, who nonetheless admitted they didn't really believe in a loving God in light of all the cruelty and suffering and untimely death in this world, frequently happening to Jews, she felt confirmed in her newfound cynicism. Would Grace become such a person as those skeptical Jews? She had always had as her closest friends, people who genuinely believed in God, including Muslim friends like Hannah and Kahlil, and Jewish friends like Sammy Cohen of the IAA, and Christian friends like Art and Marissa. Even Manny didn't question the existence of God. In some ways, the bigger question for Grace was why was she reacting so severely to the death of her mother? After all, her mother had lived a very full life. Maybe she was just reacting normally. After all, the grief process takes a while and is unique to each person. Would she deal with the grief? Would she need counseling? "Am I just getting too far ahead of myself?!"

So Grace decided to go back to the kitchen for another Bloody Mary—not a very good breakfast. But when she got up from the porch lounge, she slipped on the tiles, twisted her ankle and went down with a thump, the glass shattering on the travertine. Oddly enough, though she was not seriously hurt and could hear Manny running to her aid, Grace began to laugh heartily at herself. How silly she must look spread-eagled on the front porch in her bathrobe and slippers. If the neighbors had been walking by they might have thought she was drunk—which was not yet the case.

There is something about laughing at yourself that is healing and helpful to a grieving person. Manny inspected her bruises and insisted on carrying her indoors to a couch. He was quite surprised to be carrying a smiling wife who decided to start singing a chorus of that old Blue Oyster Cult hit, "Don't Fear the Reaper"! She kissed him on the cheek and sang out . . .

> "All our times have come
> Here but now they're gone
> Seasons don't fear the reaper
> Nor do the wind, the sun or the rain. . .

> "We can be like they are
> Come on baby. . .don't fear the reaper
> Baby take my hand. . .don't fear the reaper
> We'll be able to fly. . .don't fear the reaper
> Baby I'm your girl. . ."

Manny laughed, relieved at this new turn in Grace's attitude. With an ice pack on her ankle, Grace talked about the fact that she really wasn't feeling sorry for her mother, she was indeed feeling sorry for herself— and that's all right! Grace knew she would not return to life as normal, but to a new normal life.

~

The West house in Charlotte had certainly been quiet since Art left. Marissa was moping. She worked on her paper for a while, and then got up to roam aimlessly around the house or yard. Visiting with Joyce was good, but no substitute for being with Art. She used to be so independent; enjoying her freedom. Now she felt lost without her "other half." What was dawning on her was just how much she really loved Art, and wanted to be with him all the time. Her outlook on life changed once she got engaged. She had found her man, and she was not about to let him go. She knew they would be apart due to their different work interests, but the reality was not much fun.

Jake found her staring at a blank computer screen. "Wow, that looks exciting," said Jake Arafat, Joyce's renter, just a bit too sarcastically. "I bet I can do you one better. How about we get out of the house? Let's just say we could both use a little distraction."

"I guess we are both in the same boat, Jake. What a pair—both heartsick! You really are missing your girlfriend, aren't you?"

"You're right; I miss her. But I'll be heading down to Wilmington this weekend. Melody's afraid that absence will make the heart go wander. No way!!"

"Do you have any bright ideas to pass the time other than shooting baskets at the youth center?" asked Marissa, who was actually enjoying these court romps with Jake and the kids. She was learning some pretty slick moves under the basket, and faked out even Jake on a number of occasions. The kids found this hilarious!

"Sure! I know just the movie—*Thor*—the Marvel action flick. It should be mindless fun," promised Jake.

Marissa laughed. "Jake, you really know how to show a girl a good time! Why not?"

Joyce was invited to go along. "I was hoping you were going to suggest the movie showing at the classics theater on Providence Road—*Gone with the Wind*. But I'm game for anything. Who is this Thor, and why is he hanging out on planet Earth?"

"You'll just have to go and find out," replied Jake with a grin. "You can say it's art distracting Marissa from Art."

"I would hardly call a movie based on a Marvel comic book 'art,' but I will suspend my disbelief until we see the film," replied Joyce.

"Popcorn's on me!" promised Marissa.

11

Arch Enemies

THE NIGHT WAS HUMID, and the moonless sky was blacker than ever. The traffic around the Coliseum was light; only a few people were hurrying down the street obviously eager to get home. The scattered security guards who patrolled the Coliseum perimeter were also wishing they were home. Sergio Forte was only thinking about his new wife—and staying alive. All he had was a club and mace; guns were not allowed unless you were part of the *polizia* or *carabinieri*. Sergio was no fool, and so he stayed in the light walking his beat from midnight until 6 a.m. At five euro an hour it wasn't worth risking his life. If he saw anything drastic happening he would call the *polizia* on his cellphone.

Meanwhile, Boz and his band of painters prepared to deface yet another great landmark of Rome—the arch the Emperor Titus erected as part of his Roman triumph celebrating the sacking of Jerusalem in AD 70. Waiting until Sergio was away on the opposite side of the Coliseum, they set up the tools of their trade. The action had been carefully planned out, with the design for the graffiti drawn up in advance, and four artists selected to do the work on the backside of the arch. Boz, Marco, and Phillipo would "decorate" the inside of the arch. The area was basically locked up at night, with a perimeter fence. Boz and his boys hoped to quickly and quietly scale the fence. Dressed in black on a very dark night, they had a chance to pull it off.

The main goal was to put a ladder up inside the arch and paint over the images of the Romans carrying the menorah and other booty in the parade known as a Roman triumph through the streets of Rome. Pulling this off, right under the noses of the authorities and their security guard would be Boz's own triumph. He also planned a big floral design with the moniker for his gang on the back side of the arch as well—*B/quattrocentista*—Boz, artist. There was also inscribed their familiar slogan, "ruins are not art!"

Since this defacing was timed to happen when the sprinklers came on to water the grass, even the sound of the aerosol cans was masked at this hour. The work on the back-side of the arch, using blue and green and red and black spray paint, took about forty minutes to complete, with the four "artists" working together. But Boz reserved for himself the right to deface the most important part of the arch, where the fading image of the Roman triumph could be seen. Boz chose livid red day glow spray paint, climbed his ladder and carefully sprayed each of the figures bright red. He then used bright green to spray the menorah itself. After that, he sprayed in tiny Italian letters the words *inanimato/morte* (not living/dead).

In Boz's mind, old art is dead art, and it could only be reanimated by a great artist like himself using modern colors and modern techniques to enliven it. Just as he was finishing his so-called masterpiece, he saw from his vantage point up on the ladder two men running at full sprint down the sidewalk on the far side of the street. The first was a tall man in a suit, carrying some sort of package; the second was a black-robed man who finally caught up with the fleeing man, tackled him, grabbed the satchel and ran off into the night.

Marco and Phillipo, who were holding Boz's ladder inside the arch and serving as lookouts, saw this event unfold as well. Being curious, and since Boz was coming down from the ladder to pack things up, Marco left his post to go see who had just been mugged. Running across the street to the damp sidewalk, Marco could hear the man moaning and was relieved to discover he was still alive, for Marco was not as callous as some of his fellow artists. Much to his surprise, when he turned the man over he discovered it was Adriano Andretti, his reporter friend. Marco had often profited by slipping Adriano tidbits of news. He was still conscious and so Marco said to Adriano, "Lie still, I am calling for the ambulance. You are going to be alright. Why in the world would you be chased by a monk in a black robe? And what are you doing out at this hour of the night?"

"I was walking back to my car from Carlo's place. He's got info on that excavation behind the Vatican that you've been talking about! That monk stole my tape recorder!" complained Adriano loudly. Marco dialed the emergency number for central Rome, and explained what happened and where to come.

Marco could see that Adriano had only superficial cuts and a rising lump on his forehead. He decided the better part of valor would be to beat a quick retreat before the ambulance arrived with people asking too many questions. When he heard the sirens blaring in the distance he said, "You will be fine, the ambulance is nearly here! Don't tell them you saw me! I must fly!" And with that he ran back across the street, scaled the perimeter fence, scooted under the Arch of Titus, and followed Boz and the band.

While waiting for Marco, Boz dialed the night reporter of *Corriere della Sera* just before the paper went to press. Within twenty minutes the reporter was there at the arch taking pictures and notes, and yelling at Sergio the security guard asking where he was when all this was happening. The front page headlines read that morning, "Arch Enemies Strike Arch of Titus." The graffiti bandits had struck again.

12

Sites, Good and Bad

KAHLIL'S PHONE RANG WAKING him out of a sound sleep. It was Hannah, calling to report on Grace. Kahlil loved hearing the soft voice of his daughter. She too had persevered through much after she had been raped by her former husband only to discover she was pregnant.[1]

"I visited with her and took Samuel with me, and he was a little angel. Grace enjoyed playing with him. But I have an idea. Does this dig you are involved in have anything that would extend to her area of expertise in Aramaic inscriptions? If it does, you should invite her and Manny to come to Rome. Lord knows she needs to get out of town for a while, and it would be a good thing."

"Daughter, it is clear that Allah has been speaking to your heart, because otherwise, how could you have known what I only learned last night—that there is an ossuary with an Aramaic inscription in that tomb! Of course I will talk to Art about this, and I am sure he will agree they should come. It will cheer Grace up I am sure." The conversation continued for another ten minutes while Kahlil got out of bed and began to get ready for a day of exploring the tomb. Now he was excited about the possibility that all three of the old friends, Kahlil, Art, and Grace could be reunited through this new discovery.

Art too was on the phone, only it was with Father Salta. His meeting set for tomorrow morning was still on, but Father Peter now

1. This tale is told in the fourth Art West adventure, *Corinthian Leather*.

44

sounded less cordial, for some reason. Art was not sure why, and the good Father was not saying at the moment, but there was now some tension in the mix. Charlie was also up and about at his B&B near the Vatican preparing to pick up Art and Kahlil in the van used at the dig site. After today they would have to fend for themselves on the Rome Metro he thought, as he headed out to deal with city traffic.

The traffic was lighter than usual, and Charlie was not in a hurry on this morning. He wended his way around some of the city sites for Kahlil's sake. Charlie thought he would make a pretty good tour guide. He pointed to palazzos, piazzas, and basilicas. Kahlil shut his eyes after several near misses with the ever-present motorbikes and suggested, "Art, you need to call Grace Levine and invite her to come help us with this dig. After all, she's the real expert in Aramaic inscriptions."

"You are right about that. Maybe it will help her get over her grief. I'll call her right now!" announced Art.

The phone rang several times, and then Manny picked up. "Hello Manny, this is Art West calling from Rome. How is your lovely wife Grace?"

"Better thanks. She had a little bit of a fall on our front porch, nothing serious, but it seems to have jarred her out of her funk. When I picked her up she was happily singing 'Don't Fear the Reaper.' I hardly knew she could sing really. The last time she did that was when she fell in a hole at Corinth, remember?"

"Indeed I do. Maybe she should re-evaluate her decision some years ago not to become a rock singer. But on a serious note, do you think maybe I could persuade you two to come to Rome for a few days? We have an ossuary with an Aramaic inscription on it, and we certainly could use her expertise." There was a pause on the other end of the line, as Manny handed the phone to Grace.

"Hello, old friend. Rumors of my demise are premature. What's up?"

"It seems my friend Charlie has discovered the tomb of Andronicus and Junia, one of the first Christian power couples. The Latin inscription on the outside of the tomb identifies them as 'apostles of Christ' but here is where, hopefully, you come into the picture. The ossuary of the adult female in the tomb has an Aramaic inscription, hence our need for you to: 1) authenticate whether the Aramaic is in first century script; 2) translate the inscription accurately; and then 3) tell us its significance."

There was a pregnant pause on the other end of the line, and then, "This sounds too good to pass up. Manny, rev up the private jet, we're going to Rome for the weekend!"

"Excellent! Kahlil and I are staying at the D'Medici Hotel near Piazza Navona. We're on the way to the dig site for the first inspection. I'll call you again later today to check your schedule." Just as Art said that, suddenly the car screeched to a halt. There was a huge traffic snarl on the street that ran by the Coliseum. Police cars were everywhere, and a large number of police were busily inspecting the Arch of Titus. Something had gone wrong. There were TV crews and news teams all milling around. "Let's check this out," said Charlie, as he eased up a side street and found parking.

As they got out of the car, and began walking toward the arch they could see something had been done to the Arch of Titus. The closer they got to the arch, the more they could see bright red and green paint inside the arch at the spot where the famous relief of Titus' triumph was carved. But there were people running around the backside of the arch gesticulating and yelling as good Italians are prone to do when they are very upset. Art's Italian was not good enough to follow the drift of any of the conversations he was hearing which were going at such a clip that it sounded like machine gun fire. And finally when Kahlil, Art, and Charlie managed to get close enough to the site, and walk around the back of the arch, Art's only response was a horrified, "Oh no!" as he put his hands over his mouth in dismay. "What Italian would disrespect his own proud heritage that much?"

"The graffiti gangs who roam these streets, that's who!" said Charlie, who was equally dismayed. "Kahlil, can you imagine what would happen in Jerusalem if someone tried to spray paint the outside of the Dome of the Rock? There wouldn't just be police and photographers around; there would be riots!"

Kahlil nodded. "You are very right about that. It would be seen as a sacrilege. What a sad world we live in these days, when people spit on their own history and think they're creating art by spray painting over it. These people need to be arrested and prosecuted. They have definitely crossed the line."

Art simply said, "I think I'm going to be sick. This is going to take a sort of cleaning which will further deteriorate the already fragile relief of the menorah and the marchers in the triumph." To Art, whose love of history was so strong, this kind of behavior was incomprehensible, not to mention inexcusable.

Charlie's Italian had become good enough that he heard that the mayor was coming to make an announcement, so he said to his companions, "We should wait a few moments and hear the announcement. I imagine it's going to be a bombshell." After about another five minutes had passed, a large black sedan pulled up at the street in front of the arch, and Mayor Umberto Ferussi emerged. For an Italian, he was quite tall and tan, with his black hair neatly combed back and a carnation in his lapel. There was no mistaking the mayor. He stood out from the crowd, and there was no mistaking he was really angry. Charlie braced himself for a long harangue.

After a few preliminary remarks, the mayor launched into a tirade against graffiti artists in general and the persons who did this in particular. The mayor announced a 10,000 euro reward for information leading to the arrest of the person or persons responsible for this crime. He also announced that anyone caught defacing any public property would be incarcerated and prosecuted to the full extent of the law. He affirmed that apart from the wall set up for graffiti art, this behavior would no longer be tolerated. When this announcement was made, a cheer went up from the crowd, and even from the rather jaundiced members of the press. The mayor had thrown down the gauntlet, but it remained to be seen whether he had the will, the finances, and persistence to make his bold words stick.

"It's time to get back into our car, while the traffic has thinned a bit, and move on to our dig site," stressed Charlie.

The ride to the back of the Vatican proceeded in absolute silence, each man lost in his own thoughts. It takes a long time to create a masterpiece like the Arch of Titus, but only moments to ruin it.

13

Down in the Dig

FINALLY, THE CAR PULLED up to Charlie's reserved parking spot, and the three friends emerged. Charlie pulled out two backpacks of tools and things from the back of the van and gave one each to his companions. Charlie then crossed the street, got out his keys, and opened the steel door. Letting his friends in, he closed the door behind him and locked them all in. No one could bother them now, especially after he pushed two deadbolt locks through their slots on the inside part of the steel door. It would take a battering ram to get to them now. Flicking on the string of lights he had installed in the cave, Art and Kahlil began to adjust their eyes to the dim light, and their noses to the damp and musty smells of the tomb.

As it turned out, the tomb was larger than some family tombs, going back into the hill some twenty feet or so. Walking down the narrow corridor, Charlie stopped and shown his flashlight on a rectangular stone with a Latin inscription. "This was outside originally, but I moved it in here for safe keeping. Now everything of consequence is within this fortified cave." Sure enough the inscription in large capital Latin letters read just as Charlie had said . . .

HIC IACETUR ANDRONICUS ET JUNIA APOSTOLI CHRISTI.

There was no ambiguity about that inscription. It was as clear as one could wish. The man and woman were called apostles of Christ. Taking a few photos of the stone, Art decided he would just leave his camera out as they entered the space with the ossuaries, two small, two large. Raising his head too rapidly he conked his forehead on the roof of the cave. "Ancient people were vertically challenged," moaned Art, rubbing his head.

The ossuaries rested on stone slabs on either side of the chamber carved out of the bedrock. Inspecting the larger ones first, Art confirmed that the man's ossuary only had a toe tag inscription. The inscription on the ossuary that contained the man read in Greek . . .

> Here lies Andronicus, apostle of Christ, co-worker of Paul, loving husband of Junia, *martus Christou*

The last portion literally meant "witness of Christ" but, after Nero, had come to have the sense "martyr of Christ" as it seems to have in the book of Revelation. Looking into the ossuary itself, after Kahlil and Charlie had carefully lifted the lid, he noticed something immediately.

"Charlie, the head appears to have been severed from the spine. This surely suggests he was a Roman citizen and like Paul was beheaded. His execution is called a martyrdom. Do you reckon he was killed in the Neronian crackdown after the fire in AD 64?"

"That was my best guess, especially if these are the same persons mentioned around AD 57 when Paul wrote his letter to the Romans. Apparently they stayed here and ministered in Rome for some years, and like Paul eventually paid the price for it. But why not have them buried with other Christians in a Christian catacomb? Why here? This area did once have a necropolis but not a Christian one. Why are they here? I just don't know."

Kahlil was the first to look into the second ossuary and really there was little to see but bones arranged so they would fit in the bone box. Putting the lid back on the second ossuary, he started examining the Aramaic inscription and giving a rough translation. This one was actually on the side of the ossuary and was written in more formal script. "I don't think I've ever seen an Aramaic inscription this long on an ossuary before. This woman is certainly being lauded at length in her epitaph and that is unusual especially on women's ossuaries. It says, roughly . . .

> Joanna fell asleep in the Lord and was buried in this place. Follower of Jesus, witness of his cross and resurrection, loyal wife of Andronicus, co-worker of Paul, apostle of the Lord.

Art was dumbfounded. He had seen many ossuaries including the ones found in the tomb of Mary, Martha, and Lazarus, which he helped discover,[1] but only the Lazarus inscription had impressed him more than this one. "Notice, " said Art, "that Andronicus gets less press than this woman, presumably because she, along with someone like Peter, is one of the few original Galilean disciples who became leaders in the early church and ended up in Rome. I don't see any evidence of violence being done to her. No signs of crucifixion. Do you reckon she was poisoned?"

"Again, it's all conjecture," replied Charlie, shrugging his shoulders. "Or she could have died later and been buried after her husband was."

Kahlil had moved on to the children's burial boxes, and when he opened one of them and saw the tiny bones of a child no more than five, he began weeping. Kahlil was a tender-hearted soul, and was easily moved in the presence of tragedy. "Did they kill small children too? Were they killed just because they were part of a Christian family? It's horrible."

Instinctively he began reciting one of his favorite Kahlil Gibran poems—

> And a woman who held a babe against her bosom said, "Speak
>   to us of Children."
> And he said:
> Your children are not your children.
> They are the sons and daughters of Life's longing for itself.
> They come through you but not from you,
> And though they are with you, yet they belong not to you.
> You may give them your love but not your thoughts.
> For they have their own thoughts.
> You may house their bodies but not their souls,
> For their souls dwell in the house of tomorrow, which you can-
>   not visit, not even in your dreams.
> You may strive to be like them, but seek not to make them like
>   you.
> For life goes not backward nor tarries with yesterday.
> You are the bows from which your children as living arrows
>   are sent forth.

---

1. A tale told in the first Art West adventure, *The Lazarus Effect*.

The archer sees the mark upon the path of the infinite, and He
   bends you with His might that His arrows may go swift
   and far.
Let your bending in the archer's hand be for gladness;
For even as he loves the arrow that flies, so He loves also the
   bow that is stable.[2]

Art too took a quick look in the caskets. Only the single names
"Clement" and "Tryphosa" were etched into the end of the box. "Where
are the hand lamps you mentioned?"

Leaning up against the back wall of the cave was a small metal
cabinet Charlie had installed. He fumbled with the keys for a minute
in the dim light until he could open the box. Inside lay three well-pre-
served hand lamps, the ancient equivalent of flashlights. "Might I pick
them up," asked Kahlil as he slipped on white gloves. "It's hard to see in
the dim light here."

"Of course, just be careful," stressed Charlie.

2. This poem is from Gibran's most famous work *The Prophet*. It is in the public
domain.

Kahlil looked at each of the three more generic lamps in turn and said, "These lamps are pretty ordinary. The one distinctive feature is that they appear to me to be from the Eastern end of the Empire. I've seen lamps like these before and they didn't come from Greece and Rome, they came from Judaea or Egypt. In fact, most of the ones I've sold from my shop tested out to have been made from the clay or mud from the Nile itself. These three are slightly decorated with leaf or line patterns, but are very ordinary. It makes me wonder if they belonged to pilgrims, Christian pilgrims from the East, who came and visited this tomb. Was it a pilgrimage site?" Turning the lamps over, he did notice the small fish symbol on each one.

"Again, I have no answers," stressed Charlie. "I've just been cataloguing and being cautious because lamps and ossuaries and ancient Aramaic inscriptions are not my expertise. My expertise is in deciphering burn levels of a tel and economic levels of the people, including those buried at a site. My judgment is that these people, who could afford two rather nice ossuaries, were higher status persons."

Art was taking this all in, and added, "I need about ten minutes to take more pictures of everything, and then we can go discuss things at length above ground. I especially want to know how much you are willing for me to reveal to Father Peter when I see him in the morning."

"Yes, we must have a game plan, because anyway you cut it, this find is going to surprise a lot of people, including many in the Vatican."

Having been in the tomb for about forty minutes, when they emerged into the bright morning light, all three of the men had to squint to see for a few moments. Art immediately put on his sunglasses. The one thing he noticed out of the corner of his eye was a man in a black cowl hurrying down the opposite side of street. He did not give it a second thought, since monks and priests were a dime a dozen in this part of Rome, though he had to admit he had never seen a Black Friar here before.

14

Up in the Air

THE ADVANTAGES TO HAVING a rich husband were many, not the least of which was you could travel any time you wanted to any place. Manny's private jet was always ready to go at Tel Aviv airport. By the time they arrived Friday morning, the pilot had filed the flight plan, fueled, and taxied into position. All they had to do was walk across the tarmac and climb into the plane. Yes, there had been a security agent to clear them at the hanger, and rightly so, thought Grace. Manny had arranged a nice lunch on the plane, and they anticipated arriving at the hotel by mid-afternoon. Yes, indeed, there were many advantages to having a rich husband.

Grace's mental frame of mind had indeed changed, and she was beginning to regain some of the weight she had lost, but there was still a sadness, a pensiveness about her since her mother's funeral. Life would never be exactly the same again, and despite Manny's toothy grin and air of calmness, Grace was already fretting a bit about selling her mother's cottage. One thing that happens to a person who loses a loved one is that everything seems uncertain and tentative for a while, and one begins to worry about things one had never given a thought to before.

"So shall we begin to list the cottage for sale? We will need to do something with all that furniture Mom accumulated over the years. We certainly have no place for it in our house, even as big as it is."

"One thing at a time! There's no rush. Right now we're going to focus on a little Roman holiday, have a good time with friends, eat some fabulous Italian food, explore this new dig site, and in general forget about the last month or so when you were dealing with your mother's decline and funeral. I must say, I was impressed with your ability to sit *shiva* that whole week after the funeral."

In the practice of observant Jews, the funeral and burial are held almost immediately, within one day of death if possible. Camelia's four closest living relatives assumed the status of mourners as is the custom. Including the day of the funeral, they stayed with Grace for seven days, the period of *shiva*, helping her receive visitors.

At the funeral, Orthodox mourners traditionally rend an outer garment, a ritual known as *keriah*. The torn garment is worn throughout *shiva*. Outside of the Orthodox community, a common alternative is to wear a small torn black ribbon pinned to one's clothes. Grace and her family wore the black ribbons and accepted guests all week, although they did so from Grace's spacious nearby home, not Camelia's beachside cottage.

"I had to do that to honor my mother, but it took a lot out of me, especially visiting with all those people who came to offer their condolences. I never knew Mom had so many local friends. And as you know, I couldn't really eat much of the food the neighbors brought that week. I'm still up in the air about how to respond to the care shown me. Thank you cards seem inadequate."

"You are indeed up in the air just now honey," chuckled Manny, "and isn't that the dinner bell I hear? May I escort you to the dining room?"

"I thought you'd never ask," replied Grace as she took her husband's arm and walked carefully into the next compartment of the plane. One thing about Manny, his chef gave a whole new and better meaning to the phrase "airplane food." It was anything but "plain" food.

15

The Truth Be Told

POPE JEROME WAS VISITING Austria when Brother Tertullian discovered what was going on at the dig site behind the Vatican. Brother Tertullian, whose real name was Magnus McIlroy, was a Scottish Catholic, of the ancient order of Black Friars, and a real bulldog when it came to being a defender of Catholic tradition. Like the original Tertullian, he did not suffer fools gladly, nor was he patient with what he deemed unorthodox or heretical views of things. In his mind, Catholic Tradition and Truth, with a capital T, was one and the same thing. Zeal for the one was the same as zeal for the other. Under the heading of unorthodox views was the suggestion that women should be allowed to be priests.

Brother Tertullian made it a regular practice to follow that busybody reporter named Adriano Andretti, because he had already become infamous for several articles criticizing the Pope and questioning Catholic dogma. Tertullian saw secular reporters in general as accidents waiting to happen. Tailing Andretti the other night had proven to be a fruitful night's work.

First thing Thursday, the Black Friar had gone straight to Father Salta's office to deliver the tape recorder before returning to his spy post at the dig site. Now, he was having another meeting with the preacher to the Pope only an hour before Art's scheduled visit. "So Father Pietro, what will you do with this information?" asked the friar, sitting and sipping a cup of tea with Father Peter.

"In the first place, unfortunately, most of the conversation is a bit sketchy! I'm not entirely sure what we are dealing with here, though it sounded as though the archaeologists believe they have found the tomb of Andronicus and Junia, which in itself is not a problem. I'm actually more upset about how you came to have this tape recorder! Are you telling me you assaulted a reporter and stole his bag!? You used the seal of the confession, presumably so that I can't turn you in. Never put me in that position again, do you understand! The items must be returned!"

"Yes, Father," said the friar feigning meekness.

"You are lucky the reporter got no more than bruises when you tackled him. Seriously, this is not Christian, never mind Catholic, conduct. The end does not justify using those kinds of means to get at the truth. Indeed, using those kinds of means defiles the very cause you serve, which presumably is the truth."

"Yes, Father, I will keep that in mind in the future. But now I have to report that all three archaeologists came to the dig, locked themselves in the hole in the ground, and did not emerge for some time. I could not tell if they took anything from the tomb, but they certainly had cameras with them. That is the latest news I have. And I did wonder, might they be digging illegally on Vatican land? At least part of that hole in the ground, if it goes far enough back from the street, might be on our turf?"

"That is a question worth asking," replied Father Peter stroking his little white beard. The Ministry of Culture, which I discovered authorized this dig, has no jurisdiction when it comes to things found on Vatican property. It's ours fair and square and we would have to authorize the dig." This conversation went on for some time, until it dawned on Father Salta that Art West was due at his office any minute now. Quickly dismissing Brother Tertullian, Father Peter was lost in thought for a moment.

A Black Friar was a Dominican, not a Jesuit, not a Franciscan, and so he was of a very different order than Father Peter. Technically, Father Peter had no direct authority over any Dominican priest, only the Holy Father did. And what this meant was, he could not banish this man or send him back to Scotland. So he must reflect on whether it would be worth talking to Pope Jerome about doing so, and removing the problem of this loose cannon, or in this case, loose canon. While pondering this matter, a knock came on the door. His secretary Maria stuck her head inside the huge, thick mahogany door, and announced, "Your next appointment has arrived."

"Excellent. Show him in, and please brew us up another pot of tea, and bring some chocolate biscuits as well."

"Straight away," she said, holding the door open as Art West entered with a big smile on his face.

Art West had known Father Peter for some years now. He first met him at Asbury Seminary when he preached in the chapel and held workshops for the seminary students. At the time, Art was a visiting professor of archaeology living in Lexington, Kentucky.

"Please Professor West, come take a comfortable seat and join me," said Father Peter, "It's been too long since I have seen you. What brings you to Rome in this overly warm season of the year?"

Seating himself in a beautiful red leather chair—the twin of the one Father Peter sat down in just on the other side of a little cherry tea table—Art noticed immediately that Father Peter had a huge library in this office. There had to be at least 2000 books on the many shelves that took up every inch of the wall space in this office, except for where the one door opened. Art admired the scholarly approach Father Peter took to homiletics. His preaching workshops at Asbury were a great success. A friendship had been struck up between the two men. Peter was hoping for a frank conversation between friends on the possibly delicate matter at hand.

"First, let me thank you for seeing me on such short notice," began Art. "So I will come straight to the point. My friend, Dr. Charlie Miller, has been in charge of a summer dig beneath the street that lies directly behind the back tourist entrance to the Vatican Museum. And it has produced some remarkable findings. I am here to talk directly to you, because some of these findings may be a little hard to swallow in some Catholic quarters!"

Looking concerned, Father Peter wrinkled his brow and said, "How so?"

Handing over a photo of the Latin inscription, Art continued rather excitedly, "This was on the lintel just over the entrance outside the tomb itself." Art studied Father Peter's face.

HIC IACETUR ANDRONICUS ET JUNIA APOSTOLI CHRISTI.

Father Peter tried to stay calm despite the ominous cloud hanging over him. Friar Tertullian had certainly complicated matters. He finally took a deep breath and looked up. "This is certainly a surprise and it seems rather clear. Of course, I am familiar with Romans 16, and this would seem to confirm that the 'Junias' mentioned there is actually a Junia. Fair enough—these two must be husband and wife! But here they are obviously called apostles of Christ. There is room for debate about what apostles might mean in Romans 16—'among the apostles' or how about 'to the apostles.' The Latin here seems to favor the former, don't you think? The Latin here seems to say that they are apostles. And apostles buried right next to Vatican property, right under our noses! I know of no tradition at all in the Church Fathers about their burial spot, do you?"

"No, I don't. But if they died during the Neronian crackdown, it makes sense they were buried in or near Rome, don't you agree?"

"Actually, I do!" Silence ensued.

Then Art spoke up again. "But Father Peter, I have more evidence I want to share with you. There are four ossuaries in the tomb, two adult and two children's burial boxes. And there is an Aramaic inscription on one of the boxes. My friend Kahlil el Said from Jerusalem is here in Rome with me. His rendering of the Aramaic, not my area of expertise, is this . . .

> Joanna fell asleep in the Lord and was buried in this place.
> Follower of Jesus, witness of his cross and resurrection, loyal
> wife of Andronicus, co-worker of Paul, apostle of the Lord.

Before you ask, let me add that, as we speak, Dr. Grace Levine, one of the world's leading authorities on first century Aramaic inscriptions, is coming to evaluate this one. My guess is she will verify his translation."

Father Peter's eyes got big and he could not prevent himself from exclaiming, "Oh my Lord! Are we really talking about that Joanna? I know Junia is simply the Latin equivalent name, but really? The woman who traveled around with Jesus is buried here! And there is an Aramaic, not Latin or Greek, inscription on her ossuary! Can you imagine what the revelation of her presence here would do for our people who go on pilgrimage? But the apostolic issue is a problem, of course. Catholic liberals pushing for female priests will go ballistic when they hear about this!"

Art sat quietly and let Father Peter process this whole situation for a while. Finally, Art said, "It is possible that some of these finds are actually on Vatican property, so they would not have to be turned over to the Ministry of Culture but to the Vatican. Someone with a better sense of where the property line actually intersects with the cave will have to decide. I will tell you that the outside inscription was not on your property, but it's possible some of the ossuaries and hand lamps were. What is important is that the outside inscription is simply confirmed by the inside inscriptions on both the adult ossuaries. There is no getting around that. The truth will come out, even if it's just on the basis of the outside inscription and the pictures several of us have of what is inside the cave."

Father Peter seemed to be meditating, so Art kept gently feeding him more information to mull over. "Personally, I would prefer that these ossuaries be turned over to you folks, not the secular authorities. Someone needs to come and figure where the city's land stops and your land starts underground. And you had best double check whether the city has some sort of eminent domain law so they could claim anything found while digging a new spot for a sewer line. Do you know how we can verify the boundaries before there is a turf war?"

Father Peter slowly raised his head, "First of all, even though some of this is an inconvenient bit of news, some of it is quite exciting! We love our saints and martyrs! So I will certainly wend my way through the bureaucracy and get the answers we both need. Meanwhile, I wonder if it could be argued they were just missionaries, since *apostoloi* could mean that?"

Art shook his head. "I thought of that, but in the NT the phrase for that was apostle of a named church, not apostle of Christ, and anyway, the Aramaic inscription says Joanna saw the risen Jesus, which is Paul's pre-requisite for being an apostle of Christ, as he claims in 1 Corinthians 9."

Father Peter countered, "True, but there is room for debate on that point. Nevertheless, this is very remarkable! May I ask Art if you folks would hold your fire for a bit, until I've talked to the right Vatican people. I assume there is no big rush to publish this news, right?"

"No," agreed Art, "but every day brings danger of a leak. Anything could be claimed. But I promise you, none of us have talked to any reporters, and we will wait to hear back from you before doing so."

"Thank you for that," said Father Peter who was suddenly sweating. "I knew you were trustworthy and would tell me the truth." Father Peter wished he could say the same about himself at this point. He debated for a split second whether to tell Art about Brother Tertullian and the theft of Andretti's notes. Could he simply cover up the friar's part in all of this? The notes were sketchy but in a reporter's hands could easily be fleshed out into a fairly accurate description of inscriptions and ossuaries and the remains of Andronicus and Junia. The tape from the tape recorder revealed a Q&A between Andretti and someone who had overheard Art and others talking about the matter, presumably in some public venue. Would Andretti publish bits and pieces or hold out for a bigger story? Father Peter hoped for the latter. On a whim he suggested, "Let's get out of here and have some lunch!" Art was all for staying on the good Father's good side.

16

The Word is Out

F RIDAY'S FLIGHT TO ROME had been pleasantly uneventful, and
Manny had simply hired a limo service to drive them into downtown Rome to their hotel by midafternoon. When they arrived Art was
still with Father Peter, but both Kahlil and Charlie were there to meet
Grace and Manny, and help them settle in. Not surprisingly, Manny
booked the penthouse suite, and the hotel busboys were falling all over
themselves trying to help with the luggage and other matters.

Kahlil noticed that Grace was thinner than when he had last seen
her in Jerusalem, but her color was good, and her wit was as razor sharp
as ever. "So when are you going to give me a hug Omar Sharif?"

"Right now, of course," said Kahlil with a smile. "It is good to see
you out and about, Grace."

Charlie hated to break up the reunion, but he wanted to get Grace
to look at the Aramaic inscription right away. Pictures would not suffice, and besides she needed to inspect the ossuary itself—the shape
and size of the letters as well as the patina were all important. After
friendly banter, Charlie smiled and said, "We still have some time this
afternoon for you to see the site. I told Art I would give him a ring if
we went over there, but I think he is doing his best this afternoon to
make nice with the Vatican! Would you mind going to work for a little
while? I'm anxious to see what you think about this remarkable ancient
ossuary?"

Grace simply nodded her head and said, "Darling, I have to change out of my bling. It won't do to scuff up my shoes and jewelry in some damp cave. So you must wait for me to change into something much more suitable. If it's alright Manny wants to come as well, but I insist that he change too. Armani and Gucci will revoke our permission to stay in Italy if we visit a cave in these clothes." Charlie laughed. Grace could not be pressured, nor could she be rushed, and Manny was not used to taking orders from anyone but Grace.

An hour later the elevator opened in the old lobby of the D'Medici, and Grace and Manny emerged looking like they were ready to go camping. Grace was wearing jeans and a simple denim shirt, while Manny was wearing his usual out-of-office attire, jeans and his basketball team's jersey (Maccabee Elite). The four rendezvoused in the lobby just as the news agent arrived with a stack of the late afternoon papers. Charlie instantly grabbed one.

Charlie, who read Italian well enough, suddenly froze in place. At the bottom of page one he read, UN' APOSTOLA FEMINA TROVATA SOTTO IL VATICANO! He quickly handed everyone a paper and translated loudly, "Grave of woman apostle found near the Vatican!" Charlie looked at everyone in the circle, groaned and continued: "Now we're really going to draw attention to ourselves—all the wrong sort of attention!" He pointed to a small picture of the steel door and entrance way to the tomb. "How could this have happened? How did he get this information?" he exclaimed.

Grace sighed and coolly replied, "Well, the quicker we get in and out of there, the better. This headline is already on the net speeding around the globe. The Vatican will probably go into damage control mode. The cat is out of the bag now!"

The four jumped into Charlie's car and headed once again to the tomb. This time, they took a back route, just in case anyone was already tailing them. Charlie hoped that other reporters were just now hearing the news and he reckoned he and his companions could slip into the tomb relatively unnoticed.

This tack seemed to be working until Adriano Andretti, complete with a bandage on his head, came running towards them after patiently waiting most of the day. "*Mi scusi*! I am Adriano Andretti and I must speak with you!" But Charlie refused to make eye contact, and Manny, a large man by any standards, held the reporter at arm's length while

Charlie unlocked the tomb door. They all rapidly slipped inside, leaving Adriano to cool his heels outside.

Taking his friends directly to the back of the cave, Charlie said, "We can examine these other artifacts later, but let me set up my halogen lamp here so you can see everything perfectly Grace." This took a moment. Manny was muttering, "This place smells like my old aunt's musty basement. At least it's cool in here." With the ossuary fully illuminated, Grace began to scour the surface of it.

"This is typical ancient limestone, of pretty good quality, though it has become yellowed and pitted due to the moisture in here. There is no formal or honorific inscription on the man's ossuary, but we do have an identifier inscription, semi-honorific, on this ossuary belonging to the woman," began Grace.

"Good," agreed Charlie. "It's the woman's ossuary that will get the most publicity."

"Make no bones about it," quipped Grace, "the writer of the Aramaic inscription wants no mistakes to be made as to whose bones are in this ossuary. The Aramaic itself is middle-period Aramaic, which suits a first century date and there are clear signs of ancient patina in all the letters, but this would need to be chemically tested for confirmation. The Aramaic is not formal script, but more casual and cursive. I don't see any reference to ancestors."

Charlie concurred, "That's customary. Early Christians tended to see themselves as part of a new family, Christ's body, or brothers and sisters in Christ. Her husband is mentioned, however, which we often find with Roman epitaphs on steles and the like. The very use of an ossuary is surely rare in Rome, so these are Jews and someone bought Jewish burial boxes. The bones were kept together because of the belief in the future resurrection, and the reference to 'asleep in the Lord' was because it was believed she would awaken on the day of resurrection, refreshed and renewed as if she had been asleep in the normal sense. Death is not seen as permanent when one believes in resurrection, and so why not call it sleep?"

Grace made a mental note to compare these Christian ideas of death with her Jewish beliefs. Meanwhile, however, she remarked, "There is no doubt that the Aramaic refers to this woman as what came to be called an apostle of Christ. My guess is, this is indeed the Joanna mentioned in the Gospels as a high status wife of a Galilean estate manager named Chuza, Junia very likely being the name Jews picked for a Latin equivalent for Joanna."

Standing up, Grace dusted off her hands and said, "Yep, this is a major find, and probably does refer to a biblical figure who became a Christian apostle and co-worker of Paul. This one deserves all the ink and analysis it is bound to get, especially since the story has already been leaked in the press."

Manny and Grace were shown the other artifacts briefly and then Charlie sensed it was time for them to go.

"I'm sure I don't have to warn you that Adriano Andretti, the reporter who wrote the story, will still be waiting for us at the door. In fact, I think we will be seeing a lot of him in the next few days. I sure would like to know who gave him the story!" sighed Charlie.

Getting out turned out to be more difficult than getting in. They could only exit one by one and Adriano badgered each one in turn for a statement. But these witnesses remained silent, walked briskly to the car, and drove away quickly with Adriano left behind cursing them. Life was about to be much more complicated. At least, thought Adriano, my cameraman got shots of all of them emerging from the tomb.

17

Stirring the Pot on the Back Burner

Boz tugged on his scraggly beard and pondered his next move. While he was thrilled with the fact that he had gotten away with painting an iconic site like the Arch of Titus, he wondered what he could do for an encore. It occurred to him that if he wanted to live to paint another day, it might be wise to lay low for a while until things died down, and the security at major sites became more relaxed again. However, resting on his laurels had never been one of his strengths.

"Phillipo, I think it's time to do a bit more reconnaissance at that tomb behind the Vatican. Yesterday's headlines about some female apostle demand more attention to the site. Marco has done his share of standing around watching the site. How about you take over the sentry duties there for a while, and see what the security is like? Do a little scouting to see if there might not be another way to get into that tomb."

Phillipo, a rather pudgy short Italian who was absolutely loyal to Boz and his mission did not have to be asked twice. He was off like a shot with just a nod of his head indicating he understood what needed to happen. He would report in at regular intervals.

Boz got on his bright red Ducati motorcycle and headed away from his personal catacomb to a little *trattoria* he frequented. Boz sat outside at one of the tables in the garden reading the Saturday morning paper, and savoring the editorials that he had stirred up with his artwork. What could he do to top this? A large smile creased his face, and suddenly he realized that someone was hovering just over his right shoulder. "*Mi scusi*," said the waiter, "something to drink?"

"Amaretto black cherry granita," said Boz with a grin. "And a cornetto *per favore*." Boz had to admit that it would be hard to top what he had just pulled off. The problem for Boz was that, unlike some graffiti artists who found channels through which to sell their art, he did not have much of a head for business. Indeed, he despised business, thought it was a waste of time for an artist like himself. Day after day selling your artistic soul, euro by euro, did not appeal to him in the least. He had never been a thief, but . . .

A lazy Saturday morning slowly passed with Boz reading the entire newspaper. All of a sudden his cellphone began to jangle, and he flipped it open to see that he had a call from Philippo. The man was nothing if not dependable. "Boss, as you might imagine there is a large crowd here drawn by the report by Andretti about the discovery at this tomb. It wouldn't be wise to try anything for a while here due to all the media attention. But, I did manage to survey the top of the little slope above the tomb entrance. There is an area where one could dig, but it would have to be done quickly, quietly, and in the middle of the night. I had an idea about that. Remember the city construction crew that has been here working on a new sewer line? What if we dressed up in official looking city construction worker uniforms and pretended to be coming back to inspect our work and the conduit that leads out of the Vatican into the main sewer under the street there? This might fool the officials for a few hours."

Boz nearly leapt out of his seat. "Brilliant, Philippo, *benissimo*! This is one of your best ideas ever! Let's round up the guys and plan this back at the catacomb. See you tonight!" Putting his cellphone back in his pocket, Boz began to imagine the euros he might get hold of through this heist. "Waiter!" he hollered at the little man who was heading back into the restaurant, "One more granita, and bring me a dish of your best gelato as well! I am celebrating!"

~

The Black Friar had been in a pensive mood since his little interview with Father Peter. He was having a hard time waiting until the Holy Father returned to the Vatican the following week, and events were moving too fast. What if the artifacts in that tomb were extracted before he could stifle the story? What if they were put somewhere out of his reach? At least for now, he knew where they were. What should a good decisive Dominican do to protect his Catholic traditions? Couldn't he claim the objects in the back of that cave belonged to the Vatican and therefore they should be confiscated before they fell into the wrong hands? Wasn't this Friday's headline enough of a warning?

Magnus hadn't counted on Father Peter's cautionary approach. Was he oblivious to the damage this archaeological find could do to the arguments for the traditional male priesthood in the Catholic Church, never mind to the celibacy tradition? He didn't seem to appreciate the simmering pot of trouble. If need be, he would take action first, and then explain things later to the Holy See. He listened to the tape recording several times over, and it was clear enough they were talking about: 1) a female apostle named Junia, who 2) apparently was an original disciple of Jesus and had witnessed the resurrection appearances but ended up here in Rome and had something to do with the early founding of the church in the Eternal City. This was beyond disturbing. How could the Catholic tradition about apostles and priests be that far wrong about the history of the clerical offices? Apparently it was not just the Twelve and Paul who were apostles. For Magnus, these ideas set off a profound and visceral reaction within his whole psyche, as if his whole Catholic faith was under siege. Something definitely must be done, and soon!

Father Peter had to admit that while the tomb of Andronicus and Junia and its contents produced some worries for him, he was still intrigued enough by the Star of David and where he had found it so far, that he began to look in various other places as well. This morning he was in the tomb beneath the grotto of St. Peter, where the saint's remains were found, holding his flashlight, and combing the walls and passageways looking for clues. "Seek and you will find" said Jesus, and he was seeking. After about an hour of looking, high and low on ceilings, walls, door frames, right at the back of the grotto, where two walls came together at a right angle, Father Peter noticed something, or a part of something painted on the wall. There seemed to be an arrow pointing to the right, but the point of the arrow was partially obscured by the right hand wall. Could there be something behind this right hand wall, a chamber or passageway perhaps that had long since been sealed off? And why would it have been sealed off anyway? But what really peeked his curiosity was beneath the arrow was what looked to be part of a star, could it be another Star of David?

Father Peter came out of the tomb and sat down in one of the many pews in St. Peter's. He must think carefully. The word "aster" means star in Greek. It is the word from which comes the term astrology, the study of the stars. The Star of David, however, which is currently the symbol of Israel and the Jewish religion, would have originally had messianic connotations on the basis of both the prophecy in Numbers, and of course the star of Bethlehem.

But this was Rome. There were no such prophecies about Jews or Christians in Rome. Why then the star symbol in these odd places? Perhaps he should consider the possibility that before the cross became a major Christian symbol, Jewish Christians, which is to say messianic Jews, Jews who believed their messiah had come, may have used the Star of David symbol for Jewish Christians and their beliefs and perhaps for pointers towards their meeting places? It was only a theory, but it was the best one he could come up with on short notice. One thing was sure. He wanted to find out what was behind that wall which obscured the arrow and the star. Those symbols were not carved in the rock there for nothing. There was a feeling in the air that something momentous was about to happen, and Father Peter wanted to be prepared.

18

Eternal Treasures in Earthen Vessels

CHARLIE MILLER MADE AN executive decision. He was going to extract both the pottery lamps and the lintel sign from the tomb. So far the press had been low key, except for Adriano's annoying presence. However, better safe than sorry. Monday morning he would make sure the pieces were safely removed and stored.

For now, Charlie read back over one of his favorite Pauline passages from 2 Corinthians.

> For God, who said, "Let light shine out of darkness," made his light shine in our hearts to give us the light of the knowledge of God's glory displayed in the face of Christ. But we have this treasure in earthen vessels to show that this all-surpassing power is from God and not from us. We are hard pressed on every side, but not crushed; perplexed, but not in despair; persecuted, but not abandoned; struck down, but not destroyed.

Charlie believed that when Paul juxtaposed the idea of being a container of light with the reference to treasure in earthen vessels that he was referring to pottery lamps exactly like the one's sitting in the tomb he had excavated. Meditating on the Scripture, Charlie saw the fragile small pottery lamp as an image of the frail human form that can nonetheless contain the light of God, indeed the presence of God within. The thing about those pottery lamps was that the thinner they were, the more light got out.

So it is with us all, thought Charlie. The less I get in the way of the light in my life, the more the light shines in the darkness. Charlie had no interest at all in exploiting his archaeological find. But he was going to talk at length with various officials about how to reveal the evidence and implications of what had been found in this tomb.

Today he would enjoy the company of his friends, new and old, and then on Sunday he would go to church with Art. Having settled that in his mind, he decided to ring up Art who was resting in his room, and suggest they all go out for some of the delicious coffee and gelato to be found in the little cafes surrounding the Piazza Navona. Rather than drive, he hopped a bus from Vatican City to Piazza Navona, and met the group in the hotel lobby.

"Okay, who can tell me why the piazza is so big and so oval?!" quizzed Charlie. "Sorry Art, you aren't allowed to play! First one with the right answer gets a free gelato!"

Grace raised her hand. "It's built on the site of a gigantic stadium, the Circus Maximus of Domitian's Day."

"That would be the first century," piped in Kahlil. "So it was a big stadium for the Roman games—but which ones?"

"In the beginning, basically track and field, but eventually they had horse racing and even naval battles apparently. Can you picture 30,000 spectators sitting around this oval in marble seats."

"Marbleous," quipped Manny, "Maybe I should put marble seats in my stadium for the basketball games! But I doubt I can afford to decorate with those fountains."

"You would have to get Bernini himself to design fountains like that," suggested Charlie. "Everyone's favorite fountain is this middle one of the three, the famous Fontana dei Quattro Fiumi or Fountain of the Four Rivers. Yes, that's a genuine Egyptian obelisk rising from the center!"

"Let's walk down to the southern end," suggested Art. When they got there, Charlie described the second large fountain.

"The *Fontana del Moro* has a basin and four Tritons sculpted by Giacomo della Porta but Bernini added a statue of a Moor, or African, wrestling with a dolphin. And right over there is one of my favorite gelato shops, so let's stop and enjoy. Grace, yours is on me as promised, but I get first dibs on the pistachio!"

Kahlil was more interested in the street performers. These pantomime artists could hold a pose so well they rivaled the real statues in the fountains. But with the right incentive—a few coins in a cup—they would come "alive" and entertain the tourists. After watching intently while enjoying a coffee gelato, he said, "Okay, it's a long walk to the northern end. By that time I'll need some real coffee."

When they arrived Art was allowed to tell everyone that they were looking at the Fountain of Neptune created by Giacomo della Porta in the late 1500s. "But the statue of Neptune was added later by Antonio Della Bitta."

Despite the heat, the crowds were milling around and tourist groups abounded. Kahlil noted, "I see the tourists here are all wearing audio headsets. Those gadgets have revolutionized touring. It's so nice to be in Jerusalem without having to tune out the dueling tour guides. I don't know how the tourists ever heard what they said."

Charlie agreed. "The wireless radio guides were introduced around 2001. What a difference it has made! The visitors can listen even at a distance and not try to jockey for position near the guide. It made picture taking a lot easier too—I should know!"

"Yeah, I see you still have your trademark camera around your neck," laughed Art. "How about a few group photos! Maybe we can grab a waiter to do the honors!" The waiter was indeed willing and after some photos, everyone settled down for a good cup of espresso at one of the outdoor cafes.

The group was quickly seated under the shade of a big umbrella, and the menus were soon produced. There were so many different coffees. Grace was so intent on reading the menu that she didn't notice that the waiter with the pencil-thin moustache was quietly waiting.

"Signora?' he said as Grace looked up at him.

"Give me a large cappuccino with whip cream," she said with confidence.

"*Perfetto,*" replied the waiter with a smile.

"I'll have the same thing," said Art. Manny ordered an espresso; Charlie had his usual frothed up cup of coffee; and Kahlil asked for a cup of Turkish coffee. And everyone asked for a slice of tiramisu!

"I guess we're going to fulfill that prophecy of Isaiah 55 where it says 'delight thyself in fatness!'" quipped Art. "You know, of course, that coffee is actually a Christian beverage."

"How so? I thought it all began with Turkish coffee," challenged Kahlil.

"Nope. It all began in Ethiopia. The goats were eating the Yirgacheffe coffee beans and jumping around. Then the goatherds tried them. And then they sold them to monks in an Ethiopian monastery who were mighty cold at night. It was the monks who crushed the beans and put them in hot water, and in essence brewed the first coffee. And the news and art of making coffee travelled from monastery to monastery. Did you know that the name cappucino comes from the Cappuchin monk's hoods, which not accidentally is the same color as that little cup of Java we drink. Yes, indeed, coffee is the monastery's gift to the world, and the Turkish traders learned the art and made the most of it. The history of coffee in America is a sadder tale, but I'll save that story for later."

"In that case," said Charlie, "Let's have a little chat about what to do with the antiquities. I don't have a problem with either the Vatican or the Ministry of Culture taking care of these objects," said Charlie, "but I wonder what happens if we let the Vatican come into the tomb, take measurements and then figure out what parts belong to them? I've decided, unless someone says 'don't do it' to extract the lamps and the lintel from the tomb and secure them in a safe place. They are really the only objects that could be easily stolen."

Kahlil was savoring his coffee, nursing it along holding it with both hands. "I agree. This is a major find so you can't be too careful. My guess would be those pottery lamps will bring thousands of dollars on the open market because we know where they came from."

Charlie concluded, "Fine. Then it's settled. But I've got to figure out where to put these objects once we extract them. I do have to turn them over to someone at the Ministry of Culture or at the Vatican. First we need the Vatican surveyor to determine where the line is for the Vatican property."

Art, never one to waste time, immediately got out his phone. "Father Peter, it's Art West. I'm sitting here with Charlie Miller and the rest of the crew. I'm sure you saw yesterday's paper. We're planning to remove the objects and store them safely. Do you have any thoughts at this point?"

Father Peter replied, "I'm glad you called. After seeing the paper, I talked to our archaeology director who immediately rung up the Ministry of Culture, who immediately said that they are claiming eminent domain! I don't personally think they have a good legal argument, but our people quickly called our lawyers, and this will need to wait until next week to be resolved. In the meanwhile, the chief Minister of Culture, Rosario Pollo, assured me they will take no action to confiscate things prior to the resolution of the legal issue. You folks need to talk to him soon, however!"

Art just groaned. "Right. Charlie has a meeting scheduled for next week. Do let me know as soon as you know something about the Vatican's stand."

"Of course," promised Father Peter as he hung up.

"Well, Charlie your plan has been partially nixed due to legal wrangling. But there is nothing preventing us from temporarily extracting the small artifacts and keeping them in a safe place."

"Good. On Monday morning bright and early, we will take care of the matter." The conversation continued for a good while longer, but they were not unnoticed.

19

A Day of Rest?

SUNDAY IN ROME IS always a special day. The traffic is about half of what it would normally be during the workweek, and the town is full of the sound of ringing bells from the literally hundreds of chapels and churches and basilicas in the downtown area calling the faithful to worship. Grace, Manny, Kahlil, Charlie and Art all arrived an hour early at St. Peter's to attend the 11:30 Mass in the Chapel of the Blessed Sacrament.

The faithful were filing into the basilica past the security guards checking to make sure the visitors were properly and modestly dressed. Some were turned away. Readily admitted were a whole group of nuns in gray, a group of monks in brown, one group of French tourists, and devout locals. Promptly at 11:30 the procession began—first the acolytes to light the candles, then the crucifer to carry the cross, then the children's choir, then the regular priests, then a visiting bishop swinging the incense holder back and forth and finally Father Peter, the Apostolic Preacher, the Preacher to the Papal Household.

As the service proceeded on in Italian, with a bit of Latin here and there, it dawned on them all that while they would hear Father Peter, they would not necessarily understand Father Peter! The Scripture, however, was familiar. And art got enough of the sermon to realize it was some sort of word study distinguishing between the various kinds of love, and even referencing C.S. Lewis's *The Four Loves* at one point. Father Peter was a well-read priest and a fine preacher. Though he could not fully grasp the message, Art admired the ethos, the gestures, the voice, the delivery of the message that was obviously rhetorically effective, for people left commenting on it.

As the friends emerged into the bright noon sun, Charlie suggested they go to Bella Notte, his favorite traditional restaurant for a big meal. All was calm, and all seemed well and everyone was looking forward to Monday morning.

~

On a moonless night, a black van pulled up behind the Vatican. Two men exited the van wearing uniforms and carrying bags of tools, including drilling equipment. Putting up orange signs before and behind the van and in front of the entrance to the tomb, they began almost immediately digging and then drilling on the bank above the tomb. To the few people passing by, they looked like city workers fixing some underground problem. Everything looked official enough.

Finally, the two men broke through the dirt and rock, and cleared away the debris. Boz slipped down into the hole. The man standing over the hole did not see the dark figure quietly creeping up on him from behind until it was too late. Philippo took a heavy blow to the head. The new man in black then dropped into the hole. But he was no match for Boz.

20

Morning Has Broken

A T 6:00 A.M. A glow began on the horizon, but most things were still in the shadows in Rome. The early delivery trucks were speeding around, making the most of light traffic as they delivered their produce and papers and products to various businesses nearby. The white panel van was no longer parked behind the Vatican, though the orange plastic cones still remained. The man now sitting on the little slope above the tomb was rubbing his face and beginning to remember what had happened to him. His head ached. Reaching behind he found dried blood and a huge welt. Then Philippo heard the groans of someone in the tomb.

Peering down, he could make out nothing in the darkness. Philippo decided to try talking to the groaning man. "Is that you, Boz?" Moaning was the only reply. Philippo peered again into the hole and could see a black robe, which was enough to let him know it was not Boz! Still not thinking entirely straight Philippo stood up and realized he desperately needed to urinate. Not a man to stand on modesty, he decided he would take his revenge on his assumed attacker, peeing directly into the hole in the ground, which produced an outcry, and a burst of laughter from Philippo. Then he discovered he had been left stranded. Boz had apparently driven off without him. He had at least enough of his wits about him to trundle off to the nearest subway station, and get himself underground. But where could Boz be?

~

An early breakfast was quickly consumed, and once more they found themselves in Charlie's van heading across town. This morning the traffic was saturated with taxis and motorbikes weaving in and out of the traffic. Art was anxious about getting the precious objects secured, and he could see Charlie was feeling the same way, because when Charlie got worried about something he usually clammed up. This morning when Kahlil tried to engage Charlie in conversation, Charlie's answers had been clipped. Kahlil finally gave up. The Cohens sat silently in the back seat with Art, lost in their own thoughts.

Rounding the corner onto the street known as Stradone del Giardini, Charlie immediately noticed something was odd. There were orange cones sitting in front of the door into the dig site. No construction workers, no police, just orange cones. Snagging their normal parking space, the fivesome headed straight to the door, moving a couple of the cones out of the way. Charlie fumbled with his keys in his anxiousness to get the door open, but finally managed to open it. Immediately he noticed a change. A shaft of light was penetrating into the central chamber at the back of the tomb and he could see debris and rubble on the floor of the cave. Turning to his friends he asked, "Could you all wait here for a moment? There may be a problem."

Charlie arrived in the back of the cave to find: 1) a pile of dirt and rock; 2) the metal case broken into and left open, with no sign of the pottery lamps or the lintel sign; 3) the two small ossuaries missing; and 4) a moaning monk on the floor of the cave! Charlie called for Art.

Turning the monk over, Art recognized immediately it was the Black Friar he had met in passing at the Vatican when meeting with Father Peter. "I'm going to call an ambulance; I'll be back in a minute," promised Art. Charlie simply stood there in shock, muttering to himself, "This was precisely what I feared might happen." Standing there in shock, the monk simply moaned and seemed to smell of urine for some reason.

Stepping outside into the brighter light, Art turned to Kahlil and the Cohens and reported, "The tomb has been broken into from above over the weekend; various things have been stolen; and there's a Dominican friar lying on the floor in there! I've got to make some calls." First Art dialed Rome's equivalent of 911, and finally made the operator understand where to send the ambulance. He then rang up Father

Peter. After two rings he picked up, "*Buongiorno,*" said the deep voice on the other end of the line.

"Father Peter, it's Art West. I am so sorry to have to report there's been a break-in at the tomb, and I found that Black Friar, the one who left your office last Friday morning, in the tomb. I think he was hit with something. He's not doing well. I've called for the ambulance. But I thought you should know at once before the police charge the man with something."

There was stunned silence for a moment and then Father Peter replied, "This can only mean that Magnus was meddling in ways he shouldn't have been! I must offer apologies to Professor Miller. Would you like me to come around now? I'll just come out the back door of the Vatican and be there in a few minutes. Maybe I should go the hospital with Magnus."

"That's a great plan," said Art, "I was hoping you would say something like that. *Ciao.*" Art asked Kahlil to stay with the monk, and the Cohens to stand guard and wait for the ambulance. Returning into the inner chamber Art found Charlie standing and weeping. "This is my find of a lifetime, and look what has happened! Now it's gone—all gone!"

Giving his friend a hug, which he readily accepted, Art said softly, "Now Charlie, it's not quite a total loss. We still have the two large ossuaries that are at the heart of the find, and there is certainly a good chance we can recover the other items if the authorities act quickly. This must have happened just yesterday at some point."

At this point, Father Peter and one other man showed up in the inner chamber after stopping to check on Magnus who seemed to be suffering from a concussion or worse. Art looked up and saw them coming, smiled, and shook Father Peter's hand.

"Thank you so much for coming on such short notice!" said Art shaking his head and turning to Charlie. Introductions were quickly made.

Father Peter replied, "Thank you for letting me know there was trouble. This gentleman is Salvatore Biggio, the Vatican surveyor. He just showed up at my office this morning to talk about the tomb situation. So we came over together." Father Peter was then interrupted by Salvatore who spoke too rapidly in Italian for Art to grasp the drift of what he was saying.

"Salvatore says there can be no question. If Professor Miller has not moved these ossuaries, they are definitely on Vatican property. He'll do a detailed study later but from the moment he walked in, he was sure of the outcome of his study. The next question is, shall I arrange for the removal and safe keeping of the ossuaries, with the proviso that Professor Miller and your team can have access to them whenever you want to?"

Charlie spoke up, and said, "That was what I was hoping you would say. What this means is that only the lintel was not on Vatican property as everything else was here in the back of this cave."

Just then, Kahlil hollered, "The ambulance men are here!" Fortunately the pile of dirt and debris was small enough not to impede the medics. Not five minutes later, they had strapped the barely conscious monk on the stretcher.

As they exited the tomb, Father Peter said, "Salvatore can call the archaeology team to remove the ossuaries. Professor Miller, I assume you want to accompany them. You can make sure they pack and carry the items properly for transport. Salvatore will stay and finish his measurements for his report, but I'm sure he's right that these items are definitely on Vatican property. I have already been assured that the city of Rome's laws of eminent domain cannot be extended to Vatican property!"

"Absolutely, let's move these artifacts now! Thanks for acting so quickly!" replied Charlie as he vigorously shook Father Peter's hand. The good priest then hurried off to ride with Magnus to the hospital. In parting, he called back to Art, "Please call the Vatican police next!"

Art groaned. Police work meant paper work. But he needed the police forensic team to answer a lot of questions. To Kahlil, Grace, Manny, and Charlie he said, "Now we have a real mystery! Someone stole most of the items from the tomb, but it can't be our injured monk! So now I have to call the police, and Father Peter said I should call the Vatican police first. They won't be too pleased that we've trampled all over their crime scene and sent a suspect off to the hospital! What a way to start an investigation!"

After everyone left the tomb, Charlie lingered for a few minutes near the back wall holding a high intensity lamp. The violence done to the roof had shaken some of the years of dust off the back wall and Charlie noticed the faint outline of an arch, all filled in with mud bricks, but nonetheless an arch. And on the very top of the arch he noticed an even fainter symbol. Standing on tiptoes and holding the lamp as close as he dared to the wall itself he could just make out the outline—it was a Star of David.

21

Boz on a Ducati

WHEN BOZ EXITED THE tomb and found Philippo knocked out, but still breathing, he realized he would be no help at all. He also concluded he would be alright. Then a little light went on in his brain and a little voice said "all the more for me." Gently placing the small ossuaries on the grass beside the hole, and then the lintel, and then the small hand lamps, Boz carefully carried each of these to the panel van, placing them all on a blanket in the back of the van and he remembered to take with him the tools and other items he and Philippo had brought with them. Philippo was too heavy for Boz to drag to the van anyway, so he just left him at the scene of the crime, hoping for the best. He would call him later.

Once he was back at the catacomb hideout, Boz wrapped each of the artifacts in bubble wrap, and carefully put them into a small trailer that he towed behind his red Ducati motorcycle. His plan was to hit the road, and head to Naples, where all sorts of black market items were regularly sold and traded. Boz knew a shady antiquities dealer who could liquidate hot goods quickly and at a good price. His name was Tony "Teppista" Terranova. His nickname meant hooligan or troublemaker—a name that stuck with him since childhood.

Though Boz did not have much of a conscience, he didn't want to burn all his bridges at once, so he decided to call Philippo and let him know what was happening. The phone rang and rang and finally went to voice mail. Boz felt a bit sheepish, but nonetheless he was glad he could just leave a message and not be subject to questions from his right hand man: "Sorry about leaving you on the hill, but I checked your pulse and knew you would simply wake up with a headache. I've got some of the goods from the tomb. I'm going raise some revenue for our mission. I'll be out of town for a bit, but I'll give you a call when I can. *Ciao.*"

Breathing a sigh of relief, Boz hopped on his bike, revved the engine, put in his ear-buds attached to his iPod strapped to his arm, and found the Steppenwolf hits. Cranking up the volume, the opening heavy guitar riff buzzed through his brain as he began to sing in bad English—"Get your motor running, head out on the highway, looking for adventure, and whatever comes my way. . . .Born to be Wild!" The Ducati roared into life and tore down the little lane onto the main motorway south from Rome to Naples. It would be a long ride, but well worth it. What Boz could not afford was any encounters with the *polizia,* so despite his inclinations to race down to Napoli and unload the goods, Boz became the model citizen, never going over the speed limit, and always riding with his helmet on, in the slow lane. It was so unlike him.

Though the ride of the some 117 miles seemed agonizingly slow to Boz, nonetheless he managed to pull into the outskirts of Napoli in about three hours. He had already sent an e-mail to Teppista forewarning him he had some really valuable hot goods and to be ready to pay well. Teppista had not replied, but Boz knew he would be there as the man never left Napoli. He was as fixed to that location as the ruins at Herculaneum. Ironically, Teppista ran his underground operation out of the back of a *pensione* humorously called "Le Cozy Nostra." Hardly anyone would think to search a hostel full of young people when one was looking for missing antiquities.

The hostel was located on the south side of Napoli, within walking distance of the sea. This too was convenient for Teppista's "business" as he was able to secret hot goods onto small boats, never to be seen again in Italia. Pulling around a whole grove of Aleppo pine trees, Boz parked his bike right next to the back door. Banging on the door with his helmet, the door was almost immediately jerked open by a man who rather resembled Danny de Vito—short, bald, rotund, with a graying moustache, wearing a flower print shirt. Unshaven, unkempt, and generally disagreeable, nevertheless, Teppista grunted when he saw Boz, and said, "What you got for me this time, bum?"

Boz laughed and said, "Let's go have a cappuccino and talk about it, shall we?" Boz liked to deal with Teppista in public places where he was less liable to being pressured by one of Teppista's goons. Walking less than 100 yards down the narrow street to a café was an effort for the pudgy Teppista, and Boz simply loped along beside him. The two made an odd couple looking rather like Laurel and Hardy or Abbott and Costello or better Jackie Gleason and Art Carney.

Plopping himself down in his usual seat in this dirty little watering hole, Teppista snapped his fingers, and immediately a weary looking waitress came over and took their order for one espresso (for Teppista) and one cappuccino. "So, what do we have this time? Stolen treasures from the Vatican?" smirked Teppista.

"Close," said Boz. "In fact it is treasures from a tomb directly behind the Vatican. I have several valuable ancient hand lamps. . ."

Teppista interrupted and said, "They won't bring much."

"And also a stone lintel which refers to two ancient Christian apostles named Andronicus and Junia. Yes, that's right, a female apostle."

Stroking his chin Teppista replied, "Interesting. With the right buyer, that might make for a good sale. What else?"

"Two small ossuaries, in which presumably the children of Andronicus and Junia were buried. An ossuary is a bone box. . ." Boz began to explain.

Teppista cut him off abruptly. "Yes, Yes, I am well familiar with what they are. Fortunately for you, there is something of a market for such things these days, ever since the big splash that the James ossuary made on the scene at the turn of the 21rst century.[1] Jewish museums seem especially keen to obtain such objects. Any markings or writing on these little ossuaries?"

"Only names inscribed on the end for identification, in Latin."

"Well at least there is something that will help date them, the first or second century."

"Right. As you may or may not have noticed, a reporter in Rome already sniffed out the story of this tomb and its remarkable reference to a female apostle so I suspect the lintel will be very much in demand

1. On ossuaries including the James ossuary and their importance as a Jewish burial practice, see the first Art West Adventure, *The Lazarus Effect*.

already. And right about now, the authorities will have discovered these items missing, so the sooner we reach an agreement and you get these items out of the country, the better."

"You're right about that. I will have to make some contacts today. It will take a while. Come back and see me late this afternoon, and I will be able to tell you something. In the meanwhile, let's do what I usually do, and put the items in the locked storage shed behind the *pensione*, so you don't have to be carrying them around in case anything 'unfortunate' should transpire between you and the authorities."

Boz laughed and said, "I doubt they are much looking for me in Napoli just yet, but I agree that is a wise move. Let's shake on the fact that we will work out a deal today, and we will talk later."

Extending his thin hand, Boz embraced the little man with a frown on his face, and prepared to spend a day milling around Napoli. "I will hang around the market downtown for a while, and do a little shopping for my girlfriend back in Roma. Shall we say 5 p.m. to rendezvous?"

"Sounds like a plan," replied Tepissta as he rose to accompany Boz back to the *pensione*. All seemed well to Boz and going according to plan . . . for the moment.

22

The Return of the Holy Father

WEARY FROM HIS LONG journey back to Roma, the Pope emerged from the small white unmarked private jet at Leonardo da Vinci airport, and was met in the airport by Father Salta, two cardinals, and their entourage. There were many surprising things about this particular Pope. For one thing Pope Jerome had been an Austrian Biblical scholar and well-known theologian before he became a cardinal and then a Pope, the first ever from Austria. His recently published scholarly works on both the historical Jesus and the historical Paul had brought considerable acclaim from the world of Biblical scholars, to the surprise of many. The Pope had showed himself to be a good critical scholar and imaginative thinker, not merely repeating traditional Catholic teachings about the Bible and its key figures. Despite his reputation for being a very traditional and dogmatic Catholic priest, in fact it had been Pope Jerome who had given permission to allow lay people, including women, to assist with the serving of the sacraments passing out the "body of Christ" in wafer form to the masses. At the same time this Pope had reaffirmed the teaching that only men could be priests, which John Paul II had insisted on, partly on the basis that all the original apostles were men.

First met by Father Peter who knelt and kissed the Pope's ring when it was extended to him, Father Salta began, "No doubt you have already heard the report in the newspaper about the finding of the tomb of Andronicus and Junia. Now, Holy Father, I must sadly add that it has already been ransacked, with valuable items taken by tomb raiders, still unidentified. They did, however, leave behind the two large ossuaries, one of which identifies, in Aramaic, a woman as an apostle, her name being Junia or Joanna.

"Professor Miller, a good convert to our faith, agreed to turn these two items over to our archaeology team but there will still be the arguments with the Minister of Culture about who should have these items, considering the tomb is both within and outside Vatican land. We've had our surveyor do the measurements, and the good news is that everything but the lintel was on our property. In any case, the items left behind were quickly stored in a safe place in the Vatican, far away from prying eyes, but since the press already knows about the tomb and at least some of its contents, it will not be possible to simply ignore or bury the story. We will have to say something before too long, or face being hounded by the press."

The Pope responded, "We can surely delay them for a while by saying the items must be closely studied before jumping to any shocking conclusions. Let's set up a commission at once, including of course Professor Miller. I would like to have a chat with him!"

"Of course! But he is not alone. He has other scholars with him who have all seen and helped to evaluate these items, both the ones we have, and the stolen items. And they took many pictures of the items *in situ*. Professor Art West, I think you know, but there are also three people from Israel here. The first is Professor Grace Levine, a Jewish scholar who is an expert in ancient Aramaic inscriptions. The second is her husband Manny Cohen, a well-known and I might add wealthy businessman. And finally, there is Kahlil el Said, a Muslim who runs an antiquities shop in Jerusalem and has an expertise in ancient hand lamps."

The Pope laughed. "Quite the international think tank! Despite the gravity of the situation I will enjoy meeting all of them! I hope they feel the same about me! If possible, set it up for later this week. I need to get some rest and get over my jet lag. What you do not know is that I had to make an emergency trip to Ireland. We have another priest scandal over there and there's a cardinal who isn't handling it properly in my eyes. It seems we go from one crisis to the next these days. I stopped briefly in Austria on the way back from Ireland, to try and put a stop to the attempts to ordain women without permission there, but there was real determination to do it with, or without, my blessing. It was frustrating, and will only create more friction among the faithful there. And I fear this new discovery will only make matters worse. Sometimes one wonders about God's timing of things, you know," said the Pope with a wry grin on his face.

The journey back to the Vatican with full police escort was uneventful, but the Pope, who had insisted on Father Salta accompanying him, was lost in thought. He would rely on his team of experts and Father Peter to give wise counsel on how to proceed with this new *cause celebre*—the finding of the tomb of a female apostle. The phrase, "inconvenient truth" popped into his head. But maybe it was God's way of nudging the church in new directions. The Pope wondered how far he could push the envelope without being unfaithful either to the new revelations or to Catholic tradition. He must pray on these things.

St. Peter's Square was packed with tourists who were surprised to see the Pope roll by heading for the side entrance into the Vatican. Priests and nuns and lay people were all waving at the Pope and he waved back. "There are millions of the faithful counting on me," murmured the Pope quietly to Father Peter. "I must not let them down, even if I must share difficult news with them at some point as well."

"Yes, Holy Father, but I am sure the Lord will show you a way to do this wisely and well," replied Father Peter. "In the meantime we must devote ourselves to prayer. Perhaps holy Mary will have some guidance for us on how to deal with another devout Jewish woman named Junia?"

"Perhaps," said Pope Jerome. But he looked worried as his car pulled up to the door which opened into his private quarters. Things were going to get more complicated before they got any easier.

23

Prepping for the Pope

As a child growing up in the Boston area, Grace Levine had many Catholic friends, indeed she had attended various of her girlfriends' first communions in the Catholic church. One day at the age of eight she even came home telling her mother Camelia she wanted to be confirmed in the Catholic Church so she could wear the pretty white dress and have a party. Her mother gently reminded her that Jews didn't become Catholics. It was in that same year that she was taunted at grade school by some who found out she was a Jew. One particularly obnoxious boy told her that "Jews killed Jesus," which is why they had been cursed ever since. These sorts of memories were hard to erase from the mental data bank.

When the phone invitation from Father Peter came to all the parties invited to Rome for the Junia dig to have an audience with the Pope *at their earliest convenience*, Grace's memories of her youth came flooding back. Grace understood the ramifications for Catholic theology of finding a tomb mentioning a female apostle quite well, and so she was thinking ahead as to how to couch her presentation, telling the truth but without causing any unnecessary offense. She understood the delicacy of the matter.

"On the one hand, the truth is the truth," said Grace to Manny as they were getting ready to go to the audience. The Pope needs to hear the truth whether he is happy about it or not. There was at least one female apostle. On the other hand, there might be ways to nuance the interpretation of this discovery so it wouldn't make the church look like it was founded by folks who deliberately obscured the truth!"

Manny mulled this over as he brushed his teeth. "Well, you'd best be careful. You're in an awkward spot because it is your reading of the Aramaic on which the interpretation is going to be based."

"Yes, but don't forget the Latin words on the lintel."

"True, but someone put the five-finger discount on it, and so we don't have the tangible proof. Or will photographs be counted as proof positive, when photos can be doctored, photo-shopped, etc.? My point is you need to be your diplomatic best, without fudging the evidence."

"Right you are," replied Grace, as she pressed her lips together having applied her signature bright red lipstick. Manny had been invited to the audience as a courtesy to Grace, so she was also concerned about his feeling like a fifth wheel. Manny was used to being in charge of things.

Meanwhile, Kahlil was having a devil of a time deciding what to wear to meet the Pope. He had met dignitaries before, but none as important as the Pope, and he did not want to appear foolish. Art could tell him nothing about wardrobe protocols except to dress more formally, but Kahlil did not even own any Western style suits. He had one business suit, but it was pretty drab looking. He decided it would be best if he wore the same sort of robe, sash, and headdress he wore to Grace's wedding. Formal, but not ostentatious.

Art at that very moment was furiously ironing the wrinkles out of his best suit before he met everyone in the lobby for the ride to the Vatican. The Pope was sending over his own special limo driver with an SUV that would hold eight, if need be. Everyone was nervously getting ready including Charlie who was pacing the floor rehearsing in his mind what he would say to the Holy Father. He was so worried about this that he skipped breakfast, which was completely unlike him. Now his stomach was growling at him in disgust. He wolfed down a few crackers saved from yesterday's minestrone lunch.

Grace was the first to emerge from the elevator looking very professional in a gray dress with a gray plaid jacket and white sweater. True to self, however, she also wore a red necklace and bracelet. Trailing behind her on the next elevator down were "the boys"—Kahlil, Art, and Manny, all looking uncomfortable in their suits, and all wishing they could be comfortable in work clothes. Charlie sighed, and said, "The limo is waiting outside; we need to go now in order to be on time. And by that I mean, at least a half hour early." Grace straightened Charlie's tie and off they went.

~

As the limo departed, Father Peter was busily checking on Friar Tertullian who had emerged from his debacle with a concussion. Still having trouble focusing, the Black Friar was currently being attended to by a couple of nuns in the medical clinic in the Vatican. As Magnus sat up in bed, Peter was lecturing him, "What in the world were you thinking when you dropped into that tomb unarmed and unprepared? Did you think you were James Bond or something? Your maverick behavior has gotten you a reputation, and I can tell you it's not a good one. Remember what the Bible says about zeal that is not exercised with wisdom and knowledge? Well, you need to think about what you are going to say to your Dominican superiors. Even the Holy Father has been told about your involvement in this mess. He may personally put you on his calendar soon! Am I clear!"

"Yes, Father Peter," said Magnus grumpily. "I was only trying to help."

"Trust me you were no help. In fact, you need help. You need some counseling, to say the least. I have to go now to meet the Holy Father for an audience. Don't go anywhere without my say so!" With this Father Peter hustled out of the room, disgusted. "What do you do with monks that specialize in monkeying around?" he asked himself.

24

The Causeway Café

ON ONE OF THE many barrier islands off the coast of North Carolina lies Wrightsville Beach. It is the nearest beach to Wilmington, North Carolina, and not nearly as commercially exploited as Myrtle Beach in northern South Carolina. There are even times of day and times of year where things are rather quiet. During the summer season, however, all the local restaurants are busy, and filled with UNC-Wilmington students earning summer money to use when school began again in September. Melody Morris waitressed mornings at the Causeway Café.

Melody was Jake Arafat's girlfriend of one year. Maintaining a long distance relationship meant traveling back and forth between Charlotte and Wilmington, a 3–4 hour drive one way. Fortunately, Aunt Joyce owned a condo in her hometown of Wilmington, so Jake made the trip fairly regularly. Both Aunt Joyce and Marissa tagged along this time especially since Marissa had been promised a weekend at a warm southern American beach, something she had never experienced before.

The Causeway Café, standing in the shadow of the bridge that crossed the Inland Waterway onto Wrightsville Beach, was the highly popular breakfast spot of choice for most of the locals. It was a come-as-you-are, eat-all-you-want, no-checks-or-credit-cards kind of place. The diner specialized in crabmeat omelets, and on this morning the line was out the door waiting to get a seat inside, as it was too hot to eat on the picnic-like tables on the front porch. Melody was very busy.

Jake had come not just with a visit, but to surprise her with a one-year anniversary ring—as Aunt Joyce would call it, a "going steady" ring. Melody was definitely not ready for an engagement ring and had told Jake that she was happy just to "take things slow." Jake, who had never dated before coming to the States, was just fine with "taking it slow" but after a year things were beginning to get serious at least in his mind. So Jake figured a good-sized ring would be a constant reminder to Melody that he was her number one man.

When the oddly matched threesome of Marissa, Joyce, and Jake walked through the door, everyone's head turned and Melody beamed. She had been warned they were coming to breakfast and all morning she had her eye on the door.

It was already 11:00 and the morning breakfast crowd was mostly filing out when Melody, having served her special guests a big breakfast finally finished her shift and was able to sit down with her three really well-fed friends. "So how was the All-Star breakfast Jake? I've never seen anyone eat an omelet and sausage and grits and hash browns and two Belgian pecan waffles and wash it all down with two tall orange juices and two cups of coffee at one sitting!"

"It was a nice little snack," replied Jake with a grin. "Got to keep the calorie count up now that I'm in training for the regular season."

"Not only did he eat all that," chimed in Joyce, "he also vacuumed up the remainder of my toast and jelly, my shrimp and grits, and one of Marissa's biscuits!"

"Wow, Jake. I think you set a new record here at the café! And, trust me, I've seen some big eaters. Were you just starved?"

"Starved for affection more like," said Joyce. "He's really been missing you, Melody."

"My gosh, it's only been two weeks since we were together," said Melody. "This long distance courtship stuff is not as easy as some people claim. But Wilmington is home and I make good money on tips here at the Causeway."

Marissa spoke up and said, "If you want to talk about surviving long distance romances, Art is now in Rome, although it could have been Jerusalem, Corinth, or Ephesus. With Art it's like playing a game of 'Where's Waldo.'"

Melody took off her apron revealing a pretty white sleeveless blouse with lace on the collar. Extracting her hair from a ponytail band, her brunette locks fell to her shoulders and she began to look more like the girl Jake was so smitten with.

Jake had been waiting for the right moment, and he figured the sooner the better, because the more time went on, the more nervous he got. Looking into Melody's blue eyes, Jake said, "Melody I wanted to make clear how much you mean to me, and while I know we aren't ready for any real serious stuff quite yet, still we've been together for a year. So I was hoping we could do what you folks call 'going steady' and to make it official I brought you a little gift." Fumbling in the pocket of his cut-off jeans, he finally extracted a small brown velvet box.

Melody took a deep breath when he handed it to her. Clearly she was surprised. "Go ahead, you can open it now!" Slowly, slowly, she cracked open the box, peaked inside, and then opened it all the way to reveal a beautiful blue sapphire ring, matching the color of her eyes.

"Oh Jake, you didn't have to do this. I would have gone steady with you anyway. How did you know my ring size?"

"I called your Mom up in New Bern and swore her to secrecy. I actually think she likes me, or at least she's getting used to me," said Jake with a rather worried expression on his face.

"Relax, she's warming up to the idea that I'm dating a very tall, rather famous, Middle Eastern—well at least not your typical Southern beau!" smiled Melody with some reassurance.

"Good! So I can come around more often?" joked Jake. "In that case, how about that body surfing lesson you promised me. We all came prepared wearing our suits, so you need to go change, and we need to hit the beach!"

And as the three girls and Jake left the café, the manager in a t-shirt and bib overalls said, "You know that boy looks familiar. Is he on TV or something?"

"Come on Uncle Marvin," said the short-order cook, "You should know that's Jake 'the Cat' Arafat who plays for the Bobcats!"

"Dang!" said Marvin, "We should have gotten his picture to go up on the wall with our other celebrities."

"Oh, he'll be back, if Melody can be coaxed into coming back to work on weekends after classes start."

"Good thought. I'll work on it," said Marvin with a grin.

25

Black Market Deals

NAPOLI IS ONE OF the least appealing of Italy's cities. Tourists only come here to see Mt. Vesuvius or the ruins at Pompeii or Herculaneum, not Napoli itself. Full of crime and dirt, and sordid conditions in various parts of the city, only its museum really stands out. Boz, being no fan of history, was no fan of such history museums either. So he had taken time to go see a movie, *Captain America: The First Avenger*. Since it was dubbed in Italian, he had been able to follow the plot just fine, and got a few laughs out of the outlandish and out-sized things that super-heroes could accomplish. This had managed to burn up a couple of hours in the middle of the afternoon so now he could return to meet with Teppista without wasting any more time.

Teppista in the meanwhile had been burning up the phone lines, making deals for the "objects d'art," as he erroneously called them. Licking his chops he could see a good profit soon coming his way. Boz would believe whatever he told him about what the objects would fetch on the black market. Boz, he knew, was always desperate for cash.

The meeting transpired in a cramped office in the back of the building, an office with a desk stacked high with receipts, bills of sale, and bills of laden that had never been filed away. Smoking like a chimney, Teppista told Boz to sit down.

"So I'll give it to you straight. There are plenty of such lamps on the market. They are not in great demand, even by private collectors. I can give you 5,000 euro for all of them. The small ossuaries are also not uncommon, but they will fetch a bit better price, as they have become more interesting to collectors since the James ossuary debacle. For the two of them I can give you 10,000 euro. Finally there is the lintel, and this is the most valuable thing you brought me. I found a good buyer in a museum overseas ready to pay a pretty penny for it. I can give you 85,000 euro for it. So all in, I will give you 100,000 euro. Do you want it?"

Boz thought for a moment, thought about haggling at some length, but then said, "How about 150,000 euro and we will call it a deal?"

"Since we have a working relationship, and you've given me a few good pieces in the past, scrounged, I believe, from those catacombs you inhabit, I will do you a favor—I will give you 120,000 euro this time, final offer. But you will owe me a favor down the road. Are we done?"

Boz figured this was as good he could do, so he said, "We have a deal!" Teppista took out a small yellow padded money envelope, stuffed it with the agreed upon amount, and said, "Now go home, and when you find something else you want to unload, remember Uncle Teppista has been good to you and did you a favor when you needed some cash."

Boz sighed and embraced the man as they both stood to leave. He guessed he had done about as good as he could on short notice. What he did not know is that Teppista had been offered 1 million euro for the lintel alone by a private collector in Germany. Boz went away relieved to have unloaded the stolen goods. Teppista, waving as he saw Boz get on his Ducati, whispered to himself "sucker," and then a satisfied smile gradually spread across his face. He thought he would get out of town for a while, once he completed his sales. Life was about to get better and Teppista heard a beach somewhere calling him.

26

STAR OF WONDER

Father Peter knew he had a busy day ahead. The papal audience, for the express purpose of discussing the archaeological finds behind the Vatican, was at the top of his list. However, the whole Star Prophecy/ Star of David puzzle was still being pieced together in another part of his brain, especially since he had some biblical, even Jewish, scholars coming shortly.

They would certainly know that the Star of David, sometimes called the Shield of David, is still an important symbol for the Jewish people and Judaism in general. In fact, the term "Shield of David" can also be used to denote the God of Israel. He stared at the two triangles making for a six-pointed star or hexagram, not to be confused with the five-pointed stars prominent on the American flag. His research turned up one Jewish tradition suggesting that one triangle represents the tribe of Judah and the other triangle, the tribe of Benjamin. But why?

More importantly he was curious about the history of the Star as a symbol particularly for Judaism. Historians have traced its origins back to the 17th century with possible connections into the 14th century on Jewish flags. Before that it may have been used on Jewish amulets. A sketchy history at best, he thought, but probably a good way to separate Jews from the Christians who used the cross as their symbol.

He was beginning to grasp the real problem—symbols with no descriptive labels and written descriptions with no picture symbols. Having been in Capernaum he had seen the lintels from the second or third century synagogue which have Stars of David as well as other sorts of stars carved in them. But of course, there are no written explanations from the sculptor as to why he put them there! "So why am I finding the Star of David everywhere I look?" he mused.

As he mulled this over his phone rang. "Charlie Miller here. We are in the limousine now and heading your way. There is one thing I failed to mention to you that I discovered at the last minute on Monday morning. There is a Star of David and an arch, filled in with mud bricks, on the back wall of the tomb. It's faint, but you can make it out with high intensity light."

"Really?" said Father Peter excitedly. "Because I have recently found such symbols in the Vatican itself in several places, and I was just pondering what they could mean? It is a symbol for Jews or Judaism, of course, but did Jewish Christians use it as well? Did Jewish Christians use it to distinguish themselves and their burial places from those of Gentile Christians? Did Jewish Christians use this symbol before the cross became the standard Christian symbol? I am just guessing, but those are the best guesses I've got."

"Those are very good and logical guesses. I would love to see what you have found and talk about it further. For now, however, we have arrived at the visitor's gate!" Two colorful Swiss Guards stood on duty at the door, one with a pike-like halberd in his hands. "Don't let the uniforms fool you, my friends. They are serious about security here. Father Peter will be along to collect us as soon as we run the gauntlet!" promised Charlie.

Beyond the security check, Father Peter ably guided them through a maze of corridors. Along the way he cautioned, "Please remember that even though this is a private audience, we will observe a rather strict protocol. You do not speak to the Pope unless he speaks to you and asks you to do so. You will not be required to kiss his ring, but a bow is expected when he enters and sits down in his curule chair. When the Pope is through with the audience he will stand to leave, and we will all stand as well. Nothing should be said to the Pope thereafter. Expect the audience to last about thirty or so minutes. I mention all this because the Pope is so very friendly, that sometimes people feel they have a license to act informally."

"We get the picture. We will be on our best behavior, I promise," said Charlie as they continued down long marble corridors, their footsteps echoing against the walls and vaulted ceilings. This was going to be a day to remember. As they walked towards the Papal chambers Charlie noticed a nun in a grey habit standing in the hallway smiling at him. It was Sister Thecla, and she mouthed the words, "God Speed!"

27

Adriano's Scoop

WHILE THE HEADLINES ABOUT a feminine apostle had certainly caused a good deal of buzz in Rome, to say nothing of Monday's break-in, Adriano was still looking for ways to follow up on his big story. By Thursday, the relics had been removed; the front door was reinforced; the hole in the roof was covered with a tarp; and a burly guard had been posted. The guard went by the name of Fabio—Adriano's cousin.

Fabio was happy to see Adriano on this drizzly afternoon. He especially enjoyed talking to Francesco, Adriano's favorite photographer. Fabio considered himself a very good, albeit amateur, photographer. Francesco praised his knowledge of everything from F-stops to special lenses. He even suggested that Fabio could do some freelance work for the paper in the future. Fabio beamed.

Meanwhile, Adriano went out to buy gelato for everyone. Fabio was so surprised that his cousin brought his favorite flavor—fragaro (strawberry). Yes, Fabio was in an excellent mood and when Adriano asked if he and Francesco could take a quick look inside, Fabio couldn't think of any reason not to let the two have a peek! Fabio even offered to pull back the tarp and lower in the equipment.

What followed was a good thirty minutes of photographing and filming the entire tomb, including the faint image of the 6-pointed star on the back wall. Adriano was in investigative overdrive. Some of the bricks on the back wall within the ancient arch were decidedly loose. He began pulling at the bricks until one gradually slid out—then another and another. What he felt next was a rush of cool air. Sliding a flash light into the now 12 x 12 inch hole, he saw a barrel-vaulted passage way, with steps leading up every ten feet or so. He was not prepared for what he saw next—niches in the walls on both sides of the passage way, with some kind of boxes in them. Francesco was barely able to squeeze the nose of his camera into the hole. Pivoting to the right and to the left as well as straight ahead, he took dozens of shots.

"Okay boss, I think we have all the pictures we need. Let's get Fabio to help us out of this pit! Did I ever tell you I'm rather claustrophobic?"

"Did you enjoy your adventure?" laughed Fabio. At this point Adriano was realizing that his cousin wasn't all that bright, but he certainly was useful. He praised the young man for being such a good worker here at the dig site, and told him to keep an eye out for any suspicious characters. Fabio promised to keep alert.

Safely back in their car, Francesco opened the view-finder and began to scroll through the digital images. Adriano watched with rapt attention. "There is some sort of secret chamber behind that wall— probably another burial chamber. But why was it walled off in the first place? And who's buried there? We have a scoop! I hope you plan to be up late tonight getting this story ready," said the elated reporter. Adriano prided himself on being the first and the fastest on breaking stories—it would make the Friday morning news and papers. He knew this would only ratchet up the pressure on the Vatican to hold a press conference and provide some answers to the mysteries unfolding on their own property.

The process of editing the film for TV proved to take longer than the camera man thought, though of course the digital still shots he took with his pocket camera were immediately available for next morning's newspaper.

Adriano honed his story down to 350 words, which is what the editor required of him and ended up talking about the mysterious Star of David in the tomb, and how tomb raiders apparently had stolen various things from the tomb itself. What he was unsure of was how much the archaeologists had already extracted from the tomb, or how much they salvaged after the fact, since no would talk with him, a fact which made him fume.

The follow-up story this time did not get the same sort of treatment as the first story about a female apostle did. The headline was smaller, the column was shorter, and Adriano's byline briefer. And there was nothing at all Adriano could do about this but accept it. For a news hound like Adriano the only fully satisfactory outcome was when one's story was not only on the front page, but dominated the front page, but that only happened once in a blue moon. In fact in his twenty-year career it had happened exactly three times. The chances of it happening twice in row were slim and none. It is always a tell-tale sign of ego when the reporter of the story thinks he is bigger than, and should receive at least as much publicity as, the story itself. Such a person was Adriano Andretti, a man who longed to make the news, not merely cover it. What could he do, and should he do next, to report, or manufacture a bigger story, or make this story continue to grow? Adriano pondered this as he watched the morning papers glide off the press, be bundled, and be trucked to the various drop off points around the Eternal City. Perhaps it was time to talk to "Marco" again, and see what dirt could be dug up about the dig.

28

Confession is Good for the Soul

MARCO FINALLY REACHED THE point of admitting that being involved with Boz' gang was both pointless and dangerous. The
Mayor was now bent on a crusade to find out who vandalized the Arch
of Titus, and he was leaving no stone unturned. In fact Marco had become disgusted with the whole enterprise of graffiti art. This was not
just because of the Arch of Titus caper, but because painting had turned
to theft and graft and corruption. Dislike for the past had turned to
disrespect even for the laws of the city that most people respected and
obeyed. Marco's old-school Italian mother would have been ashamed of
what he had been doing for the last couple of years. She had raised him,
and still cooked the best meals he ate every single week on Sundays,
right after attending morning Mass. It was time to confess and put
things right.

But to whom should Marco spill the beans? The press? Probably
not. Adriano would protect his source at all cost. The police? He could
probably get immunity if he gave up the gang. Giovanni Fisconii, the
man in charge of the graffiti clean up crews? He would be the most
grateful for any help stopping Boz's team of so-called artists. So it was
that Marco put in a call to Mr. Fisconii.

Wearing his one and only decent suit and having combed his hair
back and slicked it down with mousse, Marco went to Giovanni's office
on the eighth floor of a baroque style government building overlooking
the Trevi Fountain. The building was itself steamy, as the air condition-

ing system was antiquated and could not keep up with the summer heat. This made for cranky employees, including Mr. Fisconii himself.

After waiting a half hour, Giovanni finally made room for Marco. He entered the office, hoping for some civility. But Giovanni stood there with his arms crossed, and simply said, "I'm a busy man, what do you want?"

"Mr. Fisconii, you do not know me, but my name is Marco, and for some time now I have been both an informant for a newspaper reporter about the graffiti gangs in our city, and at the same time a lookout for the leader of the most notorious of those gangs. I am not proud of the latter, well at least, not anymore, because of things that have happened in the last week that changed my mind about my part in these things. I am young, twenty-two, and have done some foolish things in my life, things I would never want my mother Rosa to ever know about.

"There are some things I know and can tell you about the graffiti gang and its leader. I know where they meet and hide out; I know how they get their supplies; and I know how they plan their attacks. I'm willing to tell you these things, *on one condition*! This information must remain absolutely confidential when it comes to the issue of who your informant was, namely me. You must promise me that under no circumstances will you reveal my name. I know that the Mayor has posted a reward for information leading to the capture of the graffiti bandits, and that reward I suppose could go to you with the information I can provide. But again, I must be left out of the picture. Am I making sense? One more thing. If you could see your way clear to share that reward with me, it would help me get established in life. I would like to start a legit business."

Giovanni Fisconii was not a patient man, and recently he had been at his wits end trying to clean up the ever-increasing graffiti that was destroying the city's landmarks. Here standing in front of him, however, was a gift just falling in his lap. He had a chance to make a dent in the problem that was overwhelming him; make friends with the police; and impress the Mayor who might even be persuaded to give him a better job. Thus, on balance, it seemed to him a worthwhile gamble to accept Marco's terms in exchange for detailed information on how to stop the graffiti madness. And if he got a reward, well it would be worth sharing a part of it.

"If what you are about to tell me proves true, you can count on me to keep your name out of it. I can't promise you that the police won't catch up with you eventually, of course! As to the reward, if it comes my way, I will see that you get a fair share."

"Fair enough," said Marco, taking a deep breath. "In that case I can also tell you that if the police apprehend our leader, they will not only get the head of the graffiti gang, they will also get the man who stole the artifacts out of the Vatican tomb last weekend!"

This revelation caused Giovanni to step back and drop into his chair with a shout of "Mio Dio!"

"Can I sit down now, Mr. Fisconii?" said Marco now feeling a bit more in control of the situation.

"Of course," said Giovanni quietly and with a lot more respect. "This whole situation has made my life miserable and I'm sorry I took it out on you!" He knew the police were desperate to crack the case of that theft. "Okay, start from the top. Who is this guy and where is he now?"

"He goes by Boz—and that's the only name I've every heard. Just the one name, Boz. And right now I don't know where he is. He left town, that's all I know. But he did tell his right hand man, Philippo, he would be back before too long. But as I said, I know where the police should set up lookouts."

Marco went on to give the exact directions to their meeting place at the catacombs. He spilled the names of the other gang members and where they lived. Picking up speed, he divulged how the artists were able to do their dirty work again and again without detection or capture. Finally, he outlined how Boz stole the artifacts to finance their operations. Marco proved to be a goldmine of valuable information, and it came spilling out of the young man for over an hour. When he was done, he felt like he had been to confession. His soul felt much lighter.

"You now have the whole story. I really can't help you anymore. Indeed, I need to disappear for a while. Boz and his disciples will put a price on my head. So I'm not leaving any address or email contact. Consider me a ghost. In short, don't call me, I'll call you!"

Giovanni smiled and said, "You've done enough. And I believe you. I'm sure the police will confirm your whole story. I will talk to them today. And I will protect you like a priest with a confessor."

29

A Papal Audience

OFFICIALLY THE VATICAN CITY State is the smallest independent state in the world. Its 110 acres are surrounded by a wall, although St. Peter's Square itself is separated from Italy only by a white line. About 800 people live and work here, including the Pope himself, yet not one of them is considered a permanent citizen. They all eventually come and go. There is no commercial economy, no army and no taxes. Vatican City includes St. Peter's Basilica, still the largest church in the world, the Apostolic Palace which includes the unparalleled Vatican Museums, and 57 acres of gardens.

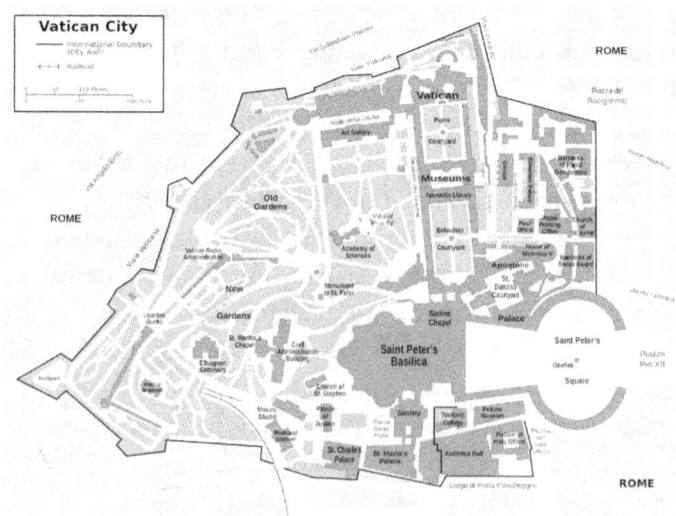

"Are you enjoying the maze of corridors?" laughed Father Peter. "When we are finished with the audience, I will give you a better tour if you wish. But I warn you the crowds in parts of the museums are impossible to navigate. But I know lots of areas less frequented and equally as interesting."

Almost in unison, Art, Charlie, the Cohens, and Kahlil said, "Yes please!"

"Right now, we are in the Apostolic Palace which contains the Pope's private quarters, lots of offices, private chapels, as well as the museums and, of course, the Sistine Chapel. Depending on the weather and time of year, the weekly audiences are held in the modern Papal Audience Chamber which seats 12,000! It's on the other side of the St. Peter's Square. Would you believe it's now covered with solar panels! We are very proud of that. Actually, I think the Holy Father is holding his audiences at Castel Gondolfo next week. But I digress! Your meeting will be in a very user-friendly room, much like the one in this picture. Do you recognize the visitor?"

"Like the picture on the wall, you will sit across from the Pope behind this ornate table, and remember you will stand when he enters and leaves, and you will not speak unless spoken to."

"This protocol sounds like the one my Mom ingrained in me when she was having bridge parties at our house in North Carolina when I was a child," laughed Art.

Father Peter smiled and nodded. "Well, consider yourself at home Art. They don't call him the Holy Father for nothing. One more thing.

If you were expecting a baroque looking room with bad lighting, no air conditioning, red velvet curtains and reams of Renaissance art, abandon hope. The meeting room is quite contemporary."

"Drat," quipped Grace, "I accessorized especially to match the red velvet curtains."

Father Peter knocked three times on a large mahogany door that was then opened by a Swiss guard. In a small antechamber, he searched Grace's purse, and confiscated everyone's cell phones. Then he ushered them into the meeting room. "The Holy Father will be here in a moment, and will come through that door. You will address him not as Pope Jerome but as Holy Father," instructed the Swiss Guard.

"I guess this is as close as I will ever get to fulfilling my childhood wish to join the Catholic Church in a pretty dress," whispered Grace to Art, who knew the stories about her childhood in Massachusetts.

"Well, it's not too late to join up," said Art with a devilish grin. At that very juncture the smaller mahogany door in the corner creaked and everyone stood up abruptly as the Pope strode confidently into the room. Father Peter made all the necessary introductions. With a warm smile and a gracious hand gesture he bid his audience to please be seated. Father Peter laid out a number of photos of the tomb on the table before the Pope.

Pope Jerome began, "Let me personally welcome you to the Vatican, though I wish I could say your visit comes under less trying circumstances. May I ask Professors Miller and West and Levine if they could summarize for me their findings in the tomb that lies at the back of and partially under our property here? You can point to the photos as you need." This request did not come as a total surprise, since they all assumed the Pope had been briefed before this audience, but presumably the Pope wanted to hear the story firsthand.

Charlie began somewhat nervously, "Holy Father, I am an archaeologist, and also a Catholic. The dig site in question was initially uncovered late last spring due to the placing of a new sewer line under the street behind the Vatican. As you might imagine, I was stunned to discover a lintel that was inscribed in Latin, 'Here lies Andronicus and Junia, apostles of Christ.' This lintel has been stolen, and we do not know where it is, but we have witnesses and pictures.

"The important point about the lintel is that it is grammatically unambiguous. It identifies Junia as a woman (the inscription does not say Junias, which in any case is an unattested male name, whereas the evidence for the female name Junia is ubiquitous), and it also identifies both her and Andronicus as apostles of Christ. This last phrase is important, because of what it does not say; for instance, it does not call them apostles of the church in Rome, which might be taken to mean they were missionary agents of the Roman church. No, it calls them apostles of Christ *simpliciter,* and therein lies a problem for some forms of our Catholic tradition that suggests that only men were apostles appointed by Christ himself.

"In addition to the lintel, deeper into the cave we found three hand lamps, two children's ossuaries, and two adult ossuaries. Most important is the Aramaic inscription on the Junia ossuary. I will let Dr. Grace Levine speak to that, with your permission."

The Holy Father simply nodded and remained silent. Grace cleared her throat and said, "Holy Father, I am honored to be part of this team, and to be here on this occasion. The Aramaic inscription on the ossuary is clear enough. It speaks of Junia but also references her Hebrew name, Joanna. It makes clear she is the wife of Andronicus, and that they both were apostles of Christ. It also adds that she was a disciple of Jesus, which, according to some definitions, would be a prerequisite for being one of his apostles. I will let Dr. West say more about the implications of the inscriptions for New Testament studies, but the main point is that the inscription on the ossuary confirms the Latin inscription on the lintel and that both should be compared to the relevant passage in Romans 16."

"Thank you Dr. Levine. I'm particularly interested in hearing about the ossuaries and lamps from an antiquities point of view," said the Pope. "Mr. El Said, apparently my archaeology staff has purchased a number of pieces from your establishment in Jerusalem! You and your daughter, Hannah, come highly recommended." Everyone's eyes open wider. The Pope was full of surprises.

Kahlil, visibly moved, began to speak in his deep voice. "Holy Father, your compliment honors both me and my Muslim family. I am equally honored to meet a holy man such as yourself.

"As for the lamps in the tomb, there can be little doubt they are first century AD lamps. The fact that they are decorated with the fish symbol strongly indicates that they belonged to early, possibly Jewish, Christians. As an antiquities dealer I can also add that Jews only buried people in ossuaries in the first and second centuries of the Christian era. Afterwards, their practices varied. This means these ossuaries have to be very old indeed, and one wonders if they were manufactured here in Rome, or were brought, perhaps by boat all the way here, and then inscribed here in Rome. If the latter, the question becomes, who knew Aramaic well enough to inscribe the ossuaries?"

Art was the last to speak. "Holy Father, I also consider it a great privilege to be here. As I am sure you know, there is a passage in Romans 16, verse 7, which reads: 'Greet with every show of affection Andronicus and Junia, my kinfolk, who were in prison with me; they are prominent among the apostles, and they were in Christ before me.' I believe that this archaeological discovery eliminates some of the ambiguity about the meaning of Romans 16:7. It becomes clear that: 1) Junia is a woman; 2) she is a prominent apostle; 3) she is in Rome with her husband and Paul wants them greeted by the largely Gentile congregation in Rome; and 4) she and Andronicus have been Paul's co-workers, and have even served time in prison with him. One of the most remarkable aspects of this packed single verse is the mention that both people were Christians *before* Paul became a Christian. That is telling precisely because Paul became a Christian very early on in Christian history, perhaps as early as four to five years after the crucifixion of Jesus.

"And, of course, Paul was the apostle to the Gentiles. The Gentile mission had not really begun in earnest before Paul's conversion. This being the case, we now understand the reference to Andronicus and Junia being Paul's relatives or kin. They are Jews, and they were likely converted in the original Christian community in Jerusalem or Judea or Galilee. And this means they are some of the earliest disciples of Jesus, likely present at Pentecost, and since Paul uses the phrase 'apostle of Christ' to refer to someone who has seen the risen Lord and been commissioned by Him directly, this presumably is what is meant by calling this couple 'noteworthy or prominent among the apostles' not merely, as some have sought to translate it, 'noteworthy to the apostles.'

"There is one more plausible conclusion. I would suggest that this Junia/Joanna is the very one mentioned in Luke 8:1–3 as a traveling disciple of Jesus, and mentioned as one who accompanied Jesus to Jerusalem for the Passover in AD 30, and was one of the women who was last at the cross, first at the tomb, and first to see the risen Jesus with Mary Magdalene. This would explain how a woman, in a strongly patriarchal culture, could come to be called an apostle of Christ, for if Christ commissioned her, who were the merely human male leaders of the church to object? I agree this was an exceptional case. Most of the apostles were men. But the point is, maleness was not a prerequisite for being an apostle.

"Now, I am no expert in Catholic theology or ecclesiology, but perhaps it would be worth considering whether being priests and being apostles are not two very different things indeed. The Levitical and Zadokite priesthood in the Old Testament, of course, involves only men. But the New Testament speaks of women deacons, women apostles, women teachers, women prophetesses. Some careful thought needs to be given to what the New Testament says about priests vis-a-vis what it says about apostles. In my view, the New Testament only suggests two priesthoods—the heavenly high priesthood of Christ himself, and the priesthood of all believers. But that is just my own conclusion. Others will differ!"

Art was about finished, but there was one more thing niggling at him. "Holy Father, I have done a lot of work on early Christianity in Rome. One thing that is clear to me from studying St. Paul's letter to the Romans is that Jewish Christians were second-class citizens in the middle of the first century in Rome. In part this was because the Emperor Claudius had banished them, or at least their leaders from Rome, and they had only returned when Claudius died in AD 54. They had only begun to re-establish themselves by the time Paul wrote Romans, and it is clear from Romans 11 that he assumes the majority of the audience consists of Gentiles, and he wants the Gentile Christians to do a better job of embracing the Jewish Christians in Rome.

"It is notable that Paul never talks about 'the church in Rome' in Romans, but presupposes separate house churches meeting in various places. One of the purposes of writing Romans is to bring together alienated Jewish and Gentile Christians before he arrives to meet with them. Romans 12–16 indicates some of the tensions in that community. What we have in Romans 16 is a list of all the Jewish Christians Paul can think of in Rome and he is urging they be shown hospitality by the Gentile Christians.

"This fact brings me to a conjecture, and it is a pure conjecture. If Andronicus and Junia lived out their days in Rome and were buried in Rome, one would expect them to have been buried by their closest Christian friends, which would surely include Jewish Christians in Rome. Perhaps, sadly, reconciliation between Jewish and Gentile Christians was never accomplished in Rome, which might be why Jewish Christians had separate burial places.

"Now, if I may, I would like to ask some questions from a purely archaeological point of view. They will require you to use some imagination," smiled Art.

Everyone, including the Pope, sat up straighter. The Pope cocked his head and said, "Well, this should make the conversation even more interesting! Please proceed!"

Art took a deep breath. "Do you think it is possible that the tomb of St. Peter, which by tradition lies under St. Peter's basilica, is connected via catacomb-like passageways to the tomb of Andronicus and Junia which we have just discovered? Could there be other Jewish/Chrisitan graves waiting to be discovered? Could this explain the remarkable Star of David Father Peter has been noticing recently in St. Peter's and in the Vatican? Imagine the implication! Holy Father, you yourself have written about the Jewishness of Jesus and his earliest followers, perhaps the Holy See reflects that heritage to a greater degree than previously imagined!"

Charlie eagerly added, "And, Holy Father, I can now tell you that the back wall of the tomb has an arch that appears to have been sealed. On the arch is the Star of David!"

The Pope had listened to all of this with keen attention, and when the team had all finally finished speaking, the Holy Father said quietly, "This is a lot to take in. I foresee more archaeological work at the dig site, years of analysis, meetings dedicated to interpreting and sharing the information, etc., etc. There are many lines of research to be investigated—the likelihood of a woman apostle, the relationship between apostles and priests, and many more I'm sure. It is my plan to follow through on these suggestions and call a major conclave of scholars, both Christian and non-Christian to debate these topics.

"No strictures shall be placed on what conclusions the symposium arrives at, if it is even possible to reach a consensus, which may be doubted. Father Peter has now secured the two adult ossuaries here in the Vatican, and so they will be available for close scrutiny. I imagine many tests will need to be done on the inscription to verify antiquity, am I correct Doctor Levine?"

"Yes, Holy Father," said Grace. "The chemical tests need to be done soon, because once an ossuary is exposed to normal air there are chemical changes in the patina and great care must be taken not to move the ossuaries around very much. We all remember what happened when the James ossuary was shipped to Toronto from Jerusalem and arrived cracked and broken. These artifacts require great care in handling."

The Holy Father smiled, "No doubt you are right. Father Peter will keep me informed on the police investigation into the theft of the articles from the tomb. Doctor Miller, you and your team can continue to study the ossuaries and the tomb itself with my blessing. So for now, this audience is ended. Father Peter, I suggest you take this amazing group to lunch," laughed the Pope.

With this the Holy Father rose, made the sign of the cross, and said, "The Lord bless you and keep you." He left the room at a slower pace than he entered it, seemingly lost in thought. Father Peter noted, "I would love to invite him to lunch with us, but that's enough for the Holy Father to chew on for one day!"

30

Interpol Interposes

INTERPOL, WHOSE FULL NAME is the International Criminal Police Organization, was established in 1923. About 190 countries chip in financially to support Interpol's $60 million annual budget. Interpol tries to stay out of politics. If a police force needs help with international crime, however, Interpol is their first choice. Everything from white collar crime to terrorism to drug trafficking is fair game for Interpol, and local authorities are happy to utilize their services.

Raoul D'Silva was a long time employee of Interpol. A 53-year-old Spaniard, he now lived with his family in Lyon, France, Interpol's headquarters. His specific task was to trace stolen goods of high importance that rarely stayed put in their country of origin. Once a stolen item left a country he could coordinate the police work. Raoul had access to computer databases crucial for dealing with international crimes.

On this morning Raoul was processing the latest requests for data that had come in over the weekend. He enjoyed his work, since it often involved unraveling mysteries and solving puzzles on a whole new level. Crime and criminals had become more sophisticated in the computer era, and Raoul actually enjoyed tracking them and their stolen goods all over Europe and the world.

When the report of theft came in from the Vatican, Raoul really took notice. He could see that it involved some precious antiquities— the digital pictures and descriptions provided by the Vatican experts and the dig team were clear and complete. The first place Raoul would look was at the list of "recently acquired art objects" provided by every major art museum in the world. On first pass through the database, nothing of relevance came to light. But he would keep checking. Objects were added to these lists every day.

~

When Teppista Terranova finished ripping off Boz, his first job was to get the lintel carefully wrapped and shipped off to Berlin. This was a delicate job and Teppista was going to do it himself, because the fewer people who knew about this hot object, the better. For a moment he even considered driving his own truck to Berlin, but he thought better of that. He needed to stay put. His cousin, Vinny, was reliable and needed the money. Four bambinos kept him living from paycheck to paycheck.

Pulling out his cellphone, Teppista rang up Gunter Bloch, a curator at the Berlin museum. "Herr Bloch, I am now prepared to send you the item we discussed two days ago. Are you prepared to pay the price?"

"*Guten tag*, Herr Terranova. Yes, we have found a donor who will pay the required purchase price. I need the bank and account numbers," said Herr Bloch efficiently.

"The Napoli Central Bank. The account number is 1009134876. The routing code is X4Y2Z3. Just to be clear, you are putting 1 million euro in the account—correct?"

"*Ja, Das ist Richtig*. It shall be done within the hour, and you should be able to check your account online. Is that satisfactory? And now you need a delivery address. It is 8899 Schwartzstrasse, Berlin. Tell your driver to drive around to the loading dock at the back of the museum, and tell him to call me at 0017897154 when he is about to arrive. Our hours are 9 to 9. Be sure to include the paperwork."

"*Bene*," said Tepissta, "We will send the item on its way today, and it will arrive tomorrow between those hours. It is good to do business with you once more."

"*Danke*, I agree. Until the next time. *Auf wiedersehen.*"

"*Ciao.*" Things were going smoothly, and Tepissta planned to unload the small hand lamps in Naples itself. There was a middle man who sold to the Naples museum, and he had arranged to deal with him. As for the two small ossuaries, he was shipping them to a dealer in Jerusalem. The buyer was one Hannah el Said. She too had demanded the authentication paperwork which Teppista, lying through his teeth, assured her he had. He claimed he bought the items from an Italian Jewish private collector who originally bought them from an Israeli archaeologist. Of course, this too was a big lie, but with computers it was easy to come up with bogus papers these days. With luck, Teppista could wrap up all these transactions this morning, and get on with celebrating his recent coups.

31

The Boz is Back in Town

BOZ HAD TAKEN HIS time getting back to Rome. He had stopped off in a couple of places along the road. Calvi Risorta had been a good time, with plenty of girls to share drinks with, and Ceprano had been even better. There was a casino there and he had managed to gamble away a good 30% of his cash at the black jack table. Thus, when he arrived back in Rome on Friday and called up to Philippo, he had exactly 80,000 euro left. The phone rang and rang, and finally a groggy but loud voice picked up and said, "Buon giorno."

"Philippo! It's me, Boz. Get up man, it's nearly noon! I'm back in town and heading for our hideout. Can you meet me there soon? I have money and news."

"Aren't you even going to ask me how my head is doing? After all, I'm the one who got clobbered at the site, not you. And you left me there!"

"I couldn't drag your sorry ass out of there. And I figured you'd get out okay—and I was right! So what's your beef? I've just been busy selling off the artifacts, and they are safely away now. So what's happening in town? Has there been much buzz about the robbing of the tomb?"

"There was an article in the paper by that pest, Andretti, and a promise of a full investigation by the police, but nothing else really. I've been recuperating at home. The swelling on my forehead is beginning to go down finally. I'll meet you out there in a bit. One thing. I haven't seen or heard from Marco in days. I've tried calling him, but there's no answer, and no voice mail either.

"He never did much care for voice mail. Maybe he eliminated it from his phone. He'll be back I'm sure. He may just be laying low for a while. See you soon. *Ciao.*"

The ride out to the catacomb via the Appian Way was pleasant. Rome had cooled off, and there was a hint of Fall in the air. Boz took off his bandana and let his long black dreadlocks blow in the breeze as he cruised along, caught up in his calculation of what to do next with the remaining money. As he rounded the last corner before the entrance to the catacomb, out of the corner of his eye, he saw a *polizia* van with two officers standing on the other side of the road. When they saw the red Ducati, they began blowing their whistles and the next thing Boz knew he had done a 180 degree turn, and was in a high-speed chase across the edge of town, trying to lose the van.

Revving his cycle up to warp speed, he tried to outdistance the van, but was having little luck doing so due to traffic on the road, so he turned to Plan B, ride through narrow streets where the van would have trouble negotiating the angles and width. Racing down the Strada del Parchi he took a sharp right on the Via del Monti Tiburtini. The street was packed with delivery trucks, taxis, and on the side of the road, fruit stands, one of which Boz partially knocked over as he whizzed by. He managed to lose the police on this street, or so he thought; but when he came out the other end near the La Spienza University, he discovered the road blocked with two more vans. Jumping the curb, and taking another sharp right he sped up the Viale Pretoriano and here he made a huge mistake. He ran over the spikes in the street that were meant to prevent any vehicles from going the wrong way down the ramp to the motorway. His front tire was turned to shreds and he banged into the ancient wall on the right side of the ramp. Jumping off his bike, bruised, but still mobile, he popped open the compartment on the back of the bike, grabbed his knapsack, made it to the motorway, and quickly flagged down a taxi. The police had stopped at the top of the ramp to avoid puncturing their tires as well. As the taxi sped away, a policeman took a zoomed in picture of the license plate of the taxi. Boz was clearly and absolutely now, a man on a wanted list, a man on the run.

32

Tunnel Vision

FATHER PETER SLEPT IN "late" Friday morning—8 a.m.! Then he hurried off to his office. Sipping his piccolo cappuccino in a demitasse cup, he began to flip the channels for the morning news. One thing about being part of a religion grounded in history, the more one dug up, the more the ground could shift under your feet, necessitating a change of view on various tried and traditional perspectives about one's faith and one's church. Suppose the church had made a big mistake when it came to women and ministry, particularly the priesthood? What then? Could this be changed? What would it require to correct it?

These were the things Peter was pondering when suddenly the news came on with an image of some sort of tunnel. The subtitles on the screen proclaimed,

> Tunnel into the Vatican discovered. Was the Vatican built on an ancient Jewish graveyard?

Yelling for his assistant, Father Sal, he asked him to bring in the papers. Punching the volume button on his TV control when that infernal nosy reporter Adriano Andretti showed up on the screen, he just managed to catch him saying, "And it looks like lots of caskets in the walls of that tunnel. Could it be Jews, killed over the centuries by Christians buried there, hidden from the public eye until now? If not, why does the back wall of the tomb of Andronicus and Junia have a Star of David on it? We all know what that symbol was used for in WWII, to single out Jews, and to stigmatize them. Or is there a less controversial explanation for what has been found in and behind that tomb? Stay tuned as we try to interview the spokesman for the Vatican about these matters soon. This is Adriano Andretti saying *Ciao* for now."

His aide arrived with the papers. Punching the off button with maximum force, Father Peter groaned. "Sal, the hits just keep on coming. I can hardly wait to talk to the Holy Father about this turn of events," he said a bit sarcastically. "One thing is sure. There can be no cover-up. That just feeds the conspiracy-theory people, who seem to be everywhere these days, blaming the Catholic Church for all the sins of the world."

∽

Art's room phone rang way too early. As soon as he lifted the receiver he heard Charlie Miller loud and clear.

"Turn on the TV right now!" came the command not to be ignored. Art caught the end of the story and said, "Fill me in, Charlie! Looks like Andretti is at it again!"

Charlie was ranting. "You know that man is not merely persistent, he's downright diabolical. We posted a guard! What went wrong this time? The only way he could have gotten that footage at all was by actually entering the tomb, prying a mud brick or two away from the arch, and then sticking a camera through the hole. And he had to have known he was on Vatican property without permission. The Church could press charges, but that might make for bad publicity.

Let's get over there and see what we can find out about that tunnel to somewhere, apparently full of dead men's bones! Man, you can't write this stuff! It's too improbable for Hollywood. Just another proof that truth is stranger than fiction, and sometimes the truth just complicates your life!"

Art tried to stay calm. "Too true, my friend, too true, but did you catch the angle that that reporter was going for—linking the Vatican to anti-Semitic pograms of ages past? That was a nasty twist. We need to find out what's going on in that tunnel, and if possible squash that story like a bug. I wonder if Grace . . . " Just when Art was saying this someone started banging on the door.

Art leaped up and opened it to find Grace herself, with smoke coming out her ears waltzing into the room. "That reporter managed to really frost my cake, and I am taking it, since you are watching the same channel, that you saw Mr. Andretti's little performance. We need to get to the bottom of this. If we don't, it will further damage Jewish and Christian inter-faith relationships. That was some of the most speculative reporting I have seen in a while. That man is a publicity hound! So when do we go and inspect the goods in that tunnel?"

"I'm on the phone with Charlie right now. We were just saying we need to get out there pronto. So get on your jeans and combat boots and be ready ASAP."

"Gotcha. I'll be ready. Manny and Kahlil were planning to take a personalized city tour today. I think they should still go, don't you? I was invited to the Vatican today to work with the archaeology team. But that can wait now."

At that moment Kahlil found the phone in his pocket vibrating and when he finally extracted it, there was a voice message from his daughter Hannah, all excited about a new purchase he needed to hear about. Punching the "reply to previous caller" button the phone rang only once and then Hannah, sounding breathless picked up.

"*Salaam alaikum* my girl. How are you and the little prophet Samuel getting along this morning?"

"We are fine, and Samuel is smiling right now, so you are missing out this week. Hope you will be home soon. Guess what? I just managed to buy two rare child ossuaries from a dealer in southern Italy. He has faxed me the bona fides and they all look good. Seems a private collector had them and needed to sell them. Anyway, I bargained my way down to a good price. You would be proud of me."

"I'm always proud of you. Who did you say was the dealer you are getting these items from?"

"He's from Naples, and his name is Rocco Ballista."

"That's a name I am not familiar with; have you heard it before? It sounds like the name of a catapult."

"Can't say that I have, but you know how it is. There are lots of dealers in other countries we have never heard of before. I just saw the ad online at an archaeology clearinghouse site for these items and contacted the man. He seemed legit, and was friendly enough."

"Well, when the ossuaries arrive, hopefully without a scratch, call me again and describe them to me, or email me some photos of them.

I can't wait to see what you've got. Maybe the Israel Museum will want them."

"Will do. These ossuaries even have names on the end of them, apparently. Will you be much longer in Rome?"

"Maybe another week, but I will have to come back for a conference later on in January. This tomb of a female apostle named Junia is creating quite a stir."

"I guess so, since the Pope doesn't allow any female priests!"

"By for now, I love you daughter."

"Love you too Father. Samuel is waving bye, bye."

Stroking his chin, Kahlil sat back down in the lounge chair in his room, and mulled this revelation over. "I don't suppose the two ossuaries missing from the tomb here have anything to do with the two Hannah just bought? It can't be!"

33

Peter, Apostle and Martyr

A FTER THE NEWS BROADCAST, Father Peter decided not to call Charlie or Art. He decided first to do some research on his own. Was there a connection between St. Peter, St. Paul, and even the tomb of Junia and Andronicus?

First of all he decided to watch a DVD featuring Art West. Popping the disk into the player he saw a familiar face sitting in a comfortable chair, talking to the host of the Discovery Channel show. Fast-forwarding through the preliminary chat, he came to the point where Art was summing up what scholars know about Peter.

> The story of St. Peter is a complex one. He is one of the few figures, along with someone like Junia or James and John Zebedee who were part of both the early band of Jesus' disciples and the later leadership in the early church. In perhaps the earliest document in the entire NT, Paul tells us that the Jerusalem Church had agreed that Peter would be the apostle to the "circumcised" (i.e., the Jews and their proselytes), while Paul would evangelize the Gentiles. Read Galatians 2.9. But this did not mean that Peter would never convert Gentiles like Cornelius, nor that Paul would never enter a synagogue and convert Jews. Apparently these were simply broad mandates indicating which ethnic group each apostle would mainly focus on converting.

> The evidence we have suggests that both Paul and Peter wandered widely in search of converts, and apparently from time to time their spheres of activity overlapped—Peter goes to Corinth,

and Paul shows up in some of the provinces that 1 Peter 1.1 says Peter evangelized, including Asia with its major city Ephesus. We do not know when or how Peter ended up in Rome. What we do know is that 1 Peter appears to have been written from Rome, and it focuses more on a theology of suffering than any other document in the New Testament. We also know that John 21 alludes to how Peter would die—like his master—violently at the hands of Roman authorities. Paul would meet a similar fate.

In 2006 the archaeologist to the Vatican Museum, Giorgio Filippi announced the finding of St. Paul's sarcophagus beneath the altar of the ancient St. Paul outside the Walls Church, which was supposed to be built on the spot where he was beheaded. Whether this is so or not, what we do know is that Romans did not tend to formally execute people, particularly Roman citizens like Paul, within the city walls, though there were exceptions. In 2009 the Pope announced that carbon dating of bone fragments from the sarcophagus confirmed that the bones in it belonged to a first or second century person, which supported the idea that these were likely the bones of St. Paul himself.

This brings us to an important point. If Peter was the apostle to the Jews and he came to Rome, and Paul was apostle to the Gentiles, and he also came to Rome (though we have no evidence they were there simultaneously), did one minister to a community of Jewish Christians, while the other to a largely Gentile congregation? This might explain why a Jewish Christian like Peter would be buried in a very different place than the apostle to the Gentiles, Paul. To what degree were Jewish and Gentile Christians "one body" or "one community" in the same city of Rome? It is hard to say for sure, but the hints in Romans suggest that they were largely separate communities, though prior to his arrival in Rome Paul was trying to get them together through his letter. The list of Christians at the outset of Romans 16 seems to be a list of Jewish Christians. Paul is exhorting his Gentile Christians to treat these Jewish Christians more hospitably!

Flipping the TV off Peter rose from his chair, having made a decision.

"Sal, I'm going over to the Basilica. If you need me, I'll be down in the crypt!" explained Father Peter matter-of-factly. "I will deal with the news story later. Be prepared to man the phones in my absence! Thank you!" And off he went to the crypt of St. Peter under the high altar of St. Peter's basilica. Along the way, he reviewed the facts and theories.

According to Origen, a Church Father of the early third century, Peter was crucified head downward in AD 64 near an ancient Egyptian obelisk—the same obelisk that now stands in St. Peter's Square. The area in question was then known as Mons Vaticanus, not one of Rome's seven hills, but a hill nevertheless. History shows that the present Basilica is built on Mons Vaticanus, hence the familiar term Vatican.

In 1939, Pope Pius X sent teams of archaeologists down under the Basilica to excavate the necropolis (graveyard) known to be there. In 1950, this same pope declared that St. Peter was probably buried in this crypt. In 1968, Pope Paul VI declared that further analysis had almost certainly pinpointed the actual remains of St. Peter himself. However, to this day there are conflicting opinions as to whether the real remains of St. Peter do exist.

Descending the marble stairs, Father Peter walked cautiously as the steps were slippery, worn from years of pilgrims coming to this spot. The chapel was reasonably well lit, but the spot directly under the altar where Peter's remains were at least thought to be was not.

The gold casket was obviously a later substitute for whatever Peter was originally buried in—perhaps an ossuary? In any case the real, though disputed, remains were still one further level down in the old necropolis. Father Peter was rehearsing in his mind as he went to the crypt the information written up in the Vatican library about the previous searches for Peter's remains.

What interested Father Peter about this report was the reference to the earlier find of bones from four persons and some farm animals, and apparently a later find of the remains of a 60–70 year old man which were identified as Peter, though without absolute certainty about the matter. Why would Peter be buried with others, and with farm animals, no less? Who are these others? Were these animals sheep, symbols of believers, with Peter as their shepherd? These were the things puzzling Father Peter as he stared at the golden casket of St. Peter. Then something came to him, like a bolt out of the blue. Maybe it was true that Peter was buried with other Jewish Christians like Andronicus and Junia. Maybe his tomb *was* at one end of the burial chamber for Jewish Christians and their tomb at the other end? But why would the long chamber with other caskets be sealed off at both ends? Contagion? Disease? Fear of the spirits of the departed?

Father Peter knew well that the practices of the ancients in regard to the cult of the dead were many and varied, and some of the Greco-Roman practices had been transferred over into the Christian practice; for example, the celebration of the birthday of the deceased by having a picnic on the tomb itself. Maybe the church put a stop to such visitations by sealing up the chamber, and sealing off St. Peter's shrine from the others, so he couldn't become the sole focus of the pilgrimages? But just as clearly, whoever created that lintel for the tomb of Andronicus and Junia, had wanted it known that they were apostles just as much as St. Peter. Tertullian mentions that Peter died during the crackdown of Nero on Christians after AD 64. What would the Christians who took his body off the cross have done with it initially? Did they follow the Jewish practice of laying it out in a cool tomb, waiting about a year for the flesh to dessicate, and then disassemble the skeleton and put it in an ossuary or sarcophagus? If he was buried by Jewish Christians this seemed likely. But that still left the puzzle of why the farm animals interred with the body? Did the ancient Christians believe that one should bury things with the dead they would need in the afterlife? It was hard to say.

Feeling his way along the wall where he had noticed the Star of David before, he came again to the abrupt juncture of two walls. Clearly, the left hand wall appeared to go behind the right hand one. Something was behind this wall that was now hidden.

Sal found him still wandering around in the crypt. "Dr. Miller called. If you are free, they would like to meet you at the dig site right away," said Sal with some urgency in his voice. Father Peter ran up the marble stairs and out through the narthex of the Basilica. He took the back routes through the private quarters to the back door of the Vatican, running past the security scanner and the guards, and out the door. Breathless, he arrived just as Charlie and his team pulled up to the steel door to the tomb. It had already been an interesting morning.

34

Tracking the Boz

A s ONLY A FEW non-painters know, paint itself has a "signature." By this is meant it has a specific combination of chemicals distinctive to that paint. An expert can normally analyze a paint sample and tell you what the name of the manufacturer is. This is even true with spray paint. And on this particularly warm day, Claudia Molinari had pinpointed exactly what sort of paint had been used to vandalize the Arch of Titus. It was a quick-drying, high-gloss paint sold by only one chain of stores in Italy—the Benissimo Presto (or "best quality quick") chain. In Rome itself there were exactly two places where it could be bought— one on the west side of town, and one on the east side of town. As it happened, one of these stores was only two miles from the catacomb hideout of Boz and his gang. Armed with this new information, the police were now going to these stores with a description of a tall lanky man with long black hair who rides a red Ducati motorcycle to see if that rang any bells. At the store on the west side of town, no one had seen anyone like the sketch shown to the employees. But at the store on the east side of town, the reaction was immediate.

"That one comes in a lot," said the shop owner, "and often he is not alone. He has a bunch of others, an entourage, trailing him wearing the same sort of black leather jackets and pants he wears. His nickname is Boz, and he always pays cash, so I have no idea what his real name is."

Phillipo was very worried. When he arrived at the catacomb early Friday afternoon, there was no sign of Boz, or anyone else. He did notice a bike tire mark turning around about 100 yards up the road. And there were car tire tracks all around the dirt entrance to the tomb. As he stared at the entrance to the catacomb, he saw a new word spray painted in large black letters on the door—*morte*—death. It did not bode well for Boz and his gang. Something bad was going down, and Philippo didn't want any part of it. He realized he needed to stay as far away from the catacomb as possible.

~

Giovanni Fisconi was not a man to let grass grow under his feet. Only shortly after he spoke with Marco on Thursday, he called the chief of Rome's police, Paulo Belladonna, and told him the news that he was looking for a particular gang led by a man nicknamed Boz. This information had been quickly spread throughout the force, particularly to the special units squad in charge of tracking down the Titus Arch vandals. Still no one knew the actual name of Boz.

At the catacomb outside the city, the investigative team extracted multiple prints. They would run this through their databases and see if anything turned up. For now, they were content to be on the right track,

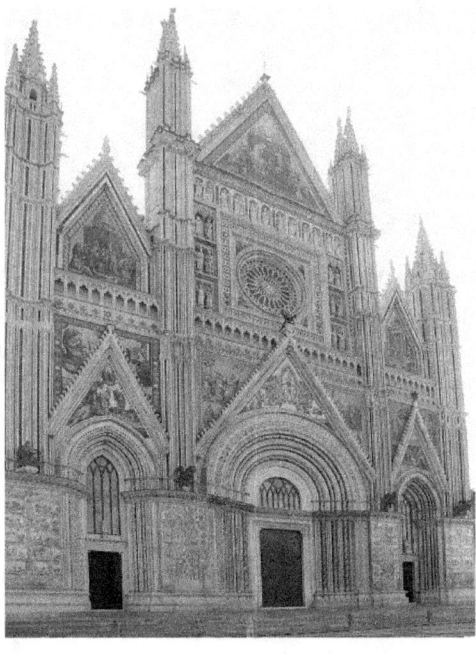

with a confirmation from two sources that Boz, whoever he was, and wherever he was, was their man.

Sixty miles north and slightly west of Rome was the beautiful hill town of Orvieto, famous for its wonderful white wines, especially the award-winning Orvieto Classico Amabile. The town was an ancient fortress, surrounded by a large wall. A magnificent cathedral graces the town square. The front of this cathedral shone in the sunlight as the tourists and residents who frequented the café across the street admired the view and sipped their coffee.

Equally impressive is the ornately decorated interior of the cathedral that illustrates biblical stories. Tourists are especially amazed by the vivid images of the dead rising up out of the ground at the resurrection. The realism is striking!

True art surrounded Boz the graffiti artist. Boz had decided to hide from his pursuers here in Orvieto after eluding the police and hopping a train north. He was staying with his second cousin Guido, son of Guido the lawyer, in his three room apartment. The story he fed his cousin, whom he had not seen in some two years, was that he had lost his job in Rome, and needed a place to make a fresh start away from the nagging voices of his parents. Guido, could sympathize. His parents had kicked him out of their home on the back side of Orvieto and had made Guido go out and get a job to support himself.

"Look, man, I need a job. How about I go out with you to the quarry and see if your boss can find some work for me," pleaded Boz.

"Yeah, there's work to do. But you better clean up your act. Dreads aren't allowed in the quarries. And then there's your real name . . ." said Guido looking at his cousin with a smug smile. Boz sighed.

Yes, the problem was he would have to show his drivers license with his given name, a name not very popular in Italy. Boz was actually Antonio Mussolini, the son of Vittorio Mussolini, the son of Benito Mussolini. Boz had come by his atheism honestly. It had been the ideology of his family since the 1930s. "I've got that covered. How about this one?" offered Boz as he pulled a fake driver's licence out of his pocket. It read, Mondriano Picasso.

"You've got to be kidding! Would anyone believe that's your real name!" said Guido laughing hilariously.

"Sure! And I'm guessing your boss won't look too close or run a security check!"

"You're right about that. But there's still the problem of all that hair," said Guido still laughing. "Let me find the scissors! Turn up the music! I do my best work listening to heavy metal—put on Damnati ad Metalla. I caught their gig at The Black Hole in Rome last week!"

Boz would disappear into his new identity, and only Guido would know the ruse. He cut his hair and shaved his face—the new Boz was a new man. He would not be recognizable to someone looking for Boz, the graffiti artist and thief.

35

The Tomb that Never Ends

THOUGH THERE WAS A hole in the roof of the tomb of Andronicus and Junia, and though the tomb was now empty, Charlie was still excited about what might be discovered behind the back wall of the tomb. Charlie cautioned his companions that they were going to need to work very cautiously and deliberately as they removed the ancient mud bricks inside the ancient arch, lest the whole thing suddenly collapse on them. And as Charlie predicted, the work was painfully slow. But Father Peter claimed he hadn't had this much fun in a long time!

Though there was plenty of light through the man-made "sky light" the light was not shining directly on the wall. Charlie had set up his halogen lamp so all could see exactly what was happening. Using long thin metal files (finger nail files actually) Charlie, like a surgeon, carefully inserted the file in the small gaps between the bricks one by one. He had brought two small braces as well in case a wall began to collapse. He was lucky, however, for this cave was damp enough that the bricks did not crumble so long as they were handled with care.

This process, of creating a walk way through the arch, without removing all the bricks or the arch itself, took upwards of three hours, with Art and Grace and Father Peter, in his "work robe" as he called it, stacking bricks about five feet back up against the side walls of the tomb. Finally, the opening was large enough that if each of the explorers carefully stooped down they could enter the tunnel like chamber.

They had three flashlights as well to assist them with their explorations. Though it was nearing noon, no one was at all hungry.

"Remember," said Charlie, "if there are sarcophagi in here, you need to wear the little masks I brought, and also the latex gloves, just in case there is something nasty lurking anywhere in there."

One by one, the team filed slowly into the tunnel, and shone all three lights into the distance. They could not see an end to the tunnel. It seemed to go on and on. Then, as they shone the lights to each side of the tunnel what they saw caused a gasp—row upon row of niches and in almost every slot, sarcophagi or ossuaries, call them what you will. The niches had been carved out of the tufa rock and sealed with terracotta.

It was Father Peter who spoke first. "I've been doing a bit of research about the finding of Peter's bones under the basilica, and as it turns out, there were the bones of four persons, and several farm animals as well. The reason I'm mentioning this is that I have a hypothesis. What we have here is a tunnel that ends up under the basilica, only it is walled off now at the other end, I'm betting. That suggests this is a Christian burial ground, with Andronicus and Junia being given a separate chamber in this catacomb because they were apostles. It's just a guess, but I think it's a good one."

As Father Peter explained his idea, Art slowly walked up the corridor with flashlight in hand, Grace right by his side. Gently, he rubbed the ends of the sarcophagi to see if there were any names on them, and sure enough, about half of them had names. He began reading off the names, some in Greek, some in Latin, none in Hebrew or Aramaic.

"This one says Ampliatus. This one is Urbanus. This one is Epanetus. This one is Maria. This one is Apelles . . . wait a minute! I know where we have read all these names in one place before—Romans 16! These are the Jewish Christians of Rome, and they are buried together here." Looking up on the wall, Art saw some sort of faint sketch or painting. Carefully rubbing his handkerchief over it an image of shepherd emerged.

"This may be the earliest image of Christ ever painted—- as the good shepherd of the sheep. This image may suggest this tomb was continually used for several centuries after the time of Christ. Christ is depicted here as bare-faced, and with Roman hair and attire. It's amazing how each generation envisions Christ as one of their own, as like the person who is doing the painting."

Though Father Peter and Charlie were listening, they were also walking rapidly up the corridor, trying to find an end. The whole place smelled musty, but the odor of death had long since dissipated. There were some spider webs, and lots of dust accumulated over the ages, but things looked remarkably well preserved on the whole.

After a walk of almost 300 yards, finally Father Peter's light shone on a wall at the end of this tunnel. All along the corridor there were loculi with burial boxes of one sort or another, but what Father Peter wanted to know was who was buried closest to what he judged to be the burial spot of Peter under the basilica. When they saw the end wall, both Charlie and Father Peter walked even more briskly right to the end. And what they saw at the end astonished them into an absolute silence. There was a large mausoleum at the very end of the corridor, on the right hand side.

Taking his hand and wiping the lintel over the entranceway into the mausoleum, Charlie shone his light directly on the lintel.

Hic iacetur Prisca et Aquila, servi Dei. Damnatio ad metalla
Charlie said in hushed tones, "Here lies Priscilla and Aquila, servants of God, condemned to the mines."

As he turned he found Father Peter on his knees thanking God. "They are all here in this place. The Roman Jewish Christian saints of the Lord. I must go back into the Vatican, into the crypt of Saint Peter. I will bang on the wall and shout, Hallelujah! If you hear me, bang on the wall and shout, Amen!" And like a flash Father Peter was jogging down the corridor humming a hymn and saying to himself, "This is a great day to be a Christian."

Charlie, Art, and Grace stood quietly, almost reverently, in the catacomb. Art broke the silence, "This mausoleum tells a horrible tale: here lies Priscilla and Aquila, condemned to the mines by Nero. So how did they end up here after that ordeal?"

36

Damnatio Ad Metalla

A T FIRST WHEN MARISSA saw the Latin phrase she laughed, translating it roughly "to hell with metal!" But laughter quickly turned to frowns when she actually read the article in *Biblical Archaeology Review* on Christians condemned to work in the mines by Roman authorities. The phrase means "condemned to the mines"—one of the many punishments Romans dreamed up for those found guilty of some crime, including believing the wrong religion.

The article specifically discussed copper mines, southeast of the Dead Sea in modern-day Jordan. Who knew there were mines like that in the Nabatean desert near Petra? She wondered when it was that Christians first found themselves condemned to such labor. The copper was mined and smelted by slaves and war captives who had been turned into slaves. "This is literally slave labor," muttered Marissa to herself.

Marissa had been reading *Biblical Archaeology Review* to distract herself from the fact that she was missing Art badly, and wanted to be in on the archaeological excitement. The article, fortunately, was fascinating enough to capture her full attention for a while. She learned about the tool kits of the Christian miners—hammers, chisels, and wedges to deal with loosened rocks. There were ropes for climbing and baskets on ropes to put the ore in, if it was a shaft mine where things were hauled out vertically. But there were also lamps, small, oil lamps used to light the scene underground so the miners could do their work.

But how did you get such slave labor to actually work, and not run off into the desert under the cover of darkness? The Romans had an answer. A garrison of foreign soldiers with no knowledge of the local languages guarded the mines and made sure the work was done and no one escaped. Sometimes the miners were even shackled to make sure they did not run off either deep into the mine, or elsewhere. It was clear enough that even the strongest person could not survive decades in the mines. To be condemned to the mines was a death sentence. They literally worked themselves into an early grave, if they were not killed by the frequent mining accidents.

It is not a surprise that when the circumstances of mining came to the attention of Greek and Roman philosophers they saw the practices as a "violation of the earth," not to mention an inhuman practice (Pliny, *Natural History*, 33.1–3). By Pliny's day in the first century AD mining had become prohibited on the Italian peninsula, not so much because of the cry of inhumanity but due to the fear of divine vengeance for violating the earth (33.138).

As Marissa read on, she discovered, with horror, that not only pagan Emperors used this punishment on Christians, especially in the third century, but even Christian Emperors used it on those they deemed Christian heretics. The report of the ancient Roman historian Strabo was believable. "In addition to the anguish of the work, they say that the air in the mines is both deadly and hard to bear. Workers are continually consumed by sickness and death" (*Geography* 12.3.40). When someone was too old or infirm to work, the mandate was that the guards would just behead the person and discard them into some shallow grave. It gave Marissa the shivers. "Life was cheap in the Empire," she said to herself.[1]

"Marissa," called the voice from the kitchen, "it's time for lunch."

"Coming Mrs. West," she said without much enthusiasm. The article had definitely spoiled her appetite. How many more days would she be twiddling her thumbs in Charlotte or Wilmington, she wondered? "I guess this is an opportunity to do a better job of cultivating the virtue of patience," she whispered to herself, as she entered the kitchen determined to put on a happy face.

---

1. On all this see the fine article by M. Najjar and T.E. Levy, "Condemned to the Mines. Copper Production and Christian Persecution," *BAR* 37.6 (Nov–Dec 2011) 30–39 and 71.

37

The Pergamon Museum

THE PERGAMON MUSEUM IS one of five museums situated on Museum Island, a piece of land in the middle of Berlin's Spree River. Built between 1910–1930, the museum amazingly enough houses full-scale reconstructed sites including the famous altar of Pergamon and the gate of Miletus. These items were hauled off from their original locations in Turkey by German archaeologists and sent to Berlin. The museum was originally built to house them. The more stunning of the two reconstructions is the Pergamon altar, which once sat on top of the acropolis of that ancient city.

While attempts to extradite these artifacts have been made by the Turkish government for years, thus far they have produced no results whatsoever. In fact this museum has its own reclamation problems, because at the end of WWII the Red Army carted off lots of the smaller artifacts in the museum and they are now still in either the Hermitage in St. Petersburg or in the Pushkin Museum in Moscow. These items have also not been returned, and the haggling has been about restitution or repayment for the artifacts. Despite its ups and downs, this museum continues to be the most visited one in all of Germany. The popularity of the museum has only increased since the two parts of Germany reunited.

Today the Pergamon Museum houses three mini-museums—The Islamic Art Museum, the Antiquities Collections, and the Middle East Museum. It was for the second of these that Herr Gunter Bloch worked, which is why he was eager to obtain the lintel of Andronicus and Junia. Known for his daring, and the ability to outbid other rival curators, Bloch's work for the Antiquities Collections had brought him considerable notoriety, not to mention regular raises in his salary.

On this Saturday afternoon, Herr Bloch stood on the back dock of his part of the museum and watched a small panel van gradually ease its way down to the rubber-bumpered dock. As the truck's back up signal beeped away, Herr Bloch smiled at the thought of his latest coup. Obviously someone in Rome would one day want it back, but as the saying goes "possession (and a legal bill of sale) was nine-tenths of the law."

Vinny, sweating like a pig, emerged from the cabin of the truck, climbed up the dock steps with his stubby little legs, holding a bill of lading that the curator must sign. In rather bad German Vinny said, "You Curator Bloch?"

"Is your English better than your German, young man?" asked Gunter sarcastically. After Vinny nodded, he continued in English, "I believe you have something you want me to sign."

Vinny handed over the document, went over to the back of the truck, unlocked the padlock on the sliding door, and gave the door a little upward push. It rolled back into the top of the truck like magic. Sitting in the back of the truck, strapped down with belts tied to either sidewall of the truck was a small immobile package wrapped in a ton of bubble wrap. Jumping onto the back of the truck, Vinny unstrapped the package, picked it up with two hands, and took it over to the curator.

"Let's trade," said Vinny but as he passed the package to the curator with his sweaty hands, the package slipped and neither man was able to prevent it from falling onto the concrete abutment on the dock.

"Well, fortunately, it was all wrapped up," said Vinny, with a sheepish grin.

"Fortunately, or I would be handing it back to you and voiding the sale!" said Herr Bloch not amused by Vinny's carelessness. Nevertheless, Vinny was allowed to go on his way with the signed bill of lading, and Bloch eagerly took the package inside the back of the museum, and headed for the preparation room where all such antiquities were first taken to be readied for showing.

When Bloch had finally managed to completely unwind all the bubble wrap and the lintel emerged, Bloch gasped. There before him was a lintel, broken in three pieces, but not shattered. The lintel had been made out of rather fragile limestone, limestone that further dried out and became more brittle under the pressure of the bubble wrap. Cursing, he realized all he could do at this point was to call in Fraulein Hilda, his restoration expert. Sighing, he also realized this meant at least a month's delay before he could advertise the new item on the website and then put it on display as a special exhibit.

"Oh well," said Bloch, "at least Fraulein Hilda can make it look almost like it was never cracked at all." But going forward he knew that this exhibit would have to be encased in a climate controlled glass container which allowed a certain amount of moisture to be in the container to keep the artifact from totally drying out and becoming even more brittle.

38

Surprise in a Box

THE UPS TRUCK ARRIVED first thing Saturday morning and parked as near as it could to the Damascus Gate. From there the driver used a hand truck to deliver packages to the various shops. The driver was a friendly Palestinian whom Hannah had known for years. He lived in East Jerusalem. Already the markets were opening along the Cardo, and already old men were sitting on little stools drinking their tea and discussing the news d'jour. Hannah opened the antiquities shop not five minutes before Salie came knocking at her door, but she had run into the back because baby Samuel had taken this opportunity to start crying for attention.

"*Salaam alaikum*, are you here Hannah?" said a friendly voice.

"Coming," said a muffled voice from the back of the store. "Just a minute, I'm changing the baby!"

Salie stood in the Cardo, watching all manner of humanity pass by—tourists, vendors, old women carrying huge bundles of greens, a man pushing a fruit cart, a mullah heading for morning prayers, two orthodox Jews hurrying off to the Western Wall, and so it went every day in Jerusalem.

"Sorry to keep you waiting," said Hannah, a little out of breath. "When the baby calls, I have to answer, even if my friend the UPS man is left waiting."

"I understand entirely, our twins keep us hopping all the time. If you would just sign here, I will hand over your special delivery package."

Hannah did so with a flourish, and Salie waved as he left her standing there in front of a biggish brown box no doubt packed to the gills with confetti or bubble wrap around something. Sliding the box inside the store, and closing the door, turning the sign around on the door so it would say SORRY WE'RE CLOSED, Hannah took her best paring knife and opened the box. Inside there were two wrapped parcels, each of them a little less than three feet long and about two feet wide—two small ossuaries, without bones in them. Boz had dumped the bones out before he put the goods into his trailer when he left Rome.

The ossuaries were intact, and so Hannah breathed a sigh of relief. They were both made of limestone, and they each bore a name on the end of the box. One said "Clement" and the other said "Tryphosa" in Greek. The script was really just a scrawl, not an honorific inscription, but a simple identifier for the person who tended the crypt in which they had been buried. Hannah had seen a lot of ossuaries, but none as well preserved as these little gems. They would likely bring a decent price on the open market.

Hannah decided to closely inspect the insides of the two ossuaries with her magnifying glass before calling her father. Lifting the lids gently off of each box, almost immediately, something caught her eye in the Clement ossuary. And it wasn't bones—there were no bones in either ossuary. Something was stuck to the right hand side wall. At first it looked like a piece of yellowed modern newspaper, but on closer inspection it turned out to be a piece of papyrus, a piece of papyrus with writing on it.

Running to get her tweezers and put on her best glasses, she could hardly contain her excitement. A bonus had come with this ossuary! She might need to use a little heat as well to make the manuscript detach from the side wall of the ossuary, so she grabbed her hair dryer as well. Snatching a high stool on which to sit, Hannah hovered above the ossuary which sat on her work bench.

The first step in the process was to test the papyrus to see if mere tweezers would peel the delicate material off the limestone inner wall of the box. As it turned out, the paper was pretty well stuck to the side wall, and would be torn if she pulled too hard. Step two was to bring out the hair dryer. She directed the gentle heat onto the outside of the side wall. Slowly and carefully over thirty minutes she extracted her prize.

The papyrus had eight lines of letters, all in Latin. Each line consisted of only capital letters, all run together with no spaces between words (what the experts call *scriptio continua*). Hannah's Latin was a little rusty so she got out her Lewis and Short's *Latin-English Lexicon* and started translating away. What emerged was a story of the Neronian crackdown on Christians in AD 65. The top part of the manuscript was missing and so it continued in mid sentence.

> . . . which he, barbarian that he was, did not refrain from do-
> ing. Even children were executed in the Circus Maximus,
> for Nero claimed they played their part in the great fire.
> His wrath focused on Jewish Christians young and old,
> for Romans were biased against the Jews.
> Petros, Paulus, Andronicus, Junia, and children
> were executed to satisfy the Beast's bloodlust.
> Some were condemned to the mines.

It appeared to be some kind of diary or chronicle of the massacre in the mid-sixties that devastated but did not eliminate the Christian community in Rome. Hannah whispered to herself, "This is a first century piece of papyrus in someone's original hand, maybe the only one we know of that is not a copy of an earlier document. The earliest fragment of any New Testament source is a small bit of John 18 from the second century. This seems to come from the first century itself, entombed with a child named Clement. This is awesome!"

It dawned on Hannah that her phone call to her Father was well overdue. Quickly booting up her computer, she discovered her father was already on Skype waiting to hear from her. It took a minute for the connection to fully work, synching up the audio with the video.

"Can you hear and see me now?' said Hannah.

"Yes," boomed her father's voice back at her. Like so many people, he assumed he had to talk louder to be heard through a computer or a cellphone.

"I have a major surprise for you. These two little ossuaries we bought came with a bonus, a genuine first-century papyrus, which I have extracted and will read to you in a moment."

"Wait until I tell Grace and Art about this!" exclaimed her father.

"I'm taking the computer camera and giving you the visual tour now of the two boxes." Kahlil got as close to the computer screen as he dared to get a good look at the ossuaries.

"They appear to be in remarkably good condition!" remarked Kahlil smiling broadly.

"They are, and now I'm coming around to the end of the ossuaries which have names scratched on them. One says Clement and the other Tryphosa."

Kahlil furrowed his brow and after several moments said quietly, "I hate to tell you this Hannah, but those ossuaries look very familiar."

"What do you mean, Father? How could you have seen them before?" said Hannah with a hint of panic in her voice.

Kahlil sighed. "They appear to be the ones stolen from the very tomb here in Rome that we are right now exploring. Remember, I told you it was robbed last Monday! I should have been more explicit. We lost the lintel, the hand lamps—and two children's ossuaries!"

"Oh no!" cried Hannah. "But the dealer sent the bona fides and assured me they came from a private collection with authentication papers. He claimed they had been in his possession for several years!"

"Remind me again, who was this dealer?"

"His name is Rocco Ballista; he's from Napoli."

"I will have the authorities here check him out. Anyway, don't go selling those boxes. They probably need to come back to Rome. The reason I know this is that Art's photos of the ends of the two children's ossuaries show the very same two names you just mentioned!"

"I apologize father! I thought I had checked well enough before buying these items. I did not know they were stolen goods," said Hannah with a great deal of anguish in her voice.

"Of course you didn't! We all know the pitfalls of buying antiquities. But on a happier note, tell me what the papyrus says."

"It's really just a fragment of a scroll and I found it in the Clement ossuary. It was in Latin so I did a translation using our lexicon."

As she read Kahlil her rough translation, he got very excited. "That is absolutely amazing! It might be a first century eyewitness account of what happened to Christians, especially Jewish Christians, during the crackdown under Nero after the fire in AD 64. That little scroll is probably worth ten times what the ossuaries are worth! But if I'm right, we both know that the ossuaries and the papyrus will have to be returned to the Vatican to be studied and hopefully displayed in their museums. What do you think?"

"I think your morals outweigh your business sense—and I'm very proud of you!" laughed Hannah.

"I will talk to Art and the gang about this shortly. If you would just fax to me here at the Hotel D'Medici pictures of the ossuaries we can verify that they are truly our missing ossuaries. And please send pictures of the papyrus and your translation. And how about copies of the bill of sale and so-called authentication papers. Isn't modern technology wonderful, daughter?"

"Indeed it is! You will have all the information shortly. Just stand by!" said Hannah happy that she took several courses to learn computer skills.

"And Hannah, kiss little Samuel for me!" said Kahlil as he signed off.

When Hannah had shut down the Skype connection, she sat stunned for a minute or two. The world was full of deceitful people. Hannah felt like she had let her father down by not doing enough checking, but then she reasoned that it could have happened to any antiquities dealer. In the end, some good would come of all this. The Vatican would get back the ossuaries. The worst that would happen is that all sorts of archaeologists and technicians and experts would argue over who gets to study the finds! People never change. Hannah finally smiled.

39

The Other Side of the Wall

A s Art stood in the bathroom he rehearsed in his mind the events of the previous day—the entering of the tomb, the removing of the mud bricks, the finding of a whole host of burial boxes, the tunnel that ended at a mausoleum of Aquila and Priscilla. The final piece of the puzzle was supplied by Father Peter who returned to St. Peter's crypt, banged on the back wall, and shouted, Hallelujah! Art, Grace, and Charlie, being on the other side of the wall, in unison responded, Amen! Sure enough, the long tunnel led straight to the crypt under the Basilica!

Picking up his flip phone Art dialed Charlie's number and with barely a "hello" urged, "We need another door installed pronto, before that nosy reporter wanders into the long tomb." Charlie, who was groggily trying to put on his pants at the time, merely grunted, agreed and hung up.

Father Peter picked up immediately when Charlie called him around 11 muttering about a door. "I'm way ahead of you. The door is already being installed, and I'm having another set of keys made for you. I'm also having the hole in the ceiling sealed over. No more snooping reporters 'dropping in' to check things out. How would you all like to have a late lunch with me here at the Vatican?"

"After yesterday, I'm up for anything relaxing," said Charlie supressing a yawn. "By the way did you catch the fact that Art found an early image of Christ, probably, as the good shepherd, looking more like Romulus or Remus than Jesus."

"Yes, I glanced at it in passing this morning as we began to install the door. I think we will need to install a climate controlled glass box around that spot, but I haven't figured out just yet how to attach it to the wall with further deterioration around the image. Charlie, I can tell you're tired. I promised to show you something that will wake you up again. Try to rally the troops. See you at one?"

"My pleasure!" replied Charlie beginning to revive. Several phone calls later, Kahlil and Art were on their way to the Vatican to rendezvous with Father Peter and Charlie. Art noticed that Kahlil was alternately smiling and frowning all the way to Vatican City—he seemed lost in thought. "Probably just tired like the rest of us," thought Art.

Grace decided to fly home for the weekend with Manny who needed to check on both business and pleasure—his basketball team.

Over a late lunch of caprese salads with a side of the best prosciutto Art had ever had, the four *amicos* began to relive yesterday's excitement; all except Kahlil who was still acting very strangely.

"And one more thing," added Father Peter. "You know that star of David in the painting by Raphael? I figured out that it is hanging directly over the Jewish Christian catacomb. And the Star is in the lowest corner of the painting, pointing down! Raphael, or someone, knew what lurked beneath the floors at that spot. And after lunch I want to show it to you."

"That about clinches the argument that the Star of David was used to signal where Jewish Christians were being buried. It was a symbol already used at Capernaum in Galilee at the synagogue there, and Peter and others must have used it as an identification marker in Rome, one that pagan Romans would not recognize as a Jewish symbol. Indeed they would have likely viewed it as an astrological symbol of some sort."

Kahlil could contain himself no longer. He finally decided this moment was right to spill the news. "I know where the two small ossuaries are, and they are in good hands, praise Allah!" Kahlil sat back smiling while he watched three jaws drop simultaneously.

"And you know this how?" asked Art as he stared with astonishment at Kahlil.

Kahlil calmly answered. "Because my daughter Skyped me this morning, and I saw the very same ossuaries we saw before, only now they are sitting in our antiquities shop in the Cardo. Hannah bought them, thinking they were coming from an honest collector in Naples. No, I am positive we have found our stolen ossuaries. And I am guessing that the Vatican would like to have them back immediately. Am I right, Father Peter?"

"Praise God! You are so right, Kahlil!" exclaimed Father Peter.

"All's well that ends well," said Charlie cheerfully. "Except you are out some considerable amount of dough, I'll wager."

"I am willing to write off the cost of the ossuaries. It is better that they come to rest where they were meant to rest—here in Rome. But there is more—a pearl of great price—maybe even priceless. A gift from Allah, I believe. Can someone order me a cup of coffee, I need to keep talking while it's all fresh in my 70-something-year-old mind." Art jumped up to find a waiter.

Everyone then sat anxiously awaiting for Kahlil to continue. The coffee came. Kahlil took exactly one sip, smacked his lips and said, "And now, the *piece de resistance,* as the French would say. There was a piece of papyrus stuck to the inside right wall of the Clement ossuary."

"No way!' said Art. "I looked in both those ossuaries and saw nothing!"

Charlie added a bit sheepishly, "But, to be honest, I just sort of peeked in."

"Exactly!" replied Kahlil. "You forget you were groping around in the dark with mere ordinary flashlights. I have been mulling this over in my head since Hannah called. I remember that the right side of the Clement ossuary was not visible to you since that was the front side of the box on the ledge where it set, and you would look in and naturally just see the back side when you shone your flashlight in it."

"So what did we miss, an advertisement for the latest gladiator contest?" joked Art.

"Close," said Kahlil, who suddenly became very somber—a true sadness crept across his face even to the point of a tear. Unfolding the piece of paper in his pocket. "This was originally in Latin, and the translation is my Hannah's rough draft of the eight lines. He read quietly . . .

> . . . which he, barbarian that he was, did not refrain from do-
> ing. Even children were executed in the Circus Maximus,
> for Nero claimed they played their part in the great fire.
> His wrath focused on Jewish Christians young and old,

for Romans were biased against the Jews.
Petros, Paulus, Andronicus, Junia, and children
were executed to satisfy the Beast's bloodlust.
Some were condemned to the mines.

Kahlil then ventured, "This is surely a first century document about the persecution of Christians. We don't have anything like this until much later, am I right? And furthermore, I believe that this is the only New Testament era document by a Christian, literally, that we have an original copy of. Again, am I right?"

"The first part may not be quite right," said Art. "Consider these words from a passage in Hebrews." Art pulled a small pocket Bible from his jacket and began flipping pages. "I like to call Hebrews 11 the hall of faith chapter. So here goes."

> Others were tortured, refusing to accept release, in order to obtain a better resurrection. Others suffering mocking and flogging, and even chains and imprisonment. They were stoned to death, they were sawn in two, they were killed by the sword; they went about in the skins of sheep and goats, destitute, persecuted, tormented . . . They wandered in deserts and mountains, and in caves and holes in the ground.

Charlie added solemnly, "The author seems to have written to Jewish Christians in the mid to late 60s as these things were beginning to happen in Rome. Good call, remembering that passage."

In the afternoon, Father Peter escorted them all around the complex to show them the Star of David symbol which seemed to pop up with regularity—when you look for it. Eventually they walked around to the back of Vatican city to check on the tomb entrance. At least six construction workers, under the supervision of the Vatican's archaeology department, were busy fixing the roof, installing new doors, and even putting a fence around the whole complex. They could hardly believe all that had transpired in the last ten days. They imagined the children's ossuaries sitting maybe once again snuggled in their niches with their parents. But they also worried about ever again seeing the lamps or the lintel.

40

A Summer's Day

THERE IS SOMETHING ABOUT the beach that really helps a person unwind. Maybe it's the sound of the ocean, or the cool, but not too cool, waters at Wrightsville Beach, or maybe it's just sitting in a beach chair and baking while reading a summer novel, but whatever it was, Jake and Melody were about as relaxed as two people could be. This was their second morning at the beach, and already Melody was beginning to have a tan, and Jake always looked like he had one. The night before, Jake wrote Melody a poem, inspired by the sand and surf.

ODE FOR A SUMMER'S DAY

The spray, the foam, the salty air;
The feel of breeze, the sky so fair;
The way the sun shines down all day;
The way the waves roll cares away.

The sand, the crabs, the shells all white;
The sound of gulls as they take flight;
The ebb and flow of time and tide;
The feel of a friend by your side.

See the young with sand castles near;
See the fisherman at the pier;
All this and more will soothe your soul;

God made it all, and made it whole.

Melody asked her artistic friend, Julia, to reproduce the poem in calligraphy. Then she planned to have it framed. Jake's birthday was coming up in a few weeks. She knew he would be pleased but embarrassed—tough athletes don't normally write poetry! After a year they knew each other's strengths and weaknesses, pet peeves and idiosyncrasies. Given their cultural differences, Jake's non-pushy approach to their relationship was very helpful. He had been living by the motto Aunt Joyce had preached: "growing a relationship is like creating a fine wine—if you rush it, you ruin it."

"So, Melody, are you up for dinner and a movie tonight?' asked Jake, while burying Melody's fingers in the sand.

"I vote for *The Best Exotic Marigold Hotel*! It's set in India and has a huge cast of stars including Judi Dench and Maggie Smith."

"Sure—ah, do I know those people?" said Jake who really hadn't seen many movies in his lifetime.

"Well, if you've seen James Bond movies, then Judy Dench now plays the spy boss who goes by 'M.' And if you've seen any of the Harry Potter movies, then Maggie Smith is second-in-command at Hogworts School of Witchcraft! She plays Professor McGonagall. Is this helping any?"

"Actually, yes! It might surprise you that I have seen those movies! But, I'll trust you—this time," said Jake jokingly. Jake would have watched Bugs Bunny and Road Runner as long as he could be with Melody.

"Good, then it's settled. I'll check the times on the Internet. Meanwhile, I am going to race you to the water! The first one who catches a wave and makes it to shore gets to pick the restaurant! Let's see how quick Jake the Cat really is!" Melody broke into an all-out sprint for the water. Jake was caught laying back in his chair, and had to play catch up. By the time he got to the water's edge, Melody was already jumping on top of a perfect wave, extending her arms in front of her and riding it into shore. Jake decided that instead of catching the wave he would catch the surfer, and when he snatched Melody up out of the water and into his arms, Melody instinctively gave him a memorable kiss.

"You really know how to sweep a girl off her feet," she said with a smile.

Down the beach two women watched from afar. Aunt Joyce smiled and said, "I'd give better than even odds I may have to deal with two weddings next year, and won't that be fun, especially if I don't have to plan either one!"

"And at least one wedding will be on your home turf –Wilmington! But trust me, you will love Istanbul," promised Marissa. "And while you're there we can give you the grand tour—to Ephesus and Ankara. Are you up for a balloon ride over the tufa hills of Cappadocia?"

"What a thought!" said Joyce a bit breathlessly. "Both weddings would have a real exotic quality about them. Jake is not merely a convert, he's a Palestinian and former terrorist! Life can take a lot of strange turns."

"Don't remind me," said Marissa with a frown. "Art being away right now wasn't what I expected." Joyce just nodded.

Watching Melody and Jake simply reminded Marissa that she was away from Art, and it was high time she heard from him again. She resolved to have a long chat with Arthur, and find out when exactly he would be heading back her way. On the plus side, while it had been a fun week getting to know Art's Mom, and hanging out at the beach, she was too much of a professional archaeologist to enjoy standing on the sidelines and cheering for her husband while she drank Cheerwine and ate hickory smoked pork barbecue with hush puppies. Marissa longed to be involved in the current adventure and intrigue he was experiencing in Rome. Besides, she had only been to Rome once, for a conference, and had never really seen the place. So Marissa was considering doing something drastic—cutting short her beach vacation and heading to Rome.

As they were driving home late in the afternoon, Marissa broke the silence and told Joyce about her plan.

"I was wondering when you would get ants in your pants and want to go and be with Art. I don't blame you a bit. We've had a good 'get-to-know-you' visit. Can I count on you to look after my son? I tell you what, after dinner, you go book your flight for Sunday night, and I'll call my son and tell him to expect a surprise package at his hotel Monday. How's that?" There was no argument from Marissa.

———————————————

The phone on the night table began buzzing, and Art did not hear it at first. But like a bumble bee returning to the same flower, it went off again and the second time Art awoke and picked it up.

"Hallo" said the sleepy voice.

"Well, son, I've done it again."

"What did you do, Mom?"

"I forgot the time difference between you and me. It's 7 PM here; what time is it there?"

"Hold on a minute. It's 1:00 AM. I was sound asleep. You wouldn't believe all the things that have happened here in Rome today!"

"I'm sorry I woke you, but I wanted to let you know that a very special package is coming your way and should arrive on Monday, so please be on the lookout for it. Now son, this package is big. It will be unmistakeably for you! So when it comes, be sure you give it your full attention!"

"Okay, Mom, but I'm a little busy just now. We found the Jewish Christian catacomb under the Vatican's property and its got all kinds of people in it mentioned in the New Testament, including Priscilla and Aquila. When we discovered this, I got so excited I nearly wet my pants!"

"That will not do, Arthur! And another thing, don't go getting trapped in some catacomb. I remember last year's escapade in Hierapolis all too well."[1]

"Yes, Mom, I hear you. I'll be careful. Gotta go back to sleep now. Talk to you later. Love you, bye!" Art decided to hang up rather abruptly before she launched into a lecture about taking care of himself, not spending time with her, leaving Marissa behind, etc., etc.

After he hung up, he scratched his head and said, "Couldn't that have waited?" Getting back to sleep wasn't easy.

---

1. A story told in *Papias and the Mysterious Menorah,* the third Art West adventure.

41

Future Plans

THE BLACK FRIAR WAS not a happy camper. Though his physical wounds had mended, his bruised ego had not. He could not believe that Father Peter and the Holy Father told him he would be disciplined. Disciplined for what! For being a faithful monk that cares about the Catholic Tradition! On this Sunday morning, instead of looking forward to Mass, Magnus was fuming.

"Don't they realize what will happen if convincing evidence of a female apostle and her burial box come to light? The pressure on the Vatican to ordain women will be enormous. Already priests are trying to ordain women without the Pope's permission. Where will it all end?"

What was really causing his clerical collar to chafe on this morning was the news that the Holy Father had decided not to see him in the foreseeable future. Worse, there would be a commission of priests set up to look into his actions to see if he should be defrocked! Would they defrock a defender of the faith? Magnus was irate, and could hardly contain himself. He thought about going to that reporter Adriano Andretti and venting, but then he realized that would only further cook his goose.

"Suppose I track down the thief who stole our holy relics. That might get me back in the good graces of the Holy Father." So it was that Magnus decided he would start a manhunt. He would call up Adriano and ask some questions. He would call up the Ministry of Culture and do the same. He would talk with the police. He would leave no stone unturned. He would redeem himself! Having something to do was always better than sitting around feeling sorry for oneself. And Magnus viewed himself as a man of action and orthodox zeal. Whipping out his cellphone, he started making some calls.

~

Teppista Terranova had to admit, he could get used to living the high life. No more living out of the squalid back end of a *pensione* in Napoli. Teppista had come up in the world, and using some of his Mafia connections, he had found out about a real estate deal that was unbeatable. He bought himself a small but comfortable furnished villa by the sea in Sorrento, left his pitiful belongings behind, and moved in almost overnight. He hired a boy to keep the pool clean, a yard man to mow the grass, a maid to clean the house, and a chef to cook his favorite Italian dishes. What could be better? Teppista left the Cozy Nostra behind for good and had no intention to return. He told his cousin Vinny to bag up and burn all the files and records and receipts in his old office. "Clean the place out, and it's all yours," guaranteed Teppista. Vinny told him he would take care of it right away.

Teppista had made so many shady deals in his life that he decided it would be smart to change his name. This he did in Napoli for a small fee, before he got around to changing it on all his bank accounts, and before he bought the mansion called *L'Summum Bonum*, the Highest Good. When he told the real estate agent he would pay cash, the agent was all too ready to make a deal, whoever the buyer might be. The view from his mansion was simply breathtaking.

And as for his new name? A devilish grin came over his face when he thought about how wise he had been to change from Teppista Terranova to Pietro Pavarotti. He renamed himself after St. Peter and his favorite opera singer, Luciano Pavarotti. Who would ever guess these two named persons were one and the same? "No one," thought Teppista, "no one at all." For years he had saved up thousands of euros from his illicit deals, until the last sale of the ossuaries and the lintel had given him more than enough ready cash to realize his dream and retire. Just in case, he had a half million euros placed in reserve in a Swiss account. For now, he was putting his past and past worries behind him. He had bought himself a nice home and a red hot car to cruise the Amalfi coastline.

He would stock up his wine cellar and find a beautiful woman who could at least put up with him. The maid showed up poolside and asked, "Another margarita perhaps sir?"

"Definitely!" said the newly minted Pietro Pavarotti. "Make it a mango—frozen—and don't skimp on the Cuervo Gold Tequila."

42

Hot on the Boz's Trail

ORVIETO WAS A TOWN famous for its wine, not its rocks, unlike Carrera where all the great marble was quarried for Michelangelo to make his famous statues. Nevertheless, there were plenty of rocks in Orvieto, and Boz at the moment had been assigned the task of breaking some of them. As he saw it, this was a good way to get out his current frustrations. He had thrown away his old cellphone and bought a new one with a new number, but when you do that, and don't tell anyone, no one ever calls, a problem for a narcissist. Truth be told, on his second day at the quarry, Boz was already bored with menial manual labor. It seemed beneath the dignity of an artist like himself. With a (phony) name like Picasso, he ought to be able to start selling some pictures soon, and then maybe he could quit his day job. He resolved to do some paintings of the front of the cathedral and make some quick cash. Silly tourists with no art sense would buy anything that looked colorful, whether it was good art or not. Boz smiled and thought, "What an irony. I'm going from cutting edge graffiti art to mediocre classical art." What a turn of events, and all to stay anonymous.

～

Since Marco's visit, Giovanni Fisconi had done some real digging and come up with some startling revelations. All of this he shared with the police who, in turn, kept the Vatican police informed.

Happy with his detective work, Giovanni wondered where exactly his informant Marco had gone. "Well, none of my business! I promised to leave him alone." But there was another name that kept popping up as a known associate—Philippo. Giovanni planned to spend Monday morning searching for this man. By now, a whole network was looking for Boz.

As it turned out, Boz was the grandson of the most famous Fascist in Italian history—Benito Mussolini! No wonder the man had a propensity for grandiose displays and self-centered actions. His record included several speeding violations on a Ducati, the same motorcycle abandoned during the chase of the man police tracked from the catacomb outside town. The bank account registered under the name of Antonio Mussolini was still open, and had recently seen a deposit of 80,000 Euros. Boz didn't get that for spraying painting the arch of Titus! So the police were now betting they would find some more of the man's fingerprints in the tomb of Andronicus and Junia. They still didn't know where Boz had run off to, but eventually, if he made the mistake of drawing on his bank account, they would be able to pinpoint his location.

~

Also on Monday morning the Black Friar dropped in on a friend who worked for the Vatican police.

"Good morning, Alberto! I'm helping Father Peter and the archaeology team with that big case involving the Big Dig outside the walls. How about filling me in," said Father Magnus with such assurance that his friend was sure he was part of the investigation. In no time, the Black Friar got a whole story about an anonymous tip given to the local authorities about a man named Boz that might be involved in both the graffiti investigation and the theft at the Vatican."

"You don't say! Father Peter will certainly want me to tell him about your suspect," claimed the Friar. And armed with that much information, he left to continue his own investigation.

~

Adriano Andretti had a good relationship with many on the local police force. It didn't take long for him to glean all the information he needed from his buddies while they stood around the water cooler sharing stories about hot cases. They told him to go interview Giovanni Fisconi, who was heading up the investigation of the defacement at the Arch of Titus. Apparently, the same man was involved—someone named Boz.

"Don't worry," boasted one of the young sergeants. "We'll find this Boz guy and string him up for both crimes."

Over mid-morning coffee, Adriano and Giovanni were comparing notes. But Giovanni did not disclose Boz's real name. That was a police matter. He knew where to draw the line when dealing with reporters, in case there was a trial down the road, and Fisconi did not want to do anything to prejudice or make difficult the conviction of this criminal. Naturally Adriano was not fully satisfied with his interview, but at least he had some leads now on this Boz, and knew enough to start combing the Internet. Another bloodhound was on Boz's trail.

43

Surprise, Surprise, Surprise!

THERE IS SOMETHING MIND-NUMBING about an overnight flight to Europe, especially one which has two connections because you couldn't get a better ticket due to last minute booking. Art had really "lucked out" in getting the flight from Charlotte. Nevertheless, dazed but undaunted, Marissa stepped off the plane at Da Vinci Airport at 4 PM Monday afternoon, ready to get into town on the train, and have supper with her husband to be. She was tired, lonely and eager to get this traveling over with. "I like everything about traveling, except the traveling," she said to no one in particular as she stood in line at passport control.

Grabbing her one suitcase, pulling up the handle and rolling through the lobby of the airport to the entranceway to the train station, she just made the five o'clock train into the central station in downtown Rome. Looking at herself in her pocket mirror, she noticed her hair was limp, her lipstick non-existent, and the bags under her eyes were about as big as the bag she was dragging with her. "Yeah, Art will be really thrilled to see me. I look like something the cat dragged in." Going to the ladies room at the station, she washed her face, gargled with the last bit of mouthwash she had in her carryon bag, brushed her teeth and hair, straightened her blouse, put on some lipstick, and in general made herself look as presentable as someone can be when traveling. Life was about to get better, and less boring, but less boring usually meant more tiring, and she was already terribly tired.

Grabbing a taxi, she inched across the center of Rome towards Piazza Navona and the Hotel D'Medici, excitement building up as she got closer and closer. It was almost suppertime, and she figured the gang would be back from work by now. She was wrong. There was no sign of Art or Charlie or Grace or Manny or Kahlil or anyone she knew!

"Harrumph!" she said. She decided she would try a bold approach. Going up to the hotel manager, she waved her left hand in the air, put her passport on the desk, and said forcefully, "I am Dr. Marissa Okur, an archaeologist from Turkey. And, just as importantly, I am Dr. Arthur West's fiancée. See, here's my passport and engagement ring to prove it! I've been traveling since yesterday—from the United States. I would really like to surprise him when he comes back from work. Could you allow me to get into his room and wait for him there? This was arranged as a surprise, so he doesn't know I'm coming."

The manager grinned and replied, "I am the manager here, but I am not Italian. In fact, I am Turkish, which is probably why I am inclined to believe your interesting story. In fact, your story is too improbable not to be true! But this is Roma. Who wouldn't be thrilled to see a beautiful Turkish woman like you here in Roma with *amore* in her eyes? I will help you, Dr. Okur!"

Coming around to the front of the desk, Rafa took her right up to Art's room and let her in. "Let me know how the surprise turns out," he said with a wink as he closed the door. The room was a wreck. The bed was made, by a maid no doubt, but Art's clothes were strewn all over the room—on the chairs, on the floor, anywhere but on a hanger in a closet.

"Oh Arthur, how am I going to live with you?" asked Marissa, but actually she was just glad to see she was in the right spot. At approximately 6:30 Marissa heard a key card sliding into the door, and so she positioned herself in the one empty chair across from the door. The door opened—and in came a barely recognizable and decidedly filthy Art West!

Blinking and doing a double-take, Marissa said "Surprise!" She ran over, stopped short, looked him up and down, and leaned in with a big kiss on his lips, the only clean portion of his entire visible anatomy.

"What in the world have you been doing today?" were the next words that popped out of her mouth.

"Oh, nothing much! You know, just your typical day at a dig site! Today it was the mausoleum of Priscilla and Aquila—on my hands and knees obviously!" By now they were both laughing and hugging despite the dirt and exhaustion.

Art finally stepped back, held her shoulders, and asked, "How in the world did you get here, and get into this room, anyway? Are you the big package my mother promised was coming? Please tell me you didn't get here in a box in the bottom of a UPS cargo plane!"

"Nope, but it sure took a while to get here. You go take a shower and get dressed. You need to treat your girl to a decent dinner in the Piazza Navona. Rafa downstairs will make a reservation for us pronto. Rafa is Turkish, by the way!"

"Ah, that explains how you got into the room. You used your feminine Turkish wiles. Nice job!" praised Art with an appreciative smile. "And just for the record, I sure am glad to see you! Tell Rafa to make us a reservation at Platia del Marina. It's a great spot next to a fountain."

"Will do, husband-to-be, will do. Back in a jiffy." Marissa raced out of the room and down the hall towards the elevator. Halfway there a tall, dark, and handsome Kahlil el Said stood in her path. For a split second, Marissa was quite afraid of the ominous-looking man.

"I saw you coming out of that room, madam, and I must say, I didn't know Art was keeping a woman!" boomed Kahlil, and then he laughed and said quietly, "It is good to see you, Marissa. Art said nothing about you coming to Rome. I am Kahlil el Said, Art's friend from Jerusalem. Do you remember me from Grace's wedding?"

"Now I do, but I must admit you gave me a bit of a fright! It is a pleasure to see you again. And, don't blame Art for not mentioning my coming; he didn't know either. This is a big surprise. I'm going down to talk to Rafa about my room and make a dinner reservation."

"Very good! You should make this dinner a private one. I'm sure you two need to catch up. Tell me, was he as dirty as I am when you found him?"

"Oh yes. I can tell you have both had a great day in the field," said Marissa laughing.

"Right! And now I will retire to 'clean up my act' as the Americans say."

Dinner proper did not begin until 8 PM and by then Art and Marissa had both cleaned up and changed. Over dinner, they ran through a whole host of topics including how she got along with Art's Mom; what was happening in Turkey at Hierapolis these days; what things Art and his friends had discovered; the theft of various items from the tomb, and much more. Now, after two glasses of wine, a full meal and some shared tiramisu and cappuccino the couple was simply staring into each other's eyes, holding hands, and Art was occasionally pressing his lips to her right hand. "What a blessed man I am to have you in my life. Sometimes I wish we were already married. I know my body wishes that as well."

"Me too," was all an exhausted Marissa could muster. She felt like she was in some kind of dream world, having been magically transported to Rome to meet her sweetheart. "Arthur, I would love to paint the town red tonight, but I am exhausted, so take your girl home please, and put her to bed."

Art paid the bill and held Marissa's chair while she stood up. Woozy from the wine, she leaned against his shoulder. Art steered her back to the hotel, towards the elevator (with Rafa watching intently from the desk), and to her room—four doors down from his. After opening the door, he picked up Marissa and carried her in.

"Practice for the wedding day," he joked.

Marissa said, "Just put me on the bed. I'm too tired to change." He took off her shoes; gently covered her with a blanket; kissed her softly; and slipped out of the room. She was asleep before the door shut.

44

Father Peter and St. Peter

FATHER PETER SALTA WAS indeed named after St. Peter, and it became something of a cliché in his family that he was destined to work, in a sense, for St. Peter in St. Peter's own basilica. When that actually happened, no one in his family was surprised. His preaching skills were recognized early. In the early 1980s he was appointed the Apostolic Preacher or the Preacher to the Papal Household, a position established in the 1500s. Only Father Peter was allowed to preach to the pope, although he regularly prayed and meditated with other senior officials in the Roman Curia.

On this morning, Father Peter was feeling the weight of the Catholic tradition on his shoulders. He had spent the night thinking about how Gentile Christians might well have betrayed, or at least failed to protect and defend, Jewish Christians during Nero's mad rampage beginning in AD 65 All those corpses, all those bones of dead Jewish Christians, were silent testimony to the fact that Nero apparently singled out the very people Paul, in Romans 16, had said the Gentile Christians needed to show every degree of hospitality to. In the end, many of them, even children, had died. Father Peter knew well the sad history of Christianity's own anti-Semitism, and now, with the revelation of there being a female apostle, was also deeply troubled about the suppression of gifted Christian women.

The Pope would take a cautious approach to the revelations from the tomb underneath the Vatican, but at least he had promised a symposium. Of course, Father Peter knew that symposiums often lead to a lot of good discussion, and not much actual change in the church, though he had been at Vatican II, and had seen real change in the way the Bible was studied and worship was conducted after that. He thought about the fact that Church life is complicated and change is slow. Father Peter remembered a little ditty Art West had once sung for him: "Like a mighty turtle, moves the church of God; brothers we are treading, where we've always trod. . ." Most importantly of all, Father Peter was trying to listen to what the Spirit was saying to him. How should he preach or teach about the truths he was learning?

Leaving his quarters and going to the altar in St. Peters, Peter knelt and prayed. "Heavenly Father, if I am a servant of your truth, then I must be honest about that truth. I know the church has made many mistakes over the years, but help me to see how I can speak and explain the truth in love about what I have learned, and not try to explain it away. These are already difficult times for our church with all the sex-abuse scandals, and now these fresh revelations will be seen by some as a threat to Catholic tradition and unity. Already there are those prepared to ordain women as Catholic priests on three continents, even though they have no Papal approval. I am a priest and yet I am called The Apostolic Preacher. Explain to me, Lord, the differences between being a priest and being an apostle. Not all priests were apostles, and not all apostles were priests. I don't really understand then what to make of a woman apostle, though I do understand that this new truth makes clear we cannot claim that we can't ordain women, because there were no women apostles. Give our shepherd Jerome the wisdom to know what to do. Guide him to speak the right words at the right time in the right way, in the name of the Father, Son, and Spirit, Amen."

Father Peter decided to inspect the progress at the tomb. As he walked out of the back door of the Vatican, he ran into Adriano Andretti, pen and paper and recorder in hand. When he saw Father Peter coming he turned on his recorder and raced over to the priest, "Is it true Father Peter that you are sealing off the tomb to hide the truth about all the Jews buried under the Vatican?"

Father Peter was so angered by this abrupt question, and caught off guard, that he replied bluntly, "No! It's not just any sort of Jews buried under there, it's Jewish Christians, and it's not just any Jewish Christians buried under there, it's some of the ones who lost their lives at the hands of Nero, including children! It's a story about pagan Romans killing Christians! So you need to stop insinuating things about the situation when you don't know the facts. Go tell the story about the theft of items from the tomb. Plead for help recovering these items. In short, do something useful! Put your desire for a sensationalism aside for once and do the right thing!"

Adriano shot back, "I will, I will! But you need to tell me more or else the world will think you have much to hide, especially when at least part of the tomb involves a female apostle. You need to come clean about all that, and soon!"

Father Peter went silent as he continued to walk away towards the tomb of Andronicus and Junia with Adriano nipping at his heels. He finally said, "You must go now. I will think about your request. You are probably right that we need to have a press conference—but not until we have our facts straight! Facts, man, not conjecture; do you understand?"

"A press conference doesn't get me a lead story," complained Adriano.

"It's not about you; it's about what's best for everyone! Please try to understand that," pleaded Father Peter.

"Then I'm guessing you won't invite me into the tomb right now," said Adriano wryly as they both arrived at the front gate.

"No, my son, I cannot do that. Please remember that I am not in charge here," said Father Peter much more calmly. Adriano turned to leave. Father Peter berated himself. "Stupid, Peter, stupid. Don't take the bait next time. Learn to just keep your mouth shut!"

When he opened the door of the tomb, standing just inside was a fetching young dark-skinned woman he had never seen before. Art stepped up and said, "Father Peter, let me introduce my fiancée, Professor Marissa Okur. She's an archaeologist in Turkey."

"Leave it to Art to dig up someone who loves to dig," laughed Father Peter as he enthusiastically shook Marissa's hand. She was quite taken with the spry priest with the gray hair and warm smile.

Just then, Charlie emerged from the back of the tomb. After greeting Father Peter and telling him that his timing was impeccable, he turned to Marissa and said with mock solemnity and a deep voice, "You are about to enter one of the most important Christian archaeological sites anywhere in the whole wide world! Be prepared to be surprised, but keep your mouth shut, or else the spiders will drop in!" So it was once more into the tomb, and one more pair of eyes to see it for the first time.

45

Same Old, Same Old Teppista

THERE IS AN OLD saying, "once a crook, always a crook." Tony "Teppista" Terranova (aka Pietro Pavarotti; aka Rocco Ballista) could change his name all he wanted, but it didn't change his nature. After several days of lazing around in his old villa, Teppista began to get restless. He began to get the itch to work another deal, to swindle another sucker, to cheat another naïve customer. The problem with being a successful thug is that you get an adrenaline rush when you score. What Teppista learned after only a few days of lethargy was that he needed another adrenaline fix.

The afternoon sun was beginning to go down over the coast of Sorrento, and while the view was beautiful, he was already getting bored with gorgeous sunsets. "Mr. Pavarotti" began making phone calls to his old cronies, including Herr Bloch at the Berlin Museum. To his surprise, he got an earful on the carelessness of his cousin Vinny. He was told that the Museum required his new address to send him a bill for the repair of the cracked lintel, something Teppista agreed to, so he could keep his profit pipeline open. Finally, he called a local antiquities dealer in Napoli—the same one he had sold the hand lamps with the fish symbols. The dealer was out, but his secretary took "Mr. Pavarotti's" number and promised he would call back.

Teppista had not avoided prosecution after all these years without being able to read the warning signs, the dark clouds on the horizon. It occurred to him after these phone calls that he should lay low for a while before attempting more sales. Things were too hot in Italy just now, both literally and figuratively. Teppista knew enough not to leave the country. By now, the authorities knew that the hand lamps, lintel, and ossuaries were hot items. So he was stumped. What should he do next? For now he ordered out for a famous Sorrento pizza, and he told the maid to open a bottle of his favorite Chianti. What good was having ill-gotten gains, if you couldn't enjoy them for a while? He would bide his time for now.

Cousin Vinny was getting nervous as well. He suspected that the lintel was the one stolen in Rome that recently made some headlines. Time to get out of town he thought. While he was contemplating this new plan, a detective showed up at his door. "Are you Teppista Terranova?" asked the policeman.

"No, I'm not! And I don't know where he is. I'm his cousin, Vinny Terranova," he replied rather hotly.

"You'll do just nicely," said Detective Ubaldo. "May I come in?"

"Umm, I'm kind of busy just now. Could it wait until say, tomorrow afternoon?"

"I don't think so," said Ubaldo smiling confidently. "I believe you had something to do with the sale of an artifact recently. And I'm pretty sure that if I wait until tomorrow, I may never see you again!" Detective Ubaldo sort of waltzed into the room while Vinny held the door open with a wide-eyed expression on his baby face. He was no match for a seasoned detective.

"What?" Vinny stammered. "I d-don't know n-nothin' about any art!"

"That's artifact, not art, young man. Interpol has identified you as the person who delivered stolen goods to a Berlin museum last Saturday!"

"What in the world are you talking about? My cousin bought that art or artifact or whatever it is fair and square from a seller. He didn't steal nothin'!"

"Thanks for mentioning your cousin Teppista again. Where is he just now?" pushed the Detective.

"I already told you—he's out of town. Gone south I think," replied Vinny already realizing he said too much.

"When will he be back?"

"I don't know. How about you just leave now," ventured Vinny.

"There seems to be an awful lot you don't know, Mr. Terranova."

"You're right. I just drove a truck and delivered an item like I was told. That's all I know! You can go now," said Vinny again, starting to feel a bit braver.

"As we police like to say, don't leave town. You are now part of my investigation. If your cousin contacts you, then you should contact me. Here's my card. Do you understand?" said the Detective regaining the upper hand.

"Yes sir," replied Vinny rather meekly. The burly detective sauntered back to his unmarked car.

Now Vinny was really scared. And he did what any really frightened person might do. He panicked. He began to empty the file cabinet, scoop up the paperwork on the desk, and throw everything into a large plastic garbage bag.

Meanwhile, the Detective was watching from a safe distance. When Vinny took the trash out to the road, Detective Ubaldo caught everything on camera. Once on the street, trash was fair game. The net was closing around Vinny, even though he couldn't feel the rope around his neck just yet.

He'd better call Teppista and ask him what to do next. Vinny had no clue. He was not a professional criminal; he was just a bum who went along with the big plans of his older cousin in order to make some euro on the side. In actuality, he was just a local fruit merchant, running a legitimate business. This didn't mean the police planned to go easy on him. There was a lot of political pressure to come up with some arrests—quickly. Both money and manpower had been allocated to the hunt, and it was now in full swing. The outgoing phone call to Cousin Teppista was traced—they knew where the man was now.

46

Storms Brewing

EARLY WEDNESDAY MORNING FATHER Peter joined Pope Jerome for a lengthy meeting over breakfast in the Pope's private quarters. Peering out the window, Father Peter remarked on the dark clouds heading in from the Mediterranean.

"I certainly don't like these articles written by Mr. Andretti," remarked Pope Jerome over scrambled eggs and prosciutto. "Just look at this headline: Vatican denies hiding atrocities; dead men's bones right under their feet! It demands some sort of explanation. Have our people prepare a press release."

Father Peter warned, "There will be further requests for interviews if we do so. May I suggest that we do much more than just have a press release?"

"What do you have in mind?" said the Pope raising his brow.

"Let the archaeologists have a press conference strictly about what was found and what was lost. That at least might stop the rumor of a cover-up involving the Vatican and Jews. There are lots of rumors swirling around, thanks to our Mr. Andretti, and my inability to keep my mouth shut yesterday!"

The Pope just smiled. "Don't feel too bad, Peter. At least this article seems a bit more restrained. It quotes you at length, I must say. He must have really pushed your buttons, as they say! But the implication of the headline isn't good. This reporter would like nothing better than to embarrass the Holy See."

"Exactly," said Peter. "Gone are the days when we can just control the media and stonewall questions. In the world of computers and cellphones and instant messages, we can't avoid commenting on controversial issues."

The Pope replied, "I realize this, but we must find a way to turn it to our advantage. Do you think we can craft the news release and set up a press conference in the next couple of days? We need to do this for ourselves, of course, but I do hope Dr. Miller will be at the press conference."

"Yes, Holy Father, I'm certain we can have our Vatican press conference and, at the same time, provide Dr. Miller with a platform to discuss the archaeological finds. So first, I'll make sure Dr. Miller is on board. I'll get on it right away and then head over to the Media Center to start the ball rolling. By the way, did you send our hot-headed friend Friar Magnus off on a spiritual retreat or some mission?"

"No. In fact I told him he would be disciplined before long."

"Well, I saw him leaving the Vatican in a hurry this morning when I came to work."

Groaning, the Pope said, "That man is a cannon just waiting to misfire. I hope he doesn't make matters worse. It's amazing what some people feel obliged to do in the service of Christ."

"Sadly, you are right, Holy Father. Do you have some time now for meditation and prayer?" asked Father Peter.

"That's the very reason your post was set up so very, very long ago. The Church has weathered many storms—thanks to prayer!" marveled His Holiness.

∼

On a good day, the ride to Orvieto only took an hour in a car from Rome. Magnus was excited. Since Monday, he had discovered that Boz's real family name was Mussolini, and many of that family's relatives lived in or around the town of Orvieto. He knew the police were also looking for Boz, but Magnus decided on a different, more personal, approach. He would go to Orvieto and find as many of his family members as possible. Maybe one of them would know Boz's whereabouts. It was a cloudy day with thunderstorms forecasted. Still, any excuse to get out of Rome for a while was worth the effort.

Magnus easily convinced himself that he was on the right track. In his mind, he imagined the praise he would get for helping to solve the crime of the missing antiquities. This would surely restore him into the good graces of the Pope, or so he hoped. When he arrived in Orvieto, and urged his little car to chug up the steep hill into the ancient walled city, it just about refused to cooperate. A lightning bolt struck in the valley below, and the first drops of rain hit the road.

Finally, his car arrived at the top of the hill, and Magnus managed to park it near the town square. In his mind he had an image of Boz with a goatee and long black hair. With a strong black umbrella over his head, he combed the streets looking for someone who fit that description, and found no one even close. There was a man with dark hair under a café awning working in oils to capture the cathedral facade, but that man said his name was Picasso.

"No, I've never heard of this guy Boz. You say he's one of the Mussolini family? Maybe he lives in the next town across the valley. You like my work? Everyone paints in the sunshine, but the clouds give the cathedral a different feel, don't you think. These are stormy times, my friend! You should sit in the café and have some cappuccino. Your pants are soaking wet!" laughed Boz.

"No time! No time! I will find this bad man!" cried the Black Friar getting more and more frustrated. Another three hours of dodging showers went by. The sky was getting even darker, and Magnus was getting nowhere. Glum, he decided to have dinner and check into the local *pensione* near the old monastery. Things were not going according to plan. As he headed down the cobblestone street from the town square, he thought he heard footsteps behind him, but when he turned, there was no one there so he dismissed the early warning signal that went off in his brain.

47

Press Day

WEDNESDAY WAS A LONG and tiring day for Father Peter. While the scattered storms bounced around Rome, he made plans for the press release and conference. First he contacted Charlie who readily agreed and put his own team into high gear. Art, Marissa and Kahlil were on board. Grace was called and agreed to fly back immediately.

Secondly, he found Father Giordano in the Holy See Press Office who helped Peter craft the press release. The facts had to be right; the tone had to be perfect. Many calls were made back and forth to the Charlie, the Vatican police, their own archaeology team, etc. etc. Any press release from the Vatican would be picked up internationally and released in multiple languages in multiple media. Every word had to be carefully considered as Father Peter well understood. When it was finished, Father Peter was quite satisfied. It read:

> The Vatican announces today the discovery of a major, pre-viously unknown, Christian catacomb with many Christian saints' remains buried in it, including familiar New Testament figures such as Priscilla and Aquila, and Andronicus and Junia. This catacomb appears to have been a place where first century Jewish Christians were buried, many of them martyrs at the hands of Nero.
>
> Found in the tomb were several ossuaries, including those of at least two children. Other items found in the tomb include

several hand lamps decorated with the fish symbol, and a lintel identifying one of the couples buried there.

The two children's ossuaries, the hand lamps, and the lintel were stolen. The Vatican is pleased to report, however, that both children's ossuaries have been recovered. Security measures have been undertaken to prevent further desecration of this new catacomb system.

The Holy Father also announces that a symposium will be convened for the careful study of the artifacts and remains found in this large catacomb. The date has not yet been set. Friday at 4PM, in the Vatican media room, a press conference will be held by Professor Charles Miller, whose team is responsible for discovering these antiquities.

Notable by its absence was any reference to female apostles, but that was a discussion and debate for later. This press release was to focus on the facts, not their interpretation. While Father Peter hoped the archaeological team would not engage in a bunch of speculation in the news conference in the afternoon, he was studiously avoiding trying to tell Charlie Miller or anyone else what they should and shouldn't say. The old days of censorship were over.

∾

When Charlie Miller, Art West, Marissa Okur, Grace Levine, and Kahlil el Said walked into the media room at the Vatican on Thursday afternoon, it was packed from front to back with at least one hundred representatives of the media, complete with all the paraphernalia of modern journalism. At 4 o'clock cameras went off leaving those at the long table where the scholars sat blinded. Charlie, in a navy blue suit and a natty red bow tie, strode to the podium.

"The protocol for this afternoon's press conference will be as follow: each of us will speak to our area of expertise, followed by thirty minutes of questioning—that's all—so please make your questions very pertinent," said Charlie with a friendly smile.

"Early last May, during the digging of a new sewer line under the street directly behind the Vatican, an entrance to a tomb was uncovered. The first thing to be discovered proved to be the tomb of Andronicus and Junia, Jewish Christians mentioned in Romans 16 as being co-workers of Paul. The lintel over the doorway was translated to read, 'Here lie Andronicus and Junia, apostles of Christ.' This lintel seems to confirm the reading of Romans 16:7 which states that 'they are noteworthy among the apostles.' Yes, we seem to have a reference to female apostles. Professor West will speak about that matter.

"In addition, two ossuaries for adults, one for Andronicus and one for Junia, plus two ossuaries for children, one for a male child named Clement and one for a female child named Tryphosa were also found. The script was in Greek, except for the Junia ossuary, which had a rather lengthy Aramaic inscription. Subsequent examination of the Clement ossuary revealed a small piece of papyrus. In addition to the four ossuaries and the lintel, we found three small hand lamps.

"As you know, the tomb of Andronicus and Junia was raided. The usual security was in place, but someone dug through the limestone roof and entered it from above in the middle of the night. I must admit, having read the stories of the Egyptian tomb raiders, who even used boiling oil to crack open huge granite sarcophagi in order to steal the gold and jewels on royal mummies, I should have realized how very persistent and ingenious tomb raiders can be. Nevertheless, we are happy to report that the two adult ossuaries were too big to be stolen; the two children's ossuaries have been located; and we have some leads on the lintel and hand lamps. All of the artifacts, except the lintel on the front of the tomb, were found under Vatican land. They are therefore the property of the Vatican as the lawyers have now confirmed. The city of Rome has no eminent domain statutes that cover Vatican land. If and when we recover the lintel, it will be turned over to the Ministry of Culture.

"Subsequent to this theft, a bricked-up archway, bearing the symbol of the Star of David, was revealed by a reporter who gained access without our permission. After removing several bricks he videotaped what appeared to be a room behind the archway. Our team completed the careful removal of the mud bricks and discovered a very large catacomb, full of burial boxes of various early Christians. It will take years for us to carefully examine these items.

"At the very end of the chamber is one large mausoleum. The sign there indicates that Paul's co-workers, Priscilla and Aquila are buried there. It appears that one or both of them were condemned to the mines and died there.

"Through the help of Father Peter Salta, we have ascertained that the far end of this chamber, which is also bricked up, reaches a spot adjacent to the crypt of Saint Peter. So it appears that Peter was buried at one end of the chamber, near Priscilla and Aquila, and Andronicus and Junia at the other end, and apparently a large number of Jewish Christians in between. Why Jewish Christians would all be buried in a special cemetery is a matter for close study. The manuscript found in the Clement ossuary seems to provide a clue."

Charlie concluded his remarks and Art West arose immediately. Wearing a tan suit, a Carolina blue shirt, and a dark blue tie, Art looked every inch the scholar. Marissa had made sure he looked exactly right for the occasion—formal but not stuffy she had said.

"What I want to stress is that archaeological work rarely finds a direct parallel to things said in the New Testament, but this dig is the exception to that rule. The names of the persons buried in that cata-comb correspond to the many names Paul lists in Romans 16, a text which calls upon the Gentile Christians in Rome to be hospitable to these Jewish Christians.

"The papyrus in the Clement ossuary was not discovered until Hannah, the daughter of Kahlil el Said, both Jerusalem antiquities dealers, opened the package she had purchased of two children's os-suaries, allegedly sold by a legitimate dealer in antiquities here in Italy, and found the piece of papyrus plastered against the inside. Hannah removed the papyrus, and translated the Latin. The papyrus was torn, at both the top and the bottom, and what remained was as follows,

> . . . which he, barbarian that he was, did not refrain from doing.
> Even children were executed in the Circus Maximus,
> for Nero claimed they played their part in the great fire.
> His wrath focused on Jewish Christians young and old,
> for Romans were biased against the Jews.
> Petros, Paulus, Andronicus, Junia, and children
> were executed to satisfy the Beast's bloodlust.
> Some were condemned to the mines . . .

"Apparently many in this graveyard, including children, were martyred by Nero. While Hollywood has fixed in our imagination the persecution of many Christians in the Coliseum, the Coliseum did not even exist in Nero's day. It was constructed during the reign of

Vespasian and his sons. At the end of the first century AD, Tacitus, a notable critic of Nero, wrote in his famous *Annals* the following:

> Yet no human effort, no princely largess nor offerings to the gods could make that infamous rumor disappear that Nero had somehow ordered the fire. Therefore, in order to abolish that rumor, Nero falsely accused and executed with the most exquisite punishments those people called Christians, who were infamous for their abominations. The originator of the name, Christ, was executed as a criminal by the procurator Pontius Pilate during the reign of Tiberius; and though repressed, this destructive superstition erupted again, not only through Judea, which was the origin of this evil, but also through the city of Rome, to which all that is horrible and shameful floods together and is celebrated. Therefore, first those were seized who admitted their faith, and then, using the information they provided, a vast multitude were convicted, not so much for the crime of burning the city, but for hatred of the human race. And perishing they were additionally made into sports: they were killed by dogs by having the hides of beasts attached to them, or they were nailed to crosses or set aflame, and, when the daylight passed away, they were used as nighttime lamps. Nero gave his own gardens for this spectacle and performed a Circus game, in the habit of a charioteer mixing with the plebs or driving about the race-course. Even though they were clearly guilty and merited being made the most recent example of the consequences of crime, people began to pity these sufferers, because they were consumed not for the public good but on account of the fierceness of one man. (*Annals* 15)

"Scholars have tried to minimize the persecutions of Christians by Roman authorities, and indeed the persecutions were not systematic, but rather sporadic and local in the first century AD. This does not mean they were not horrific, and did not involve a significant number of Christians. What we learn from this catacomb is that Tacitus was not exaggerating, and the particular focus of Nero's wrath seems to have been on Jewish Christians. Anti-Semitism was already rife in the Roman Empire, and Nero would be picking on a favorite punching bag, the subject of ridicule and ethnic prejudice already for many years in Rome.

"But there may be another sadder sub-text. The Christian community in Rome was largely divided along ethnic lines. This division was reinforced when the Emperor Claudius expelled Jewish Christians, or at least their leaders like Priscilla and Aquila from Rome (see Acts 18). When they returned in AD 54, a mere decade before the fire and persecution, it must have been difficult for them to get re-established in Rome. Paul in AD 57, writing Romans, tries to push the Gentile Christians to show every degree of hospitality and affection towards their returning fellow Christians who were Jews. I would argue that the list in Romans 16 names all Jewish Christians that the Gentile Christians are asked to embrace. What this separate Jewish graveyard probably sadly attests is that Jewish Christians took the brunt of the persecution, and some or many Gentile Christians faded into the woodwork and provided little help for them in their hour of need. This is a conjecture based on the text of Romans and the findings at the dig.

"One last thing, about women apostles. The apostolic office was separate from, and not the same as the later Christian priesthood. Thus, to call Junia an apostle certainly means she was an early Christian leader of note, one who likely saw the risen Lord and like Paul was commissioned by him to preach and teach. She is not called a priest in either the New Testament or in this new archaeological evidence.

"Different scholars will argue differently about whether the original apostles were priests. I would argue they were not, unless you are simply referring to what is meant in a metaphorical way in 1 Peter, that all Christians are priests, offering themselves and others up to God. I am an Evangelical Protestant and my view would be the New Testament knows nothing of a class of clergy or priests. The only priesthood in the NT is the priesthood of all believers, both men and women, and the high priesthood of Christ himself in heaven. That is all. If this is correct, it creates problems for Catholic theology and tradition that has closely associated the apostolic office with the priestly office, and said that only men were called by Christ to it. In my view, this is a historical mistake, but these things will be viewed differently by different scholars. Thank you."

The reporters could hardly take notes fast enough. Nothing like this press conference had ever transpired in the Vatican before, and it was raising as many questions as it was providing answer. Next up to bat was Grace Levine, wearing a stunning hunter green business suit and her usual red glasses and spiked heels.

"As a Jewish scholar, I count it a privilege to be here, and to be part of this team, and I want to thank our hosts for their gracious welcome of both me and my husband for these last few days. As you know, the relationship between Jews and Christians has not always been cordial; indeed, it has often involved much hostility. But this graveyard is *not* another historical example of Christians persecuting Jews. This is an example of Jews, specifically Jews who were followers of Jesus, being persecuted specifically by pagans. Some of the recent headlines in this town have been completely irresponsible in their innuendo that the Vatican was covering up some Christian persecution of Jews. Absolutely false!

"My area of expertise is ancient epigraphy, in particular ancient Aramaic inscriptions from the early part of the Common Era. The Aramaic inscription on the Junia ossuary literally says, 'Joanna/Junia fell asleep in the Lord and was buried in this place. Follower of Jesus, witness of his cross and resurrection, loyal wife of Andronicus, co-worker of Paul, apostle of the Lord.'

"Junia is the Latin equivalent of the Hebrew name of Joanna, and the phrase 'disciple or follower of Jesus' probably does mean this is the Joanna who was formerly married to Chuza, Herod Antipas's estate manager in Galilee. Thus Andronicus would be her second husband. She was likely divorced by Chuza because she kept going on 'walk-about' with Jesus and the male disciples, which would have been seen as scandalous. The reference to her being an apostle of the Lord probably refers to her having been one of those who claimed to have received an appearance of the risen Jesus. What we know is that according to Luke she was there at the cross, at the empty tomb, and Luke 24 says she also saw a vision of angels.

"This is an important woman, sort of the female equivalent of Peter, since she was both a disciple of Jesus and an apostle in the early church. As a high-status person she was probably literate as well. The fact that she was in prison with Paul may suggest she was incarcerated for her public evangelism of people, and so was jailed for the same sorts of reasons Paul was. Paul seems to have worked with several important couples: Andronicus and Junia, and Priscilla and Aquila being two of them. In my judgment there is no doubt that this is a first century Jewish ossuary with a genuine first century Aramaic inscription. Finally, yes, there is evidence that the Star of David was already a Jewish symbol in antiquity. The evidence is found at the synagogue dig in Capernaum, and dates at least to the third or second century of the Common Era. I will now hand the presentation over to Mr. Kahlil el Said."

Kahlil cut a very different figure from the previous presenters. Beside his daunting physical appearance, Kahlil had decided to wear his formal turban, a long muslin robe, and his ceremonial purple, red, and yellow sash around his waist.

"Unlike my friends at this table, I am not a true scholar. I hold no doctoral degrees. I am an antiquities dealer, but I have learned much in the school of business experience, and one of the things I have learned the most about is pottery lamps, especially first century clay pottery lamps, the ancient equivalent of flashlights.

"Unexpectedly, my daughter Hannah became involved in this when she quite innocently made a purchase of two ancient burial boxes, which turned out to be the very ones stolen from the tomb of Andronicus and Junia. God has a sense of humor when it comes to his providence. The thieves could not have known they were selling the boxes back to people who would return them to the Vatican!"

Laughter swept briefly through the room and then Kahlil added, "Now as for the lamps themselves, they are certainly early Christian lamps, as they all have the primitive symbol of Christianity on them, not the cross, but the fish. The fish was a Christian symbol because of the Greek word *Ichthus* being used as an anagram for '*Iesous Christos theos uios soter*' or Jesus Christ Son of God Savior. These lamps are quite typical in their size and shape and clay composition. There is nothing ornate about them, except the fish symbols on their bottom sides, and a little line marking on the top. Here is a picture of these top

of the lamps. Unfortunately, I do not have a picture of the Ichthus symbol on the bottom. They were stolen before I took a picture. So here is where I make a plea for their return." Up on the screen came this image.

"I imagine by now you are on information overload, so I will simply conclude by saying, I have no doubt these are first century AD pottery lamps. We will now take a fifteen minute break, before we resume for the Q and A session."

Father Peter, observing from the back of the room was pleased, though he wished that Art West had not pressed the most thorny of the theological issues, the relationship of the apostles to priests. He thought it was understood that the theological issues were to be left for another day. "I don't think the Holy Father will be too pleased about that," he mused.

But still overall he was pleased with all the presentations. They provided a good backdrop and context for an ongoing discussion. What they did not do was lessen the pressure on the Vatican to consider ordaining women! "Oh well, we are used to pressure and undue media attention these days," said Father Peter with a sigh.

48

Found, One Lintel

INTERPOL WAS NOTHING IF not persistent in pursuing leads. And Raoul D'Silva on this morning was following the maxim, "Just follow the money." What he had learned was that there had been a very large bank transfer of funds into the account of a Mr. Terranova in the Central Napoli Bank, and that the funds came from the Pergamon Museum in Berlin no less. It did not take a rocket scientist to conclude that the Museum was paying for some precious relic or artifact. Could it be one of the stolen objects from the tomb in Rome? Mr. Terranova had a reputation with Interpol for shady dealings, and indeed for Mafia connections, so Raoul was not prepared to give the man the benefit of the doubt. Indeed, it had been Raoul who put the local Napoli police onto the trail of Terranova.

On this morning Raoul was ringing up the museum in Berlin. Fortunately, Lyon and Berlin were in the same time zone. Raoul discovered online that Dr. Gunter Bloch was the curator that he needed to speak to. The phone rang for a while, and then a secretary picked up. "*Guten Morgen, Wie gehts?*"

"I'm fine," said Raoul. "I am Raoul d'Silva from the Lyon office of Interpol. I need to speak with Herr Gunter Bloch."

After a wait of about three or four minutes, a somewhat irritated Mr. Bloch picked up the phone. "Yes, how can I help?"

"Herr Bloch, Interpol is conducting an investigation. I need to know if you recently purchased an expensive item from a dealer in Naples whose last name is Terranova."

"Naturally all our sales are confidential. Many of our sellers do not wish to have their names disclosed to anyone; indeed, it is often a condition of the sale, which is the case in this instance."

"So, without saying so in so many words, you are not denying that a Mr. Terranova sold you something recently?"

"Right, I am not saying so, but I am not denying it either," hedged Gunter.

"Good. Because the hypothetical object of this sale was stolen from a tomb in Rome. It belongs to the Vatican! The same Vatican that houses a museum with which you have cordial relations, I believe. I imagine you would like to continue in their good graces, considering you recently had a major exhibit of Vatican art and artifacts that brought a good sum of money into your coffers, I gather!"

"I see your point," said Bloch nervously.

"Good. So I will ask you directly, do you or do you not have a lintel with the following inscription on it, *HIC IACETUR ANDRONICUS ET JUNIA APOSTOLI CHRISTI*?"

There was another long, awkward pause. "I have a lintel. We made a legal purchase; we have the bona fides; we dealt in good faith; and possession is nine-tenths of the law, as I am sure you are aware."

"Yes, I am aware of this sort of illogical logic used to justify bad behavior, but I'm also aware that you would like to keep your job, and I wonder what the director would say about your lack of investigation into the origins of the lintel and your quick purchase. The news is full of the story of the stolen lintel right now. Surely, that hasn't escaped your attention!"

"Perhaps not," said Bloch who was sweating now.

"I suggest that you pack up that lintel and return it to the Vatican Department of Archaeology. Otherwise, I shall go over your head and report that you were not cooperative with the law, that you say you have nine-tenths of on your side! Am I clear?"

"Crystal clear. But you might want to know that the lintel in question did not arrive intact—it arrived in three pieces! And I assure you that was not our fault!" claimed Gunter already planning on how to retrieve his money from Teppista.

"That is unfortunate. Regardless, when I receive confirmation that the lintel has been received at the Vatican, I will drop the case, and not trouble you further. *Verstehen sie*?"

"*Ja, Ich verstehe sehr gut.*"

"*Danke, auf Wiedesehen.*"

49

Q & A

A T THE Q&A SESSION, there were so many questions, many of
them unanswerable, that there was a sort of frenzy in the room.
Reporters all wanted sound-bites, McNuggets of information, and these
scholars just weren't biting. There was this nuance and that nuance,
and this qualification and that qualification. Marissa began to laugh at
the number of reporters shaking their heads in confusion. When one
reporter asked Grace to explain why she knew this was a first century
inscription, she launched into a 25-minute discussion about patina
in the letters, the shape of the Aramaic letters, ancient Jewish ossuary
burial practices, Jewish beliefs in resurrection, and so on!

The one piece of advice Father Peter had given Charlie was, make
sure no one recognizes Adriano Andretti. He didn't deserve that kind
of favor after the headlines he had cooked up on the basis of so little
information. Marissa got especially tickled watching Adriano on the
second row jump up and down to get attention. He did everything but
rush the stage and tackle Charlie who kept smiling and pointing to
other reporters for questions. The clock was now approaching 6:30, the
press conference Q&A had gone on an hour longer than advertised,
and Charlie realized everyone was getting tired and a little irritable.

"We will take one final question," said Charlie emphatically and
pointed immediately to Laurie Goodstone of the *New York Times* who
had flown over for the press conference.

"I recently wrote an article for my paper on the various attempts, by Catholic priests themselves, to ordain women. Professor Miller you are a practicing Catholic, I believe. . ."

"Yes," quipped Charlie. "I will keep practicing until I get it right!' This prompted a huge laugh, which relieved some of the tension in the room.

"As I was saying, you're a practicing Catholic and also a scholar. Do you think the revelations from this tomb might prompt a rethinking of Catholic policy about women priests? And if not, why not, since we seem to be dealing with hard historical evidence here?"

"That's a very fair question, and one I expected you would ask. My basic answer is, I just don't know. We do live in an age of surprises. For example, recently the Pope said that belief in limbo was no longer a matter of Catholic doctrine or dogma. I would never have expected that sort of announcement when I was younger. I think you need to understand that the Holy Father and the Curia are men of devotion, and they do believe in listening to what God's Spirit is saying to the church today. But as Professor West said, the sticking point would seem to be about the relationship between being an apostle and being a priest. The Old Testament is clear about only men being priests. Of course, this differed from Greco-Roman practice where there were women priests. On the other hand, if Romans 16 does refer to a Junia who is an apostle, and so does this tomb's evidence, well then a thorough reconsidering of the argument 'since only men were apostles, then only men should be Catholic priests' is required.

"There are fundamental theological questions that need to be addressed before your question can be answered. For instance, what is the relationship between the apostolic office and the priestly office? I personally would not take the same view of the priesthood as my friend Art West would. He could be right, and I could be wrong, or vice versa. It's a matter for debate. I am sure, however that this archaeological find will give more urgency to such a debate, and to that end the Holy Father has called a symposium for next January. You should all come back then, and see how it turns out. In the meantime stay tuned for more revelations about those buried Jewish Christians beneath our feet! Thank you so much for your time and attention."

General applause broke out briefly, and then reporters raced to the door to begin filing their stories. It had been an interesting afternoon. Father Peter came up, embraced each one of the panelists, and thanked them for their time, time that they had given graciously and gratis. "And now the Holy Father wants me to tell you all, including you Marissa, that dinner is on him. Though he is unable to join us, I have a Vatican van waiting and we are all going off to Piccolo Ristorante. Any objections?"

"Not a one," said Grace. "I need something, anything to revive me after all this talk about dead Jews."

Father Peter agreed with a smile. "Let's go improve Jewish-Christian relationships right now over a vintage bottle of Italian wine."

"I'll drink to that," said Art.

50

This Car is a Bomb

MAGNUS WAS SURE THAT Mr. Picasso was Boz, the man he was searching for. For the past few days he buzzed around Picasso trying to trick him into giving up some piece of incriminating evidence. Question after question was hurled at Picasso who slipped up enough to convince Magnus that he was indeed the graffiti artist. Boz couldn't help but brag, and gave away just too much information as he praised the "artistic gang" that recently decorated the Arch of Titus. He found the Black Friar quite amusing. Besides he kept Boz supplied with good Orvieto wine and bought a number of his cathedral paintings.

While Boz continued to paint in the town square, Magnus continued to spend money he didn't have to keep tabs on Boz. Saturday afternoon, Magnus decided it was time to go home to Rome. First, he called his friend at the Vatican police.

"Alberto, I'm about 90% sure that I have tracked down the man who stole the artifacts from the new catacomb. Remember, he goes by Boz, but his real name is Antonio Mussolini. I think he's in Orvieto—his family home—and he goes by the name of Mondriano Picasso. Can you believe that!? Anyway, he thinks he's a painter now. I also think he's on to me and, truthfully, he's a scary kind of guy."

"Thanks, Brother Tertullian. The gossip around the office says the team is closing in on this Boz guy. I'll tell them that you think Boz is in Orvieto. I hope you enjoyed the wine while you were there. But now, I think you should get out!"

Magnus wholeheartedly agreed. He packed up his things, paid the bill at the *pensione*, and headed down the cobblestone street to the car park. Along the way Father Tertullian was thinking, "I have an alias too. Sometimes I forget my real name is Magnus McIlroy."

The sun was beginning to head for the horizon when he got in the car and started it up. The little engine chugged into life. Magnus pulled out into the street that wound around the back of the city and headed down the long incline to the main highway. Along the way, he noticed smoke coming out from under the hood of the car, and he assumed his radiator had overheated.

Magnus pulled to the side of the road, turned off the car, and opened the hood. All of a sudden there was a rumble and a huge explosion that knocked Magnus off his feet, down an embankment and into a vineyard. He lay unconscious, but alive, under lots and lots of grapes, sour grapes, as it was not yet the October picking season.

The blast of the homemade bomb could be heard in the town square where most people were saying things like "O my God!" or "What was that?" With a Mona Lisa smile, Mr. Picasso just kept on painting. "Imagine me being the cause of a monk going to heaven. Who would have thought it?"

∼

The red hot car that Teppista bought was actually a Ferrari Testarossa. In some quarters it was the most popular Ferrari model, and one of the most expensive. Teppista bought his second hand from a shady car salesman who owed him a favor and was all too happy to get the car off his lot. The sales documents named Teppista as the buyer, although the registration used the alias of Pietro Pavarotti.

On Saturday, Teppista drove into Sorrento to have lunch, do a little shopping, and in general make himself useless. He was bored. He noticed one of the waiters humming opera, and so he burst out into song, "*La donna è mobile. . .*" (the lady is fickle). And the waiter immediately sang the next phrase, "*qual piuma al vento*" (like a feather in the wind)—and came to his table smiling.

"Ah, you are singing for your supper!" boomed the waiter.

As "Pietro" sat and ate his little Sorrento pizza and drank a glass of wine, two men in black and white uniforms were busy checking out the Testarossa. Just when Teppista was about to order a cappuccino and some dessert, his just deserts showed up in a different form.

"Mr. Terranova? I am Officer Gianitelli. My partner is waiting outside," said the tall mustachioed man holding out his identification card.

Teppista spit out his coffee and said with a flourish, "I'm afraid you've made a mistake! My name is Pietro Pavarotti!"

"No, *signore*, the mistake is definitely yours. That red Testarossa you are driving was bought by Tony Terranova, who goes by Teppista. And you, *signore*, must come with me."

"And why is that? I bought the car legally," sputtered Teppista.

"Perhaps. But there is a warrant out for you. You are under arrest!"

"But I am Pietro Pavarotti!" shouted Teppista. "I want my lawyer!"

"I heard you sing, and you are no Pavarotti. But I am the law, and the law of Italy says I can arrest you now and you can call your lawyer later from jail."

There was a moment of struggle, but Teppista was no match for the taller officer who quickly handcuffed him. The red Testarossa shone in the evening sun, all alone, without a driver, having blown up the criminal career of its owner.

51

The Vatican Library

THE VATICAN LIBRARY IS one of the most important collections of texts in the entire world. Formally established in 1475, just before Columbus headed for the New World, it currently holds some 75,000 manuscripts and over 1 million books. Recently renovated and then reopened in the Fall of 2010, the library has a rich and varied history

Through the years, this library has become a magnet attracting other collections and libraries to this spot. For example, the entire royal library of Sweden ended up in the Vatican collection. It was bought in 1689 by Pope Alexander VIII from Queen Christina of Sweden, and a good thing too because the library of Sweden burned to the ground in 1697. The Palatine library of Heidelberg was simply given to the Vatican in 1623 by Maximillian, the Duke of Bavaria. Amidst the many ancient, rare, and precious manuscripts and books in this library, Father Peter finally had time to do some research. He wanted to know more about the ancient martyrdoms and about the Star of David.

Father Peter was met at the door by Father Rafelle Farina, a librarian that specialized in early Church history. "*Buongiorno*, Father Peter! You're up early after all the excitement at the press conference yesterday. I'm sure we will get the full transcript to put on file here in the library somewhere! But that's not my area of expertise."

"There's no end of historical trails I could explore after everything that has happened in the last few weeks! But you are right. Today I want to explore the traditions about St. Peter's death," said Father Peter trying to stay focused as his eyes roamed about the beautiful room.

"Good! I have set out the books by Eusebius for you to begin with. He said that Peter was martyred in the thirteenth or fourteenth year of the reign of Nero, which would put it at AD 67 or 68." Rafelle had indeed laid out for him the reference in Eusebius, *Church History* II.25.

"Note that Eusebius stresses, 'But I can show the trophies of the Apostles. If you care to go to the Vatican or to the road to Ostia, you can find the trophies of those who have founded this Church.' I think the word 'trophies' refers to the graves of the Apostles right here in Rome on our own Vatican Hill. So St. Peter, who was executed on the Vatican Hill, was also buried here—right under our Basilica, or so we believe. Eusebius also refers to 'the inscription of the names of Peter and Paul, which have been preserved to the present day on the burial-places there.' By that he means Rome, I'm sure.

"Now we turn to Chapter 40 in the second century AD document called *The Martyrdom of Peter* which is also included at the end of the document called the *Acts of Peter*. Here is the relevant passage.

> And Marcellus not asking from anyone, for it was not possible,
> when he saw that Peter had given up his spirit, took him down

from the cross with his own hands and washed him in milk and wine: and cut fine seven minae of mastic, and of myrrh and aloes and Indian leaf, and perfumed (embalmed) his body and filled a coffin of marble of great price with Attic honey and laid it in his own tomb.

"Now we do not know where this tomb of Marcellus was, but Eusebius seems confident it was here at the Vatican. Who is this Marcellus? The *Acts of Peter* document portrays him as a Roman Senator, and so an elite person and apparently a convert. Now this tradition of his entombing Peter is found also in the *Actus Vercellenses*. There are various texts of the *Acts of Peter*, and in the one called the 'Marcellus' text there is reference to some men from Jerusalem arriving and with Marcellus burying Peter at the Vatican hill (Marcellus 63). There are more and later traditions about his martyrdom, but suffice it to say that the traditions about where Peter is buried are reasonably clear. There is nothing about his being buried with others, though nothing is said against such a notion either."

"Thank you, Father Rafelle, that is quite helpful. But what about the early traditions about Jewish Christians in general in Rome?"

"I knew you would ask that, and there is this passage from Ambrosiaster's commentary. In the preface to his *Exposition of Romans*, written around AD 375, Ambrosiaster commented on the character of early Roman Christianity. Look here at this text.

> It is established that there were Jews living in Rome in the time of the apostles and that those Jews who had believed [in Christ] passed on to the Romans the tradition that they ought to profess Christ but keep the Law. . . . One ought not to condemn the Romans, but to praise their faith, because without seeing any signs or miracles, and without seeing any of the apostles, they nevertheless accepted faith in Christ, although in a Jewish manner [*ritu licet Judaico*].

"Now what makes this testimony so interesting is that Ambrosiaster, writing at a time when the church was overwhelmingly Gentile in character, freely admits that there was a significant Jewish Christian population in Rome who had an effect on various Romans. The Satires, written by Juvenal, and other documents ridicule Romans who considered getting circumcised, or keeping Sabbath, or observing food laws. It was a hard go for Jews in Rome, never mind when you add the offense of a crucified savior which Jewish Christians believed in. But the point about the Ambrosiaster reference is that it helps us to understand a text like Romans 14.

"Why was Paul talking about varying worship practices, and varying food practices to a congregation he did not found and had not yet visited? It must be because he knew that the Roman Jewish Christians were mostly keeping themselves separate and keeping kosher, and so Paul is pleading with his largely Gentile audience, as the apostle to the Gentiles, not to judge them, but rather to embrace them, and accept their different practices without compelling them to follow the Gentile practices. It is a heart-felt plea. Paul finds himself betwixt and between—not exactly agreeing with either side of the debate, since he thinks the whole thing is a trivial matter. Christians were not required to keep Sabbath, not even Jewish Christians, in his view."

Father Peter added, "It makes sense to read Romans 16 as a letter of commendation not just of Phoebe, but of Jewish Christians who returned to Rome in AD 54. Gentile Christians are asked to embrace them."

"That seems the best hypothesis to me. If only we had more direct evidence of what happened during Nero's nasty crackdown," mused Father Rafelle.

Father Salta said, "But now we do with the fragment found in the Clement ossuary. It seems clear from this new Jewish-Christian catacomb that they took the brunt of the blow during the great persecution, and it looks like the Jewish Christian population never fully recovered in Rome. I had not thought of this before, but maybe one of the underexplored reasons why Gentile Christianity triumphed, and Jewish

Christianity gradually faded out was persecution, at least in Rome and Asia. This needs exploring. Okay, finally what about the Star of David? Do you realize I think I even found this on the painting of the School of Athens?"

Father Rafelle frowned. "I don't know how to explain that unless Raphael was secretly of Jewish Christian extraction, but the six-pointed star is important in rabbinic literature.[1] They say it is a symbol of a sort of Trinity of the Jewish soul, God, and the Torah. The triangle, of course, became a symbol of the Trinity itself."

At this point, Father Peter hypothesized, "Suppose early Jewish Christians, who believed God expressed the divine identity as Father, Son, and Spirit used the Star of David symbol in a Christian way? After all, they took over other symbols familiar from their Jewish heritage. Suppose for them it was a symbol of Jews who believed in the Trinity?"

"So, in that tomb under the Vatican, and at the door of the crypt we have not just a Jewish symbol, but a symbol embraced by Trinitarian Jews, Jews who believed in Father, Son, and Spirit?" mused Father Rafelle. "It's an idea with some merit. After all Peter himself may have seen this symbol at the synagogue in Capernaum. So may have Junia, and other Galilean disciples. Let's remember that Judaism in the first century was a legitimate religion; Christianity was not. It was classified as a mere superstition. Identifying your burial ground with a Jewish symbol might make it less likely to be vandalized or robbed. Jews were to be left alone by Romans according to the Roman law."

"There is so much here to ponder, and my brain is about to burst. So I will call it a day at this point. Thank you, Father Rafelle, for a very enlightening morning!"

"You are most welcome! I'll keep digging through the archives; you keep digging under the Vatican!" laughed Father Rafelle.

The two men left quietly together through what is called the Sistine Chapel library hallway, and Father Peter looked up in admiration at all the beauty that surrounded him. And yet he had come to this place to discuss suffering and persecution and martyrdom and prejudice. Christianity was well and truly an underground religion in the first few centuries of the Christian era. It even had its meetings in catacombs

---

1. See Chabad.org and the article by Naftali Silberberg, "What is the Mystical Significance of the Star of David?" The Star of David picture is from that article.

and underground cities. Using his pocket New Testament Father Peter quickly turned to Hebrews 11:35–38

> Others were tortured. . .others suffered mocking and flogging, and even chains and imprisonment. They were stoned to death. . .they were killed by the sword, they went about in the skins of sheep and goats, destitute, persecuted, tormented—- of whom the world was not worthy. They wandered in deserts and mountains, and in caves and holes in the ground.

"I'll bet this was written to Jewish Christians in Rome to urge them not to turn back to simply being Jews and abandon their Christian faith! It was probably written by a Jewish Christian like Apollos in the 60s, before the martyrdoms of the apostles began. Maybe we *do* have a record of things in early Jewish Christianity in Rome in Hebrews! Hebrews 13 goes on to urge the audience to visit Christians being tortured and in prison, but the book also says that none of the audience of this sermon had yet been martyred." Father Peter then wondered if the line about wandering underground was about *damnatio ad metalla.* Could it even be an allusion to the fate of Priscilla or Aquila?

A whole new vision of early Jewish Christianity in Rome was coming into view for Father Peter, and it made him realize just how indebted all Christians were to these early Jewish Christians, including the fact that they wrote almost all of the New Testament. He left the library with a copy of a book Father Rafelle handed him: Peter Lampe's *From Paul to Valentinus,* a book that chronicles the development of Christianity in Rome in the first and second centuries AD "Looks like I need a whole new education," said Father Peter, "one book at a time."

52

The Blackened Friar

FOR WHAT MUST HAVE seemed an eternity upon later reflection, Magnus lay unconscious in a vineyard with no one taking notice. When the fire truck came to put out the fire in the car, they could find no one around. No one at all. Magnus had managed to roll under the grape arbor and could not be seen from the road at all. It was not until the following morning when one of the vineyard workers was going down the rows tending the vines that he found a monk with a sooty face and blackened neck lying on the ground, still unconscious. He still had a pulse, and his wallet had not fallen out of his pocket. So it was that Sunday afternoon the Vatican got a frantic call from a priest in Orvieto, asking if they were missing a Black Friar. The call was eventually routed to Father Peter.

"This is Father Giuseppe in Orvieto. Are you perhaps missing a monk named Magnus? He was found lying under a grape vine with burns on his face and neck, and he is still in and out of consciousness. We have taken him to Sisters of Mercy Hospital here. Apparently, his car blew up and he tumbled down a hill into a vineyard. The police here suspect a bomb. Someone was trying to kill the man, God bless him."

"I will come with one of our officers! And I'll try to find out what he was doing in Orvieto," promised Father Peter.

Hanging up the phone Father Peter realized he had one errand to run before he left. His new friends from Israel were going home today. He had promised to pop over to the D'Medici Hotel and say goodbye to Grace and Kahlil who were heading back on board a private jet. "It must be nice to have one's own air transportation," thought Father Peter.

The trip to Piazza Navona only took about twenty minutes, and Father Peter found both Grace and Kahlil standing at the front desk, their suitcases beside them.

"You wouldn't leave without letting me say goodbye would you?" chided Father Peter. Grace walked over and gave the priest a hug, which caused him to blush. Kahlil decided on a firm handshake.

"You can count on us coming back in January for the symposium. We wouldn't miss it for the world," said Grace.

Art and Marissa emerged from the elevator. Art had just caught this last remark and so he added, "And you need to put a wedding on your calendar, Father Peter. Marissa and I are getting married next June, probably in Istanbul, so be prepared to leave your duties for some fun in Turkey."

"And believe me, Turkey can be lots of fun," added Marissa. "I should know; it's my country."

"How can I say no to a proposition like that? Maybe I can get away to see Ephesus and some of the other biblical sites."

"We'll count on seeing you then. We are planning on staying here for about three more days, helping Charlie tidy some things up, and get some other things started. Then Marissa and I are going to explore every nook and cranny of this eternal city."

"Excellent decision," said Father Peter. "The longer you stay in Rome, the more you realize there is always one more thing to see."

"Speaking of travel and sightseeing, don't forget to visit us in Jerusalem," stressed Kahlil to Art and Marissa. "You promised to see my grandson, Samuel. You can't turn down an invitation to see a prophet in miniature!"

"So we did," replied Art, "and we don't renege on our promises, do we Marissa?"

"Not on your life," she replied.

Father Peter, Art and Marissa all walked their friends to the door to say final goodbyes as the limousine pulled up to take them to the airport. "Oh I forgot," said Father Peter, "Hannah's ossuaries have arrived, and I just got word the lintel is in the mail as well! Things are looking up."

"Great news," said Grace as she hopped into the car. "Keep us posted on further developments. Off to Siberia."

"Will do," said Father Peter. "Siberia?" But before anyone could ask any questions the car pulled away from the curb. All this time Charlie had been quietly watching this whole scenario of farewells play out and thinking, it sure is good to have friends who will come and help you in your hour of need, and they don't even have to be Christians.

53

News Fit to Print

THE NEWS CONFERENCE HIT the newspapers: Rome's *la Repubblica*, Turin's *La Stampa*, Milan's *Corriere della Sera* to say nothing of the international press. Over the weekend, there was also a story from Sorrento about the arrest of Tony "Teppista" Terranova. Andretti managed to put two and two together and after haranguing his source at the police department had discovered that yes, this was the guy who bought the stolen goods from the tomb raiders. So Adriano was off to Sorrento to follow that angle of the story that wouldn't go away.

The general reaction of the press had been positive. They found the full disclosure and candor of the archaeological team refreshing, and their willingness to answer an hour and a half of questions very commendable. It sounded like the Vatican really meant to study the issues in depth and without secrecy. Who knew what the implications were for women becoming Catholic priests, but in any case it seemed clear there had been women apostles. Some columnists saw this as the wedge that would help open the door for women in the Catholic priesthood.

In the United States, media focus had been given to Charlie Miller and Art West, noting the interreligious cooperation between a Catholic, a Protestant, a Muslim and a Jew. This became a big sub-story in the age of multi-culturalism and increasing religious pluralism in America. There would be interviews to do when Art and Charlie got home.

"Time to make another trip to our tomb," said Charlie to Marissa and Art over brunch late Monday morning.

"Hopefully not *our* tomb, though I'm *dying* to see it again!" said Art with a silly grin.

Charlie rolled his eyes. "I suggest we just do one thing this morning. Let's take a random sample of several of the burial boxes. Look in them; see if there are bones, etc."

When they arrived at the tomb it was strangely calm and quiet on the street. No reporters snooping around; no construction workers; no sewer workers installing more pipe. The closest activity came from the lines of tourists entering the main doors of the Vatican Museum down the street.

As they passed through the now two doors, they were greeted with a new light system that had been strung over the weekend. That would make their investigation down the dark corridor much easier.

"Where shall we begin, Charlie. It's your call!"

Charlie took a deep breath, and pointed, "That one. Look, there's a name on it—Urbanus—'city boy.' Maybe he grew up here in Rome."

It took all three of them to gently lower the ossuary to the floor and even more gently to slide off the cover. Shining his flashlight into the box, Art saw bones, and more bones. And then he saw something else. The head had been severed from the neck. "It looks like Urbanus may have been a Roman citizen. He was beheaded."

"Or he too was executed at the mines when he was no longer useful," said Charlie. "Don't forget that's how they got rid of them quickly at the mines." Marissa took photos and ample notes before they recovered the ossuary and moved on to the next box of Charlie's choice.

Art read another Latin name —"Ampliatus. I'm remembering an Ampliatus from Romans 16. Marissa, my pocket NT is—in my pocket, of course. Can you fish it out and check the reference?"

Marissa read Romans 16.8: "Greet Ampliatus, whom I love in the Lord."

Charlie said, "Well, this could be our man, but I recall from Church History that Ampliatus, by tradition, became a Bishop somewhere in Bulgaria! Regardless, he's considered one of the 70 disciples. I believe. So I doubt it's the same one."

When Charlie looked in to the box he also found something he had not anticipated. The ankle bone of Ampliatus had a spike driven through it. In fact, the ankle was now separate from the rest of the bones in the box. There was silence for quite a while, and Marissa found herself with a tear rolling down her right cheek. "He was crucified wasn't he?" she asked quietly.

"Yes, definitely," said Charlie. "Ampliatus got the 'extreme punishment' as the Romans called it."

"I'm sorry but I find it so hard to fathom how people can be so brutal to their fellow human beings," she said.

"It's even harder to figure out if you are one of those people who think all people are basically good and mean well and there is no such thing as sin and The Fall," said Art.

The next two caskets they opened also contained bones. Each was carefully photographed and recorded.

Then Marissa suggested, "Can we open Priscilla's sarcophagus?"

"I was wondering when someone might suggest that. Do you realize we didn't even look at the bones in the Junia box yet? It's in the Vatican somewhere!" exclaimed Charlie.

"Too little time, and too much to do," replied Art.

As they came up to the mausoleum of Priscilla and Aquila, Art felt led to say a prayer: "Lord we don't do this out of mere curiosity or disrespect for the dead, but because we want to understand our heritage. Please guide us to do these things in a reverent way, Amen."

Both Charlie and Marissa echoed the Amen.

As they pried open the rather large, long sarcophagus marked with Prisca's name, it took all three of them to take the lid off. Shining two flashlights into the bone box, Charlie exclaimed, "Well, I'll be!"

"Never saw anything like that before," exclaimed Art shaking his head.

"Me neither!" said Marissa wide-eyed.

Priscilla was buried inside a sheep skin. Though much deteriorated, there were still small bits of wool on the skin. "This probably means she was sown into the skin of this animal, and then thrown to the lions. They would pick up the sheep smell, tear it apart, and maul the body." Charlie involuntarily shivered. "I'm amazed there are as many bones left of her as there are, though, now that I look close, there seems to be one arm missing." But the other arm was intact, and on the hand was a surprise.

She wore a ring—a ring with a symbol on it. Charlie carefully extracted the ring from the bony finger, and looked at it closely under the flashlight. He held it up to the light for all to see the Star of David pattern.

"This is a fitting point to call a halt for now to our explorations. I reckon you should take the ring and turn it over to the Vatican. They will handle it with care. This probably means it was just Aquila who was sent to the mines, but Priscilla did not escape persecution and death either."

"You read my mind," said Charlie still in shock over the findings.

By now it was late afternoon. Time had run out for the archaeologists. For them, it was the last time they would enter the tomb this season. The Vatican archaeologists would take over from here and carefully record, for the first time, the fate of many of the earliest Jewish Christians.

54

Picasso's Last Stand

Mondriano Picasso as he had dubbed himself, was no Picasso. For that matter, he was no Mondrian or Kandinsky either. He was a hack when it came to painting. But the human ego knows no bounds, and Boz's ego was bigger than most. And his dark side was darker than most. He had not lost any sleep worrying about whether or not he might have killed another human being with a bomb. In fact, he assumed that he had done so, and this brought him a sense of relief about his own fate. What he did not know was that Marco ratted him out, Magnus reported his whereabouts, and Guido was about to give him up.

The police found the flat rented by Guido Mussolini, Boz's cousin. They waited until Boz left, palette and paint brushes in hand. Another officer followed him. For sure, the man who just left the little apartment bore no resemblance at all to the pictures of Boz they had. This man wore a beret, had no beard or long hair, and did not wear leather. The transformation to native street artist was remarkable.

Three policemen knocked on the door. "Open up! We have a search warrant!" they announced. No answer. So they pushed in the door, and came in ready for action. Guido was trembling in a bathroom closet, an appropriate spot since he wet his pants when he heard the police rushing in. They found him in less than two minutes. Dragging him out of the closet and sitting him down in a kitchen chair, the inquisition began.

"So Signore Mussolini, I gather you've had a guest at your apartment recently?"

"I don't know what you're talking about," said Guido squirming in his seat. "I'm not a criminal and I pay my taxes."

"You also have two shaving kits and two tooth brushes in your bathroom. Do you have a split personality, Signore?"

"Very funny," said Guido. "So what if I do have a friend visiting. He's out."

"Did you know it's against the law to harbor a criminal, friend or not."

"I didn't know Boz was a criminal!" exclaimed Guido inadvertently giving up his cousin.

The policemen just smiled. Sometimes it was too easy. "Well, would you believe it is Boz we are looking for. Or should I say Antonio Mussolini. Or maybe Mondriano Picasso—now that's a good one," replied the lead detective sarcastically. "Would you like to be in jail for protecting this man—he's wanted for vandalism and theft?"

"Don't forget the attempted murder charge," piped in his partner.

"Of course not! Don't be ridiculous!" said Guido, who really didn't know what kind of trouble Boz was in.

"Good! Then answer the question. Is your cousin Boz staying with you? Is he masquerading as Mondriano Picasso, the local street artist? Is he the same man that just left the apartment and headed toward the main square? Now you know we can go up there to your bathroom and take fingerprints and do this the long, hard way, or we can do this the easy way. Which is it going to be?"

Guido was tired of protecting Boz just because he was family. "I prefer the easy way. Yes, of course, Boz lives here and he is my cousin. But what has he done other than a little graffiti here and there?"

"Among other things, he stole not one, not two, not three, not four, but five priceless antiquities. He sold them to a dealer in Napoli who will be prosecuted. He made a good deal of money actually. He's been holding out on you, Guido!"

"No way! He never mentioned any of this to me!"

"Maybe so; maybe not. Take a look at this bank statement."

Guido squinted at the statement and then a look of anger came over his face. "Over 80,000 euros! That sponge has been living off me when he had a wad of money in the bank. That weasel! He's down at the town square pretending to be another Picasso, with easel and palette and beret. You can have him!"

This was all the police needed, a clear confirmation they had the right man. Two of the policemen went back up the street towards the piazza; the third man circled around on a parallel street. They surrounded the little café where "Picasso" was painting. But when Boz saw the three policeman coming at him, he threw his palette at one of them, turned suddenly, ran into the café and out the back door, heading for the funicular, the little train that chugged up and down the hill to Orvieto. As he was running and running and running, and looking over his shoulder, what he did not see coming was a large vegetable truck, until the very last minute. Brakes squealing, the truck driver tried to avoid the running man, his rear wheels slipping on the wet cobblestone. As Boz attempted to dodge at the last minute, he was clipped by the tailgate of the truck which in turn flipped open the back sliding door of the truck and all of a sudden about 5,000 tomatoes descended upon Boz and buried him well and truly.

The police got to the scene of the accident only moments later, and the truck driver jumped out of his truck cursing a blue streak. "Congratulations! You have just caught a wanted criminal for whose capture there is a reward. Your tomatoes have done the job that the police couldn't do!"

"What? This man is a criminal that I clipped and buried?"

"Indeed, he is even the descendant of one of Italy's most famous criminals—Mussolini!"

"You are joking, of course!"

"Oh, the joke is on Signore Antonio Mussolini, who still has not emerged from all that tomato sauce."

"Seriously? There is a reward?"

"Yes, indeed, and it will do more than cover your losses!"

"Jesus, Mary, and Joseph! I have just hit the jackpot."

"Now if you don't mind, let us see if we can extract that man from under your vegetables."

The process took a while. Boz was unconscious under a high pile of tomatoes. When he was finally uncovered, they put him on a stretcher to be transported less than a block away to the hospital—the same hospital where Magnus was recuperating. Those standing around could not help laughing. One of the policemen had stuck a big red tomato on

Boz's nose, making him look more like Bozo the Clown than Boz the street artist.

As Boz was being lifted into the back of the panel van, Guido arrived on the scene. One of the policemen who had interrogated him, walked over and said, "Look, kid, I don't think you had anything to do with your cousin's crimes. We aren't taking you in."

"Thanks for your vote of confidence," sad Guido dejectedly. "It serves Boz right though. He even cheated his own flesh and blood."

"I'm sorry, son. Try to stay clean. As the Bible says, 'thieves are jealous of each other's loot, while the godly bear their own fruit.'"

And it *was* a godly man who was bearing some fruit in the small Orvieto hospital. Father Peter was visiting with a living and repentant monk named Magnus.

"Father Peter, I'm sorry that you had to come all the way up here for this black sheep of the family. I was only trying to make things better, and I did call the police to tell them Boz was here."

"You did, and I know you meant well Magnus, but as the Good Book says 'zeal that is not according to knowledge' is dangerous. It gets people hurt, and in this case you got yourself hurt and nearly killed."

"You mean Boz tried to blow me up?"

"That's exactly what I mean, and the good news now is that attempted murder is a more serious crime than mere theft, so it's likely he will be going away to prison for a very, very long time."

"Well, that at least is a relief. Is there any chance of our getting those precious objects back?"

"We've tracked down all of them except for the small pottery lamps, which we may never find. Such lamps are so common and most of them look alike unless you look very carefully. I doubt we will ever get them back. It's alright. I am glad you are on the mend, and we are getting you back, but hopefully a wiser version of you."

"Definitely. I know I'm in trouble," sighed the monk.

"You're both a Scot and a red head; no wonder your boiling point is low," quipped Father Peter which a grin.

Magnus began to laugh and then said, "Don't make me laugh I've got a few broken ribs here and there."

"Just so your head and heart aren't totally broken."

"No. The nurses say, I should make a full recovery, praise God, but it will take a while. I will be sent to a rehab center in Rome soon. Will you visit and pray with me? I need that."

"Of course. And I have a lot to tell you about that tomb. The story is complex and fascinating. It will take years to study the catacomb. And don't worry! The Catholic Church is not going to fall apart because of the revelations of this tomb. There may be some changes we need to make, but change can be good. For instance, change in your approach to serving the Lord."

"Amen to that."

"Until I see you again, may the Lord bless you and keep you and mend you and heal you." With this Father Peter left the ward and walked out into the street heading for his car. He noticed police cars, a truck, and a pile of tomatoes just down the street. Father Peter walked down to survey the damage.

"What is that—some kind of street art?" asked Father Peter to the veggie man supervising the cleanup.

"No, but it was used to catch a thieving street artist" said the man with a grin, "and I got a reward for bombarding him with tomatoes!"

"Really? You caught a criminal with those tomatoes? I don't suppose you know the name of the criminal."

"In fact I do. Mussolini was his real name; Boz was his nickname. Apparently he was wanted for defacing property in Rome, stealing some treasures, and even trying to kill someone here with a car bomb recently—quite a list!"

Father Peter doubled over in laughter. "God sure does have a sense of humor. The man who tried to spray paint Rome's treasures red, ends up red all over, and pretty soon he will be read about all over in the papers!" And with that, Father Peter, whistling a happy tune, got in his car, cranked up the engine and headed back to Rome.

55

September in Siberia

GRACE LEVINE WAS COLD; the average temperature for this area in September is about 48 degrees. While in Rome, she received a phone call from the Irkutsk Orphanage for Young Girls. She and Manny headed for Siberia as soon as she got back. Once again, having a private jet made the trip easy.

"I realize this is not cold weather but I was just enjoying a Roman summer. I'm glad we won't be around when people like me turn into popsicles," said Grace shivering in the foyer as they waited for the orphanage director to fetch them.

"Or in this case 'momsicles' since you are about to become a mother," quipped her husband.

Grace laughed and thought back to the day in April when she received word from the Irkutsk Orphanage that for a hefty sum, she and Manny were going to be allowed to adopt a 12-year-old girl named Yelena Yevtishenko. Nearly five months of paperwork ensued. Quietly, even secretly, Grace and Manny planned for this day without telling a soul. Leaving Rome, she had let slip to their friends they were going to Siberia, so excited was she about this whole endeavor.

Grace had heard too many tales of adoptions falling through at the last moment, especially when you were adopting from a place like the Irkutsk Orphanage, and especially when those in charge knew you were a Jew. But in this case Jewishness turned out to be a bit of a plus, since Yelena was also of Jewish extraction. Grace paced the floor as the vivid images passed through her mind of her quiet visit to this place in June to meet her possible "daughter." Ever since she had reached the age where it was no longer safe to have children, Grace's non-biological adoption clock had been ticking. Now it was about to strike midnight.

Unbeknownst to Grace, Manny behind the scenes had been greasing the wheels of this deal, bringing indirect influence to bear on a local judge who had jurisdiction over the case. Turned out the judge had a son who played basketball and was quite good. Manny had promised the "kid" a try out and a contract to play on his Maccabee team if he fit in well with the team. The judge, of course, would disavow that his approval of this adoption case at record speed had anything to do with the fact that his 6'9" son had proved he could play ball with the best of them in the Israeli league, and had just weeks before signed a rookie one-year contract with Manny's team. And Manny had said nothing about the adoption at all to Judge Ivanov, but the judge was shrewd enough to realize that it might help his son if he approved the adoption.

The senior woman in charge of the orphanage emerged finally from behind the twin doors with opaque glass windows, appropriately painted cold blue.

With a smile on her wrinkled face, Natasha Kirilenko came over and shook Grace's hand saying in her broken English, "Is almost ready. Just some last minute packing. Yelena is very excited. She has been practicing the English she learned in school." Grace too had been practicing. She had been taking in large doses of the Rosetta Stone course in Russian over the last three months. Natasha had been the *babooshka*, the grandmother, of all the 47 girls in this orphanage, and it was bittersweet to see one of them leave. But, finally the moment of truth arrived.

A thin but sturdy blonde haired, blue-eyed girl, about 5 feet tall emerged from behind the doors dragging two medium-sized suitcases. Manny immediately leapt into action taking the suitcases from Yelena who quite cutely smiled and said, "*Spasiba*—thank you." Grace was thrilled to hear this little voice, so full of warmth. Walking over and leaning down, Grace found two thin arms reaching up to give her a hug and then she heard, "You will be my new mother, *da*?"

"*Da!*" said Grace, "*Slava boga* [praise God], from now on." Truth was, it was hard to tell who was happier—a little girl who longed to get out of the orphanage and have a real family ever since she had been brought here at the age of five, or Grace who longed to have a child ever since she had married Manny.

This scene of celebration could have gone on for a quite a while except, all of a sudden, and unexpectedly, Grace's purse began to make musical noises. It was her cellphone playing the old Beatle's tune, "All You Need is Love."

"Boy is that tune apt just now," said Grace as she grabbed the phone from the depths of her gigantic purse.

"It's Art West, so I'd better take it," said Grace, handing Yelena off to Manny for the moment. After a couple of minutes of listening and saying "yes" three times, she finally said,

"Well, Art, I guess it's okay to spill the beans now. I just became a mother today! I'm in Irkutsk, Siberia."

There was silence at the other end of the cellphone and then even Manny could hear, "What in the world . . . ?"

After a couple of minutes of explaining Grace told Art, "We'll talk again soon, but from now on you will have to address me as 'Mother Superior' or at least 'Superior Mother.'" Hanging up Grace laughed and said, "Let's go home, husband dear."

"Your wish is my command, as long as we are all together."

"Together we shall be from now on," pronounced Grace with confidence. "Come Yelena take my hand, we must go."

Manny turned back to Natasha, shook her hand firmly and said, "Thank you so much for all you have done to raise Yelena, and we promise we will do everything to continue the good, gracious work you have done for the last seven years."

Wiping her own tears from her eyes, Natasha attempted a smile. "Is hard to let go. Yelena was special child, a good girl. You will be blessed and a blessing I am sure."

As the couple and their new daughter walked out the door to the waiting rented black Mercedes a new chapter began in the life of this now complete Jewish family. The last thing Grace mumbled to herself before she got into the car was, "I sure wish my mother could have lived to see this day. She would have been so thrilled to finally have a grandchild."

As they sat together in the back seat of the Mercedes that was already speeding along toward the local airport, Yelena looked up into her new mother's eyes and said, "What is grandchild?"

Grace smiled and replied, "That would be you honey. You are a *grand* child. In fact, to me you are a miracle child. But seriously, 'grand-child' means you have a babooshka, a grandmother. Only, she just passed away."

As Yelena saw the momentary cloud pass over Grace's face at the thought of her mother Camelia's passing, she squeezed Grace's hand and said, "Is okay, she is in God's hands as I am in yours," and she smiled so sweetly that Grace had to wipe her eyes once more.

"You came along at just the right time."

"No," said Yelena, "You came along at just the right time. In six months, I would have to leave the orphanage, but with nowhere to go."

"Yelena honey, I'm thinking maybe my friend Art West is right when he keeps saying that God works all things together for good for those who love him." And with that the airport where Manny's plane was parked, came into sight on the near horizon. Rosh Hashanah was only a week away, and Manny said, "What a perfect way to start a New Year. Just perfect!" The "head of the year" would find the Cohens heading in a new direction, as parents.

56

The Melody Remains the Same

FALL MEANS MANY THINGS in North Carolina. For one thing, it means college football, though the Seahawks of UNC-Wilmington didn't much figure into the news on this front and Melody wasn't into that sort of sports in any case. Her school schedule had her taking four difficult courses—Bio 362 (Marine Biology), Bio 366 (Ecology), Bio 333 (Genetics and Genetics Lab), and as an elective Eng 420 (Shakespeare's Sonnets). Melody knew that she was going to really have to buckle down this term. Three of her four courses were in her major, and she wanted to do well in that. The jobs in Marine Biology were not that plentiful.

Deep inside, however, Melody had a hard time concentrating on all this because anytime she looked down, there was the beautiful ring that Jake had given her. As a Christian girl she did a lot of praying about her future with Jake. How was this relationship going to blossom and grow when for about 100 days out of the year (or more if the Charlotte Bobcats were in the playoffs) Jake would be nowhere near Wilmington? Texting, tweeting, phoning and Skyping were all fine as far as they went, but none of that gave Melody a feeling of real closeness to Jake. You can't really hug over the phone.

Melody decided she was not going to worry about her future occupation as she figured God would show her a way to work that out when the time came. The Lord would open the right doors at the right time. She had always believed that, and she continued to trust in that belief. What she was actually more concerned about was getting engaged to Jake, eventually getting married, and the thought of having a family was not tucked very far in the back of her mind as well.

Closing the door on her little Honda Fit, and putting in her ear-buds, with the Ipod tuned to Chris Tomlin's new worship songs, she began her usual walk through the pines and magnolias that graced the front of the UNC-Wilmington campus, humming along to the music. It was 8:30 on a beautiful September morning and the birds were singing in the trees. Her first class was not until 9 a.m. and so she thought she'd surprise Jake with a call.

The cellphone range once, twice, three times, and just when Melody was about to flip her phone closed she heard a sleepy, "Hello."

"Hey there, sleepy head, aren't you supposed to be up and heading to practice by now?"

Jake snapped to attention. "Melody! What a nice surprise. I was out late last night playing pickup ball over at the Bethlehem Center with my posse. I'd promised the kids I'd come. I've neglected my crew, what with spending all that time at the beach with you. Anyway, we had a great game, and I didn't even twist my ankle this time. Hooray!"

Jake was his usual effervescent self when he got engaged in a conversation with Melody. Increasingly, he ached to be with her all the time. Even in a crowd of kids he was lonely. He needed to keep busy just to keep his mind off her. Aunt Joyce had told him he was looking like a love-sick puppy. He reckoned she was right.

"So Melody, how about we plan to get together two weekends from now in Wilmington. Then you can come back here the following weekend when the regular pre-season schedule begins in October. That way, you can actually see me play a bit."

"And protect you from all the female fans," teased Melody.

"Trust me, babe, the only woman I have any time for is you, just you. Unless, of course, you count Aunt Joyce who has decided I need to get the ladder out this morning and clean the pine straw out of the gutters."

"Well, I'd much rather you have your hands in those gutters than your mind in the gutter," joked Melody. "Sorry, honey, I gotta run. I have a class in five minutes." After they hung up, both of them were thinking that life was shaping up rather well.

Melody, however, was looking further into the future. How fast things would develop and whether marriage could wait until she finished college were unanswered questions. For now, she was content to know she had been blessed with a reliable Christian man in her life, and her future looked as bright as the promises of God.

57

Love and War

IT WAS BOUND TO happen. Art and Marissa were having such a good time on their last day tour of Rome that something had to go wrong. The argument began innocently enough over who would decide where they would eat that night. He wanted to have one more meal at his favorite restaurant in Rome, and she wanted something entirely different her last night in Rome.

And then, as they headed for the Roman Forum, they began to argue about whether Marissa was coming back to the States with Art, or going straight home to Turkey. Art knew it was getting serious when she called him by his full name. . .

"Arthur James West! I have already spent plenty of time visiting with your Mom, which was fine, and then I came all the way over here to be with you, not that you asked me to do much of anything or contribute to the archaeological discussion. And now you want me to go back to Charlotte? I don't think so! I need to see my family. I need to get busy with the wedding plans. My mother has been emailing me every day with questions. I'm tired and stressed out already, and we are still almost ten months from the wedding! Are you getting the picture?"

"But honey. . ."

"Don't honey me right now. . ."

"But Marissa, you came well after most of the archaeological work had been done here. Okay, I should have been more thoughtful and asked you to do something specific along the areas of your expertise."

"It's not like I've never dealt with graveyards before!"

"I know, I know! I'm sorry! I wasn't thinking!"

"You'd better be sorry. How are we going to work together as professionals if you treat me like I'm only your girlfriend?"

"Well, more than girlfriend—my fiancée at least," said Art, but the attempted joke made Marissa scowl. "I get the picture, really I do. I'm sorry and I repent in dust and ashes. But I was just hoping to be with you for a bit longer. Just a little bit longer. I mean I know you need to get home, and start working on the wedding, but how complicated can it be?"

This question produced the biggest explosion yet. "You must be joking! Planning this wedding will be an international undertaking—requiring a lot of diplomacy. A lot can go wrong. You don't want to go to war over our wedding, do you?" threatened Marissa.

Art could smell the smoke coming out of Marissa's ears, and knew he was just digging himself a deeper and deeper hole. He really knew nothing about planning a wedding. The last one he attended was for Grace and Manny, and that seemed to go well. How hard could it be? Finally he said, "Today is my screw up day. I'm too ignorant about these things. I apologize, and understand why you need to go home now."

There was an awkward silence as they walked by the ruins of the Temple of the Vestal Virgins. Slowly Art slid over towards Marissa and held out his hand. After a moment, she took it. Nothing was said for the next five minutes. They just walked on and on towards the Mamartine prison where Paul may have spent his last few days.

"You sure you don't want to lock me in there?" asked Art.

"Not for very long, at least," claimed Marissa. "Remember, I need to leave."

"And you need to go home to Turkey from here."

"Right."

"Which is certainly closer than from Charlotte."

"Exactly."

"Makes sense."

"Indeed it does."

They kept on walking through the Forum.

"So, shall we spend some time in the museums and then go have some supper—your choice?" promised Art.

"Let's check out the Arch of Titus. Then we can stop in at St. Peter's in Chains. Finally, we can stroll up the Via Cavour and just eat at the first *ristorante* that catches our fancy—in short, let's not plan our dinner at least!"

"I like that plan," said Art jokingly. "You know, they say that you can't really tell you're in love until after you've had your first big fight. If that was it, then I still love you."

Without realizing it, they had walked all the way through the Forum to the Arch of Titus, which had been very carefully cleaned of the paint liberally applied by Boz and his gang.

They both stopped and stared up at the fragile remains of the arch where the procession was depicted. "There goes the menorah from the Temple in Jerusalem, along with all those dejected Jewish prisoners. One man's triumph is another man's tragedy."

"Except, of course, when sacrificial love does not insist on its own way and wins by giving in," reminded Marissa.

"And I thought I was the theologian in the family. Marissa you need to help me love more like Jesus loved. I really want to be that way. Truly I do."

"And so do I. We're on a journey that will refine us both, hopefully in only good ways."

"Well at least today we checked one thing off the 'to do' list."

"What's that?"

"According to the marriage manuals, you have to learn how to fight and make up. Are you ready to make up?'

"In fact, I'm ready to make out!" proclaimed Marissa.

To the ordinary Roman passerby, it might have appeared that Art and Marissa were just another couple sitting on a park bench, full of passion and *amore*. Looks can be deceiving. For this was not just any couple. It was a couple like some very famous loving couples of long ago—Priscilla and Aquila or Andronicus and Junia—partners for life—servants of the Lord.

THE END.

POST SCRIPT

THE CRYPT OF ST. Peter is a real historic site. The tomb of Andronicus and Junia, and the catacomb under St. Peter's is the fiction of this novel. Those Jewish Christian martyrs were buried somewhere in Rome, and Vatican Hill is one very plausible spot. We noted that St. Peter was apparently found buried with several others.

The story about Andronicus and Junia (minus the tomb part) is not merely plausible, it is likely, based on the information in Romans 16. Junia was probably the first woman apostle, and the arguments have been convincingly mustered in Eldon Epp's, *Junia. The First Woman Apostle* (2005).

All of the descriptions of Rome, Orvieto, Sorrento, and Napoli are based on our travels to these beautiful cities. Our descriptions of Vatican City are based on our visits as well, although we have not been in the papal quarters or library! Obviously Pope Jerome is not the real Pope, but a fictional character. Peter Salta is partially modeled on the real Preacher to the Papal Household whom I had the pleasure of meeting at Asbury Theological Seminary—Reverend Father Raniero Cantalamessa.

The stories about the theft of precious antiquities are based on real cases and real ongoing problems in dealing with our history and our treasures, including our Christian ones. There are many shady dealers like Teppista Terranova in the real world. As for early Jewish ossuaries, you can read about the burial practice which virtually ended in the second century AD in the book I co-authored with Hershel Shanks, *The Brother of Jesus* (2003).

As for the graffiti artists, this part of the story is sadly all too accurate.

As for the adopting of a Russian child by Manny and Grace, this suggestion is based on the suggestion of the prototype of Grace, Dr. A. J. Levine of Vanderbilt University, who insisted that Grace should have a child somewhere in the course of these novels!

As for the lust for new antiquities by curators of major world museums, and their willingness to bend their own museum's rules about collecting to obtain something rare and precious, see the article in the August 12th, 2012 edition of the *NY Times* "Museum Defends Antiquities Collection," by Randy Kennedy.

Finally, the title of this novel is based on what Rome was often called in antiquity—the Eternal City. Viva la Roma! What a great city it is to this very day.

www.ingramcontent.com/pod-product-compliance
Lightning Source LLC
Chambersburg PA
CBHW070838030726
47504CB00005B/1139